The Damnation Affair

Books by Lilith Saintcrow

DANTE VALENTINE

Dante Valentine (omnibus):
Working for the Devil
Dead Man Rising
The Devil's Right Hand
Saint City Sinners
To Hell and Back

JILL KISMET NOVELS

Night Shift
Hunter's Prayer
Redemption Alley
Flesh Circus
Heaven's Spite
Angel Town

ROMANCES OF ARQUITAINE

The Hedgewitch Queen
The Bandit King

As Lili St. Crow

THE STRANGE ANGELS SERIES

Strange Angels
Betrayals
Jealousy
Defiance
Reckoning

The Damnation Affair

LILITH SAINTCROW

orbit

www.orbitbooks.net

Orbit
Hachette Book Group
237 Park Avenue
New York, NY 10017
www.orbitbooks.net

Originally published as an e-book by Orbit Books
First print on demand edition: February 2013

Orbit is an imprint of Hachette Book Group. The Orbit name and logo are trademarks of Little, Brown Book Group Limited.

The publisher is not responsible for websites (or their content) that are not owned by the publisher.

ISBN: 978-0-316-25159-4

Contents

Chapter One 1

Chapter Two 14

Chapter Three 23

Chapter Four 31

Chapter Five 39

Chapter Six 49

Chapter Seven 57

Chapter Eight 63

Chapter Nine 72

Chapter Ten 81

Chapter Eleven 89

Chapter Twelve 99

Chapter Thirteen 105

Chapter Fourteen 111

Chapter Fifteen 118

Chapter Sixteen 126

Chapter Seventeen 134

Chapter Eighteen 142

Chapter Nineteen 150

Chapter Twenty 157

Chapter Twenty-One 165

Chapter Twenty-Two 172

Chapter Twenty-Three 179

Chapter Twenty-Four 183

Chapter Twenty-Five 187

Chapter Twenty-Six   195
Chapter Twenty-Seven   201
Chapter Twenty-Eight   208
Chapter Twenty-Nine   213
Chapter Thirty   222
Chapter Thirty-One   230
Chapter Thirty-Two   237
Chapter Thirty-Three   243
Chapter Thirty-Four   248
Chapter Thirty-Five   252
Chapter Thirty-Six   259
Chapter Thirty-Seven   263

Extras   **269**

Por Gaetano mio.
Te absolvo.

Chapter 1

The stagecoach creaked to a stop, fine flour-white dust billowing, and Catherine Elizabeth Barrowe-Browne gingerly unlaced her gloved fingers from her midriff. Her entire body ached, both with the pummeling that was called *travel* in this part of the world *and* with the unremitting tension. Her nerves were drawn taut as a viola's charter-charmed strings.

For a moment, the sensation of not jolting and shuddering over a bare approximation of something that in a hundred years' worth more of wear might possibly be generously called a *road* was exquisite relief. Then Cat's body began reminding her of the assaults upon its comfort over the past several days, with various twinges and aches.

Also, she was *hungry*. A lady was far too ethereal a creature to admit hunger, but this did not make the pangs of fleshly need any less severe.

"*Damnation!*" the driver yelled, and the coach creaked as the two men hopped off. The fat, beribboned woman in mourning across from Catherine let out a tiny, interrupted snore, spreading herself more firmly over the hard seat.

Ceaseless chatter for nigh unto fifty miles, me jolted endlessly backward because her digestion won't permit her to share the forward-facer, and now she sleeps. Cat grimaced, smoothed her features, and heard murmuring voices. The town was not very large, Robbie had written, but growing.

Growing enough for a schoolteacher, apparently. Otherwise her plan would not have progressed nearly so smoothly.

"Damnation!" the driver yelled again, and the stagecoach door was violently wrenched at. Catherine's fingers took care of pulling her veil down securely and gathering her reticule and skirt. There were other thumps—her trunks, sturdy Boston leather, and thank Heaven for that. They had been subjected to almost as many assaults as Cat's temper for the past few days. "One for Damnation, ma'am!"

Yes, thank you, I heard you the first time. She slid across the seat, extended her gloved hand, and winced when his fingers bit hers. Feeling for a stagecoach step while half-blind with dust and aching from a bone-shattering ride across utterly God-forsaken country was a new experience, and one she had no intention of savoring. Syrupy golden afternoon light turned the dirt hanging in the air to flecks of precious ore, whirling like dreams of a claim in a boy's fevered head.

Oh, Robbie, I am just going to pinch *you.* Her point-toe boots hit dry earth, the burly whiskered stagecoach driver muttered a "Ma'am," as if it physically hurt him to let loose the word, and she took two staggering steps into the dust cloud. *Is there even a town here? It doesn't* look *like it.*

Any place a coach halted would have charterstones and a mage to hold back the uncontrolled wilderness. Still, the sheer immensity of the empty land she had glimpsed through barred train windows and the stagecoach's small portholes would trouble anyone properly city-bred. Across Atlantica's wide heaving waves, the Continent was not troubled by the need for charterstones; but even after almost two centuries on the shores of the New World, civilization was uneasy.

She reclaimed her hand, quelling the urge to shake her most-certainly-bruised fingers. "Thank you," she murmured automatically, manners rising to the surface again. "A fine ride, really."

"Miss Barrowe?" A baritone, with a touch of the sleepy drawl she'd come to associate with the pockets of half-civilization she'd been subjected to in the last several days. "Miss Catherine Barrowe?"

In the weary flesh. "Yes." She even managed to sound crisp and authoritative instead of half-dead. "Whom do I have the pleasure of—"

"She's here!" someone yelled. "Strike up the band!"

The dust settled in swirls and eddies. A truly awful cacophony rose in its place, and Cat blinked. A hand closed around her arm, warm and hard, and it could possibly have been comforting if she had possessed the faintest idea whose appendage it was.

"Hey, Gabe," the stagecoach driver called. "No trouble all the way."

"Thanks, Morton," her rescuer replied. "Those her trunks?"

"Yes indeedy. A very polite miss, glad to've brought her. Mail's there, picked up a bag of it in Poscola Flats. And the chartermage's order—"

"I see it, thanks." Now he sounded a trifle chilly. Cat had the impression of someone looming over her—dust coated her veil, and she blew on it in what she hoped was an inconspicuous manner. The sun was a glare, sweat had soaked the small of her back, and she devoutly wished for no more than a chance to relieve herself and procure some nourishment. *Any* food, no matter how coarse. "Godspeed."

"Yeah, well, from here to Tinpan's a long ride and the country's fulla bad mancy and walkin' dead." Creaking, as the driver hefted himself up. "See you." The whip cracked, and the stage began to rumble.

Oh yes, mention living corpses! That is just *the thing to do before a journey.* Cat's skin chilled, and she had the distinctly uncharitable thought that if the stagecoach *was* attacked by those who slept in unhallowed ground, at least the hefty woman in mourning would awaken for the event.

Or at least, so one hoped.

"Moron," the man holding her arm muttered. "As if he's not going to stop at the livery and pick up Shake's whiskey. Well, you look rattled around, miss. Let's get you through this."

Her veil and vision both cleared, and Cat found her rescuer to be a lean, rangy man of indeterminate age, a wide-brimmed hat clapped hard on his head and a star-shaped tin badge gleaming on his black vest. Guns slung low on his hips, and the chain of a charing-charm peeked out from behind his shirt collar, glinting blue. The guns gave her a moment of pause—not many in Boston carried them openly. Her own charing-charm, safely tucked under her dress, cooled further.

At least with the charing she could be certain *he* was not of the walking undead. It was faint comfort, given the way he scowled at the retreating stagecoach's back. He looked stunningly ill-tempered.

The cacophony crested, and she realized with a sinking sensation that it was meant to approximate music.

"Good heavens," she managed. "What on earth is that noise?"

The corner of his thin mouth twitched up as he glanced down at her. He was quite *provokingly* tall. "Your welcome committee, ma'am. I'll try to see it don't last too long."

How chivalrous—and ungrammatical—of him. *Oh, Robbie. I am just going to pinch you*, she thought for the fiftieth time, and braced herself.

The town center was a single street framed with raw-lumber buildings, a wide dirt thoroughfare that probably was a sheet of glutinous mud if it ever rained in this hellish place, and the greenery-cloaked mountains in the distance might have been pretty if they had been in a painting. Instead, they were hazy, oppressive shapes, grimacing in distaste.

An attempt at bunting and colored ribbon had been made across the front of a building whose sign proclaimed it to be the Lucky Star Bar Saloon, a smaller sign depending from it creaking as it swung and whispered Whiskey Scales Hot Baths. For a moment she wondered just what whiskey scales were, but the sight of the crowd arrayed on the saloon's steps under the bunting and spilling into the dusty street managed to drive the thought from even her nimble brain.

A gigantic banner flapped in the moaning-low, sage-scented wind, and a cord snapped. The banner, its proudly painted length folding and buckling, began to descend upon the motley collection of men beneath it playing instruments with more enthusiasm than skill.

Welcome to Damnation, the banner read, as its leading edge dropped across a man playing a fiddle and continued its slow descent.

"Oh, dear." She tried not to sound horrified, and suspected she failed miserably. "This is not going to end well."

He gave a short sharp burr of a sound. Was that a *laugh*? It sounded altogether too painful to signify amusement. "It never does around here, ma'am. Jack Gabriel."

"I beg your pardon?" She watched as the banner continued its majestic downward crumble and the music hitched to an unlovely stop. People scrambled to get out of the way, and one or two children crowed, delighted.

So there *were* children in this Godforsaken place. Miracles did occur. Of course, who would she be called upon to teach if there were none?

"Jack Gabriel. Sheriff. Your servant, ma'am." He even touched the brim of his colorless, sun-bleached hat. "I thought you'd be older."

Oh, really? "I am very sorry to have disappointed you, sir." She reclaimed her arm with a practiced twist. "Thank you for your assistance. I suppose I'd best restore some order here." She took two steps, found her balance and her accustomed briskness, and stalked for the milling group on the saloon steps.

"Oh, Hell no," the sheriff said, low and clear. "Can't restore what never happened in the first place, ma'am." He fell into step beside her, and she might have been almost mollified if not for the swearing. "My apologies. I just meant, well, we were prepared for…something else."

Prepared? This doesn't look prepared. She tucked her veil back, summoned her mother's Greet The Peasants smile, and told the pressure in her bladder it was just going to have to wait.

The crowd was mostly men, in varying stages of cleanliness; the few women were in homespun and bleached-out bonnets. She suddenly felt like an exotic bird, even though she'd left everything impractical or *very* fashionable at home in Boston.

Home no more. Her chin lifted, and the smile widened. "What a lovely reception!" she gushed, as the banner finished its slow descent and wrapped another portly, bewhiskered fiddler, who was almost certainly drunk, in its canvas embrace. The resultant package blundered into a man with a drum slung about his neck, and the two of them careened into a trio of men holding what looked like kitchen implements.

The first fiddler seemed to think this was an infringement upon his honor, and—uttering a most ungentlemanly oath—swung his fist at a bystander, a man in red suspenders and a stovepipe hat, a moth-eaten fur on his skinny shoulders. Who also turned out to be a mancer of some sort, since he promptly snapped a crackling flash of energy off his thin fingers and knocked his attacker backward.

"Oh, *Hell*," the sheriff said, with feeling, and Miss Barrowe's reception turned into something the locals told her later was named a "free-for-all." A tall, broad-shouldered, and very bony matron in brown descended on Cat and ushered her across the street, toward a lean wooden building—HAMMIS'S BOARD-INGHOUSE, according to the sign hanging from an upstairs balcony railing. It was squeezed disconsolately between two other nondescript buildings, one of which seemed to be some variety of shop.

"Very sorry, miss. It is *Miss*, isn't it? I am Granger, Mrs. Letitia Granger—"

Yes, we corresponded; you are on the Committee that hired me. "How do you do?" Cat managed, faintly. Behind them, the brawl spilled off the steps and into the dusty street, and the sheriff bellowed *most* impolitely. Charm and mancy crackled uneasily, the dust whirling in tight circles, and her charing-charm warmed a little, sensing the flying debris of malcontent.

She couldn't even care, she was suddenly so desperate for a few moments alone to relieve herself.

Oh, I hope they have some manner of plumbing, or I am going to explode. She reached up to straighten her hat, and Mrs. Granger whisked her inside the boardinghouse, which did have a small room for her to freshen herself. That paled in comparison to the watercloset down the hall, of which she availed herself with most unladylike haste.

The room given to her temporary use was an exceedingly small cubbyhole; the vicious sunlight pouring in through a small, dusty glass window had already scorched and faded everything in it. It could have been a palace, though. For one thing, it was not moving. For another, it was *private*, even though she could hear the brawl outside and the furious yelling as stray mancy bit and spread. Much of it was language she would have been shocked to hear, had Robbie not taken deep delight in teaching her certain phrases and their meanings.

Dust had crept into every fold of her dress, and she was far too fatigued to charm it free even if she had a moment of privacy to do so. Instead, she pinned her veil back and stretched with rare relief, and wondered if this would be her lodging. They had mentioned something of a small house—and just then the noise outside faded, and she suspected she was taking far too long and there might possibly be a prospect of something to eat by now. She checked herself in the sliver of mirror, decided she looked as proper as circumstances allowed, and eased out of the tiny room and down the stairs.

As soon as she reentered the hall leading to the boardinghouse's parlour, her hat repinned and some of the dust swept away, she was almost bowled over by a lad of perhaps ten, with cornsilk hair and an engaging gaptooth smile. "*BOXER!*" he yelled, and the slavering biscuit-colored streak behind him was obviously a dog. "They're in here, boy!"

The dog nipped smartly past her into the parlour, feathers exploded, the boy let out a crow-cry and hopped down the hall—and a chicken, its wings beating frantically, knocked over a lamp and tried to flap straight into Cat's face.

The schoolmarm was in blue, with a smart hat perched on slightly wilted brown curls and a smile fixed on her barely pretty face like she smelled something bad. Gabe didn't blame her—Damnation was none too fragrant even on the best of days. Well, *fragrant*, maybe, but certainly not *pleasant*. But even he hadn't been prepared for the melee when Collie Stokes took a swing at Em Kenner.

It was a good thing Gabe was quick *and* light on his feet, especially when it came to dodging flung charms and stray mancy. He didn't have to squeeze off a shot to get everyone's attention—it was never a good idea to start shooting in Damnation—but it was close.

It took a good half hour to restore order, but fortunately Mrs. Granger descended upon the girl and swept her across the street to the boardinghouse. It was, all things considered, the best place for her…but still, they'd be lucky if that lolling drunk Pete Pemberton didn't scare her off completely. She'd probably be back on the next coach to Poscola Flats and on the train to Boston without so much as a *how do you do*, and Gabe didn't much blame her.

When he had finally calmed everyone down—including Em Kenner, who was righteously indignant even at the best of times—and had Collie safely stowed in the jail and someone dealing with that fool banner, Gabe settled his hat more firmly on his head and set off for the boardinghouse. The occasion of a New Arrival was giving everyone the jitters, and he silently prayed that big, bony Granger wasn't frightening the poor girl even more.

He clumped up the steps and through the squeaking door, straight into another maelstrom.

He'd forgotten about the chickens the Hammis family kept behind the boardinghouse.

Well, honestly, the chickens weren't bad at all, except for when Boxer was chasing them. Somehow they had all gotten *inside* the boardinghouse, probably one of Tom Hammis's practical jokes on a day when the entire town was all het up.

That kid was gonna be trouble one day.

Gabe's temples were tight with an incipient headache. He later found out Pete Pemberton was safely in an alcoholic stupor upstairs, and that was how Boxer had gotten loose. He also further found out that little Tommy had used a simple chicken-leading charm to bring the poultry inside, thinking it'd be a grand idea to scare his harried mother.

A tornado of feathers engulfed him. The new schoolmarm had Boxer's collar, the mastiff straining against her grip and scrabbling on bare wooden flooring. Mrs. Granger was ranting, and Keb and Lizzie Hammis were trying desperately to corral the charmed fowl. Poor round Lizzie, her red face even redder, swatted at a prize hen. "Oh, for Pete's sake…Keb, grab that one—*Tommy, get down here, I am gonna take you behind the woodshed for sure!* Oh, miss, sorry, Boxer don't bite—"

"*Honestly*, Lizzie Hammis, the *one* day we ask you to be respectable!" Granger had her skirts clutched back as if one of the chickens might foul or bite her.

Gabe almost wished one would.

Boxer made snuffling, grunting, pleading noises, lunging against the schoolmarm's grip. Her hat was askew, and she was flushed. The extra color did wonders for her face, and her wide dark eyes flashed almost angrily before her jaw set and she hauled back on the mastiff's collar again. "*Down*, boy!" she snapped. "I think if we can get him—*oof*—outside, we can restore some—*ouch*—some order here." She brightened as her gaze lighted on Gabe. "You! Get over here and help me!"

It had all the bite of a command, and he decided it wasn't a half-bad idea, either. So he was already moving, striding across the raw lumber, the pale-green rugs askew and everything in the parlour rattling dangerously as Mrs. Hammis started searching for a counter-charm to gather up the chickens and get them quiet. The entire boardinghouse shook with stray mancy as the chickens sent up an ungodly noise and Boxer started moaning. Charing-charms glowed—the marm's bright and clear, Letitia Granger's a glitter of indignation, Lizzie Hammis's sparking as she sought for a bit of mancy, and Keb's barely limned with foxfire since he had no mancy at all. Gabe could feel his own warming dangerously, and didn't have time for a breath to calm it.

He grabbed the mastiff's collar, the schoolmarm worked her gloved fingers free, and in short order he had the dog outside on the front walkway. Onlookers crowded, but he made shooing motions and they hung back. "Someone find Tommy Hammis for me," he remarked, mildly. "The boy's gonna hafta give his Ma a reckonin.'"

"The new miss, is she mad?" Isobela Bentbroad hopped from foot to foot, looking scrubbed and miserable in her Sunday best. Her lank brown braids flopped.

"Well, if the music didn't frighten her off, Ma Hammis's chickens might. Just wait, Izzie. And the rest of you, don't cross these steps 'til we've got things calmed down."

Boxer set up a wail as Gabe finished clipping his collar to the chain bolted to the porch. Most of the time, the dog kept Pemberton out of trouble. But he had a regrettable yen for chasing chickens. He hadn't caught one yet, despite fowls' inherent stupidity, but he was the original Tip Mancinger in the old nursery rhyme—he just kept *trying*.

"I mean it, now," the sheriff said. A murmur ran through the crowd.

He squared his shoulders and strode back into the fray.

Granger was still going. "And *furthermore*, the drapes in here haven't been beaten since this building went up, they're *stiff* with dust! Honestly! *Chickens*, in the *house!*"

The schoolmarm stood against the parlour wall, no longer flushed but very pale, staring at the potbellied iron stove. She cast a single imploring glance at Gabe, and he was only faintly relieved to see the chickens had been dealt with.

"This is *not respectable!*" Granger was getting herself worked up but good. Keb Hammis, his meek face cheese-pale, had his shoulders drawn up like he wished he could vanish, his best suit straining at the seams. Lizzie was probably getting the chickens back into the coop, but she'd be no use here either.

Oh, Hell. Gabe sighed internally. A mastiff was one thing, Letitia Granger another entirely.

"Mrs. Granger, ma'am." He had his hat in one hand, running the other back through his hair. "Thank you. That'll be about enough."

It was probably the wrong thing to say. Letty glared at him, her bosom heaving. The cameo pinned at her throat was a sailor on stormy waters, to be sure. The charing-charm on it flashed blue, then green. She didn't talk about where her original charing had gone, but Russ Overton had once commented that it was no wonder Granger was so sour; anyone with her hard luck would be.

Gabe let his hands fall. "Keb. That boy of yours around?"

The new schoolmarm piped up. "Is he about ten, very blond, and quite agile?" The clipped, educated precision of the words made the entire parlour look shabby.

Well, we do as best we can, Gabe reminded himself. "That'd be him, yes."

"I saw him heading down the hall, that way." She pointed, her reticule swinging. "I believe he has perhaps made his escape. Will you be placing him under arrest?"

For one mad moment he thought she was serious, before the glint in her dark eyes caught up with him.

Jack Gabriel surprised himself by laughing out loud. Keb Hammis outright stared with his mouth open and his colorless eyes wide, and Mrs. Granger was mute with astonishment, thank God.

"He's a handful and no mistake, ma'am. I don't pity you having him in school." It didn't come out quite the way he wanted it to—he sounded sarcastic instead of amused. "I think we might be able to show you the house now, if you're so inclined. Garrett's already taken your trunks."

Mrs. Granger harrumphed. The house was a sore subject. Or not precisely the house, but the hired help.

The sparkle in Miss Barrowe's eyes was gone. She reached up, twitching her hat back into place. "Yes, I'd quite like that, thank you."

And Jack Gabriel, abruptly, felt like a goddamn fool, for no good reason at all.

Chapter 2

The house was small and trim, freshly painted white and green, and at the very edge of the "town" proper, though no doubt inside the charter-boundaries. Cat kept her back straight with an effort of will, and groaned internally at the thought of more welcoming committees. There had been a crowd of people, some of them scuffed and bruised, all coated in dust and a layer of sparkling mancy, standing agoggle outside the boardinghouse. Stray mancy still vibrated in the street, and her charm was warm again. Sweat slicked dust to her face, her dress would perhaps never recover from the double assault of dirt and feathers, and her entire body ached. The sharp bite of hunger under her breastbone threatened to make her well and truly irritable.

If she never again sat in another rocking wooden contraption pulled over ground by terribly apathetic nags, she would be *ever* so grateful. Mrs. Granger rocked back and forth in the seat behind them, either too mortified to speak or holding her peace for other reasons.

The sheriff pulled the horses to a stop. "It's small, but it's safe. The town charter covers a couple miles out past here, so you don't have to worry about any bad mancy or otherwise. Plus the girl working here, well. She's a fair girl, in her own way, except she's Chinee. You don't mind that, do you?"

Behind her, Mrs. Granger sniffed loudly. It wasn't quite a harrumph, but it was close.

That's right; they did mention a girl to charm the laundry and do the cooking. "Mind? Why on earth would I mind?" The meaning behind his words caught up with her. "A Chinoise girl?" *Does he think we've never seen them in Boston?*

"Name's Li Ang. She's a widow. Good girl, will cook and keep house. She gets half Sundays off, and she's a fair seamstress. Knows some English. Glad you don't mind." It was by far the longest speech he'd given, and he looked straight ahead at the horses while he did so. "There's good people here, and our charter's solid." Still staring forward, as if he couldn't bear to look at her. "May not be what you're used to, but—"

"Sir." She wished she could remember his name. It wasn't like her to forget such a thing, but a day such as this would strain even a mentath's wondrously unshakeable faculties. "If I held the comforts of civilization so highly, I would hardly be here. I am *quite* prepared for whatever this town holds."

For some reason, that made his mouth twitch. "I hope so, ma'am. Hope we ain't scared you off yet."

"It would take far more than this to frighten me, sir. On the contrary, I am roundly entertained. Shall we proceed?"

His only answer was to hop down from the cart. Mrs. Granger cleared her throat. The woman was a serious irritant. She reminded Cat of Mrs. Biddy Cantwell in her everlasting black and disapproval, jet jewelry and her habit of lifting her lorgnette and peering at anything that incurred her considerable and well-exercised displeasure. Biddy's daughter had been a success in Season, and could have had her pick of beaus, but Mrs. Cantwell had driven every suitor off one way or another. It had been the tragedy of the year and was still bemoaned, and Miss Cantwell—none dared unbend enough to address her as *Eliza*, especially in her mother's hearing—was now officially a spinster and would quite probably be her mother's handmaid until said mother shuffled off the mortal coil.

Mrs. Granger shifted her weight, and the cart rocked. "This was not my idea, Miss Barrowe. The girl *is* mostly respectable. She's a widow, and a Christian. But her condition—"

Thankfully, the sheriff again intervened. "Mrs. Granger, ma'am, let's not go on. Miss Barrowe's probably worn down by all the excitement." He offered a hand, and Cat accepted his help. The landing on hard-packed earth jolted all the way through her, and she longed for a bed. Or some cold chicken and champagne. "You look a little pale."

"Quite fine, thank you," Cat murmured. "Merely unused to the heat. Is it always this warm?"

"Except when it's raining. Sometimes even then. And winter's snow up to your…well, that's why the town was named, maybe. For the weather."

"Really?" Now *that* was interesting.

"No. Just my personal guess. This way, ma'am. We repaired the gate." He said it as if he expected a prize, but Cat only had the wherewithal to make a small sound that she hoped expressed pleasure at such a magnanimous gesture. It was difficult to keep her balance, for the ground was swaying dangerously underfoot, as if it had thrown its lot in with the stagecoaches of the world.

The gate in question was painted white, and opened with only a single guttural squeak. There was a sad, spiny attempt at a garden, cowering under the assault of heavy sunshine, and a pump that looked to be in working order. She hoped beyond hope that there was a little more in the way of plumbing *inside*, and swayed as the ground took a particularly violent turn underneath her.

A hand closed around her elbow. "Miss Barrowe?" The man now sounded concerned.

"Quite fine," she muttered. Her stomach twisted on itself, and she hoped it wouldn't growl and embarrass her. "Thank you."

"You don't look fine, ma'am. Let's get you inside. *Li Ang!* It's Gabe, open up!"

The stairs tilted most disagreeably, but she received the impression of a small, lovely porch with white railings, blessed shade enfolding them. The sudden darkness almost blinded her. There was a sound of bolts being drawn back, and she swayed again.

"Aw, *Hell*." Gabriel, she remembered. Gabriel was his name, a herald of woe, and his fingers suddenly bit into her poor arm. "Granger, come on up here, she's about ready to—"

Everything went fuzzy-gray, as if she had been wrapped in a fog-cloud. Her stomach made an indiscreet grumbling noise, and the embarrassment flushed the gray with rosy pink.

Cat returned to herself with a thump, half-reclining on a black horsehair sopha which had seen much better days. The cushions were hard as rocks, and someone held a cup against her lips. It was sweet water, and she drank without qualm or complaint.

Her vision cleared. A scrubbed-clean little parlour met her, lace under-curtains and brocaded green over-curtains, a small table with curved legs, and threadbare carpet worked with faded pink cabbage roses. The sunlight was tamed as it fell past the lace, and Gabriel the sheriff proceeded to try to drown her with the remainder of the water from a battered tin cup.

Cat spluttered in a most unladylike manner, and an exotic face topped with shining blue-black hair rose over the sheriff's shoulder. Sloe-eyed and exquisite, the Chinoise girl was in a faded homespun frock that did *nothing* for her, and the high rounded proudness of her belly suddenly made all the talk of widowhood and respectability much more comprehensible. Mrs. Granger hovered near a doorway cut in the white-plastered wall, her long jaw set with a mixture of what looked to be resignation and apprehension. Feathers stuck to the big woman's bonnet and her quaintly cut brown stuff dress; a completely inappropriate desire to laugh rose in Cat's throat and was ruthlessly quelled.

"Oh, my." She tried not to sound as horrified as she felt. "I am *ever* so sorry."

The sheriff's face had turned interestingly pale, but he snatched the tin cup away and didn't offer an explanation for tossing its contents over the lower half of her face. The Chinoise girl moved in with something like a handkerchief, dabbing at said face, and that was how Cat Barrowe began her stay in Damnation.

The regular card game upstairs at the Lucky Star was usually blessedly monosyllabic, except when there was news of a surpassingly interesting nature.

It was just Gabe's luck that the schoolteacher's arrival was extra-wondrous. It had replaced Jed Hatbush's fence as the preferred topic of gossip, at least.

Stooped Dr. Howard, in his dusty black, dealt with flicks

of his long knobbed fingers. "Little Tommy Hammis, the snot, charmed the chickens into the boardinghouse. And set that damn dog loose."

Paul Turnbull, silent owner of the Star, smoothed his oily moustache with one finger. He was a heavy man, stolid in his chair, but quick enough in a saloon fight. And he dealt with Tilson, who ran the girls and handled the day-to-day operations of the Star, well enough. At least, he kept Tils mostly in line, and that was a blessing. "Wish I'd seen Letitia Granger's face at that."

It was a sight, Gabe silently agreed, scooping up his cards. Not a bad hand. The whiskey burned the back of his throat, and he tried to forget the dazed look in Miss Barrowe's eyes. Big dark eyes, and surprisingly soft once you got past that prim proper barrier of hers. She probably thought they were a bunch of heathens out here, and she wasn't far wrong.

Russell Overton, the town's official chartermage, scooped up his cards with a grimace. Dapper in his favorite dark waistcoat, dark-curled and coffee-skinned, when he was sitting down you didn't notice he was bandy-legged and had a stiff way about him. You could, however, *always* tell he was aching for a fight, like most short men. "That woman could sour milk. So, what's she like, Gabe?"

"Granger? Still sour." He picked up his own cards, his charing-charm cool against his throat. The schoolmarm's was a confection of lacy silver and crystal; his own was a small brass disc with the orphanage's charter-symbol stamped on the back. There couldn't be a better illustration of just how much she didn't belong here.

Stop thinking about it. It won't do any good.

Dark eyes. Brown curls. Not like blonde, blue-eyed Emily.

Stop it.

"Not Granger, you buffoon." Russ chomped the end of his cigar as if it had personally offended him. Smoke hazed between the lamps. "The schoolmarm. From Boston, yes?"

"Far as I know." Gabe's mouth was dry. He took another jolt of whiskey, eyed the cards. The room was close and warm, the saloon pounding away underneath them with rollicking piano music and a surfroar of male voices. Every once in a while a sharp feminine exclamation, as the saloon frails and the dancing girls went about their business. It was, Gabe reflected, almost like a steamboat making its way upriver. The noise made it seem like the place was rocking.

"You're asking Gabe? You should know it's like pullin' nails." The doctor showed a slice of yellowed teeth as he examined his cards. "She *is* from Boston. Highly recommended, according to Edna Bricketts. Why a miss consented to come here, only God knows. She's a little thing too; I couldn't see much in the melee. Seemed a bit prim."

I am so very sorry, she had kept saying. *I don't wish to put you to trouble, Mr. Gabriel.* After nearly fainting, for God's sake. He was willing to bet it was a combination of hunger and nerves; someone should hold her down and feed her something fattening. Little and birdlike. And she acted like a pregnant Chinee girl was no great shakes, offering her hand to Li Ang and murmuring *How do you do* just as she had to him.

He laid his offerings down. "Two."

For a few minutes, each of them focused on the game. Doc took the round. "Well, I heard Joss Barker's already sayin' he's in love with her. So's Eb Kendall. Two."

"His wife won't like that. Two and a half."

"His wife don't like nothin'. Three, and call."

"You'd feel the same way, married to Eb. Look at this, two Dominions and a Pearl."

Gabe laid his cards down. He took the round, with the remaining Dominions, two Espada, and a Diamond. There was a good-natured round of cussing before he accepted the greasy cards and began to shuffle. "Who else?"

There was a brief silence. Maybe they didn't understand. So he added a few more words. "Barker, Kendall. Who else?"

More silence. He glanced up as his fingers sorted through the winnings, blinking a little, and Doc hurriedly looked away. Turnbull's mouth was open slightly; he shut it with a snap and became suddenly very interested in his own pile of seed corn.

"Nobody," Doc finally said. "You know how Barker is. Mouth two sizes too big for the rest of him."

Well, that's true. He searched for something else to say, a thing that might paper over the uncomfortable silence. "Last thing we need is some damn thing else happening to scare away the schoolmarm. Had a hard enough time finding one as it is, what with recent events."

Meaning the boy, and the claim in the hills, the cursed gold, and the incursions. Since closing the claim, though, the rash of walking dead had gone down quite a bit. Even if some damn fool sooner or later would be tempted by the rich veins lurking under the claim's black mouth. Or the bars, each stamped with that queer symbol, just waiting for the unwary to carry them home.

Another uncomfortable silence.

"Well, then." Doc watched Gabe's hands as the cards slid neatly into their appointed places, no motion wasted. "Bad mancy, to talk about women at a card game."

"Aw, Hell," Russ piped up. "What else we got to talk about?

Whiskey and donkeyfucking, and claims up in the hills."

"Not to mention undead. How's the charter holding, there, Russ?" Turnbull grinned, and Gabe sighed internally as the chartermage and the saloon owner glared at each other over the cards.

"Charter's holding up fine." For once, Russ heroically restrained himself. It was probably too good to last. "No howlings from the hills that I can tell. Gabe?"

And from there it was all cards and business. But Gabe caught the doctor looking at him speculatively, especially as the night got later and Paul and Russ started sniping at each other again. The night ended as it always did—Paul a little behind, Russ a little ahead, Doc and Gabe largely breaking even.

And the saloon below them rollicking on.

Chapter 3

It was such a welcome sensation to sink into a bed; Cat almost squeezed her eyes further shut, rolled over, and dove back into sleep. But sunlight gilded the window, and she heard a queer tuneless humming floating somewhere in the house.

I am here.

Where was Robbie? Had he seen her, in yesterday's comedy of errors? It wasn't like him not to join in a joke. She'd half-expected the banner to be *his* idea, of course. How it would have warmed his heart. If anyone loved a prank, 'twas Robert Barrowe-Browne.

Cat pried one eye open, wincing as her body protested even such a simple movement. The humming was actually quite pleasant, and she deduced it must be the Chinoise girl. Her charing was blessedly cool, and she rolled over, blinking at the plastered ceiling and stretching gingerly.

All things considered, she was quite well. Merely hungry enough to do shockingly unladylike damage to a platter of breakfast, and sore clear through.

The larger bedroom was at the end of a tiny hallway; the

smaller was tucked to the side and held a low corncrib and some few bits of fabric draped on the walls to provide a bit of cheer. Cat made a mental note to find at least a *chair* for the poor girl, and made her way downstairs on slippered feet. The slippers had been set neatly by her bedside, and yesterday's gown hung to air on a press, charmed neatly enough that no dust or feathers clung to its folds.

Which was a most welcome surprise.

Her nightgown made a low sweet sound as she tiptoed along the back hall, following the humming to its source. Which was, as she had suspected, the kitchen.

The Chinoise, her slim back betraying little of the proud belly in front, was humming as she scrubbed, elbow-deep in suds, at something. The kitchen, bright and airy, was full of a wondrous scent. There was a stripped-pine table, two chairs, a steaming kettle, and a washtub to the side. The stove, its heat enclosed in an envelope-charm, spun a fresh globe of golden glow aside; the globe, drifting through the kitchen, bumbled merrily out the open top half of a door leading to a porch and a short breezeway. It bobbed along, the mancy on it crackling, and would eventually rise into the sky, safely dissipating away from anything flammable. 'Twas an elegant bit of work, and a relief. At least the house would not burn down around them.

It was a great relief that charterstones and charings would make mancy work reliably even if one was not properly native-born. The great influx of those from other countries seeking a better life, or merely drudgery in a new environ, could practice such mancy as was native to them within charterstone's bounds. After the Provinces War, the discovery of gold in certain wasted places and the determination to bring the railroad to every corner of the New World had brought all manner of folk to these shores.

It was even quite *quite* to have an exotic as a servant, preferably indentured. The Barrowe-Brownes had not, preferring solid German and French maids, but often her father had spoke of perhaps engaging a Lascar as a manservant, merely to give her mother the vapours.

The Chinoise girl raised a dripping hand, and soap bubbles drifted free into the breezy kitchen. It was a simple charm, meant to amuse, and Cat answered before she could help herself. Her own fingers tingled, and the mancy slid free—light glinting between the bubbles, striking rainbows glittering-sharp as diamonds.

Cat's Practicality was in light; Robbie's had been…well, *otherwise*. Light was a very acceptable Practicality in a young lady, indeed, and the Chinoise girl's Practicality was plain as the bubbles drifted on the swirls and eddies of clear air. For a moment the two charm-streams intermingled, light and water a happy marriage—not like air and fire, or fire and water, though true fire Practicalities were rare, and a good thing too. Metal and earth Practicalities were common, and wood was eminently respectable for a gentleman but *not* a young lady. A stone Practicality was considered rather boorish, for it meant one could pass paste jewels for real; a mechanical one was almost as bad as being in trade. New Practicalities shaped themselves as Science and mancy moved forward.

Soon, there might even be Disciplines, as in Englene and the Continent.

The bubbles popped, the rainbows drained away, and Cat found herself facing a pale, heavily pregnant Chinoise girl in a dun frock, who refused to quite meet her nominal employer's gaze.

In short order there was breakfast on the table—Cat gave it

to be understood that she wished to eat here instead of in the postage-stamp parlour, and perhaps the girl looked relieved? With a modicum of gesturing and facial expressions, Cat asked if the girl had eaten breakfast yet; receiving a small shake of the sleek dark head, she marched to the cupboard with what she fancied was great determination, fetched a second plate and cup of thick, durable earthcraft, and set it down on the small table as well.

In any event, Cat tucked in with a will, and there was even strong fragrant tea.

Their first breakfast passed in companionable silence, and the Chinoise girl looked rather less pale and peaked by the end of it. Cat settled back with a cup of tea—the cup was actually porcelain, and painted with blue flowers, very fine save for its lack of matching saucer—while the girl collected the dishes and returned to her washing.

So far the morning had proven very satisfactory indeed. The breeze was fresh and smelled of sage, fragrant tea and bacon aromas filled the kitchen, and Cat was beginning to feel almost *quite* again when a shadow fell across the back step.

The Chinoise girl whirled, inhaling sharply. Her little hand flashed out, grabbed a knife that looked more fit for repelling pirate boarders than cooking, and hissed something in her native tongue. Cat let out a pale shriek and started, almost dropping her cup, and Jack Gabriel peered over the half-door, reaching up to his hatbrim. His hazel eyes were bright and wide, and he ducked a glowing ball of heat drawn from the stove.

"For God's sake, Li Ang, put that away. Figgered I'd—well, hello, ma'am. Pleased to see you looking better."

Heat raced furiously up Cat's cheeks. "*Sir!* I am not even *dressed!* Were you never taught to knock before entering a house?"

"I did. Don't reckon you heard me." He took this in, and actually, of all things, *smiled*. "That thing you're wearing could qualify as a winding-sheet, miss. *Avert*," he muttered, right away, flicking his hat to brush away bad mancy or ill-luck. "Beg pardon, ma'am. I'll wait in the parlour."

Cat, her heart pounding, swallowed a most unladylike urge to shrill like a harridan. Her mother would know exactly what to say to this man to cut him to size. "Very well," she managed stiffly. "Perhaps you would care for a cup of tea, while I arrange myself."

He shrugged, leaning lazily on the half-door. Li Ang had gone back to washing, and Cat suddenly noticed the girl's ankles were swollen. Definitely a chair, and some provision must be made for the baby as well.

"I prefer coffee, but thank you kindly. I'll wait."

"I was unaware I had an engagement today," she floundered.

"Thought you might like to see the schoolhouse. But I can understand if you'd rather rest, ma'am. Yesterday was prob'ly enough to turn a lady's nerves to ribbons."

What a gruesome image. Thank you, sir. "I am made of sterner stuff than most, sir." Why was she possessed of the sudden feeling that she was coming off very badly in this conversation? "Good morning."

"Morning." He didn't say another word as she retreated, crimson-cheeked and acutely aware she was practically *barefoot*. Her bare ankles were brazenly revealed. And she was in a *nightgown*, of all things, in the kitchen with a servant.

And the day had been going so well.

Li Ang offered him two biscuits and some leftover bacon on a plate; he took it, so as to be mannerly. Besides, his breakfast had been bolted before dawn, and now he couldn't even remember what he'd shoveled in before heading out to ride the charter-circuit with a sore-headed Russell Overton. "How you feelin'?"

She shrugged. She understood far more Englene than she could speak. Not much escaped those dark eyes of hers, either. She returned to her work, moving slowly, and Jack sighed, leaning against the door while he reflectively chewed on the bacon. He gave it a few minutes' worth of silence, to let her get comfortable.

And also to let himself think about the schoolmarm. Bare-ankled and lost in a nightgown that looked big enough to swallow two or three of her, with her dark hair anyhow and falling out of its braid. He hadn't seen a woman like that in a few years.

Not that it would help him to think about it. He'd spent years not thinking about women at all, and more years trying to forget one particular woman.

It never got easier.

"Any trouble?" he finally persisted, after giving her a decent time to compose her nerves.

Li Ang looked into the washsink like it held gold dust, shook her head. The long braid of glossy black hair bumped her back. She rinsed a plate, then half-turned, pointed at the hallway, and nodded once, decidedly. "Good," she said, in a high, thin, piping child's voice. She thought for a moment, finding the word in her mental storehouse. "Good charm." Another nod. "Good sense."

Well, that was as close to an unqualified vote of confidence he'd ever heard Li Ang utter. He felt the need to qualify it himself, so she wouldn't think he was...what was he? "Bit prim, that miss." *Kind enough, though, and didn't lose her head in*

Hammis's parlour. "You! Take him outside." Least she's practical.

Made of sterner stuff, eh? Well, we'll see. Been too quiet around here. May be another attack soon. "Keep the doors bolted," he finally added, taking a bite of biscuit. She made them doughy, did Li Ang. For all that, they were food, and he didn't want her to feel poorly. He'd refused to eat her cooking once, and her face had crinkled like she might cry. He still felt a mite guilty over that. "Darkmoon comin' up."

Li Ang shrugged and brought him a tin cup of water, which he swilled gratefully. He wished for some coffee, but Miss Barrowe hadn't precisely offered, and Li Ang was probably mad at him for scaring the bejesus out of her. That knife had come within a hair of being flung, and he had a healthy respect for her aim. "Hate to scare her away," he added, mostly because he suspected the Chinoise girl liked having him make some noise so she could be sure he wasn't sneaking. "Hard enough gettin' a schoolmarm out here, and the young'uns is right savages."

Li Ang made some remark in her native tongue. She could have been calling him a dogfaced monkeylicker, for all he knew; all Chinois sounded the same to him. But at least she said it nicely enough.

"I don't worry so much about little Hammis or some of the othern. It's the older ones." He popped the last bit of biscuit in his mouth. "Like Tommy Kendall, for example. Or that Browis boy. Like to send her home in a sobbing heap. Maybe I should have a quiet word, you think?"

Li Ang shrugged and made another short comment. Jack sighed, scratching at his forehead. "Well, they're likely to take that nose in the air as a challenge. Quiet word might sort it out, or might make 'em nastier. God*damn*, Li Ang, why do I always end up talking around you?"

"Lo-nu-lee," she half-sang as she charmed the water in the washsink afresh, sparks of mancy crackling. "Jack is lonely."

Well, shit. I knew that. His mouth pulled sourly against itself, and he balanced the plate and cup on the door. *I should just shut up while I can.*

It took the schoolmarm a damnably long time to get ready, and his mood didn't grow any brighter. At least he refrained from opening his fool mouth anymore, and Li Ang collected his plate with a dark look and shuffled away.

By the time he heard a light step in the hall, he was half-ready to tell the Boston miss something had come up and he wasn't available to squire her around all damn day. His mouth was dry and he'd already wiped his hands on his pants, cursing himself as the bacon grease made itself felt.

She looked cool and imperturbable in some sort of flowered dress, a pale ruffled parasol at her side and her hat perched smartly on brown curls. As if she was about to go stepping out on a Boston street instead of sitting in a dusty wagon with him, going to look at a one-room schoolhouse that was probably as fine as a chicken coop to her delicate sensibilities.

"Good morning, Mr. Gabriel." She was even wearing *gloves*, for God's sake. She offered her hand as if she'd never met him before. "I must apologize for my previous disarray. Shall we?"

His brain froze like a hunted rabbit and his mouth decided to mumble. "No trouble." Under the gloves her fingers were slim and fragile.

She don't belong here. He swallowed, dryly, and her dark eyes mocked him for being dirty and shapeless. Jack Gabriel reclaimed his hand, jammed his hat back on his head, and mumbled something else.

It didn't figure to be a pleasant afternoon.

Chapter 4

*M*iss Bowdler's Book of Charms For Frontier Living had been quite adequate so far, but *Miss Bowdler's Book For Schoolteachers* had not prepared her for a ramshackle barn of a building still smelling of raw wood probably hauled from the distant, frowning mountains with a tiny outhouse tucked behind it like a secret. It had a bell, certainly, and a very new slate board. Fine gritty sand drifting over the floor, riding drafts that bore a striking resemblance to a maelstrom. The long rickety seats looked decidedly uncomfortable, and the desks sloped a bit. A rack of pegs for coats and the like, a boot-scraper near the door, a pot-bellied stove that would perhaps be beyond her powers to keep lit, and precious few windows added to the general air of "barn."

But she essayed a bright smile. "This will do very well, I think. Was it much trouble to build?"

He gave her a look that suggested she was perhaps a trifle soft in the head. "Got to build everything, out here."

Well, of course. Slightly irritated, she forced her fingers to unclench. "So it *was* trouble." Ill-tempered of her, of course, but she had the idea manners were perhaps missing in this quarter of the country. Or if not, they were certainly lost on this *inhabitant* of said quarter. "I apologize."

"Didn't mean that, ma'am. Just meant, we were afraid you'd be offended. Not quite what a Boston miss might be used to."

There are slums in our fair city, sir, that would put this to shame. Though she had never gone a-treading them. It was not the thing for a young lady; but Robbie had brought back blood-curdling stories more than once.

In the absence of a clear trail to Robbie's whereabouts, the least she could do was attempt the employment she had pursued and was expected of her.

Perhaps a peace offering to this uneasy man would not go amiss. "It seems solid enough. I am greatly heartened."

"Thank you kindly."

An uncomfortable silence fell. How had she set herself wrong with him? If he disliked her so thoroughly, why had he elected himself to show her this place? Mrs. Granger would have been a far better choice, being on the Committee of Public Works as she was, and a matron Quite Respectable to boot.

Abruptly, Cat realized she was alone with a man, miles from civilization, and she had not even asked for a chaperone. How forward did she appear? She took a few nervous steps away, her skirts making a low sweet sound, and a stream of golden sand creaked from the rafters as the wind shifted.

"Damn dust," he muttered, swinging his hat. "Pardon, ma'am. It'll be less thick in here after the rains. Roof's sound, at least, and some of us will come out and stopper up any drafty bits before winter gets bad. We was fair excited about your arrival."

Oh, good heavens, rain. If God is merciful, I might not be here at the advent of such an event. She tried another bright smile. "I am glad to have been anticipated. Now that I have some idea of the facilities, shall we—"

"I reckon I might need a dipperful. Well's out front, ma'am. I'll be back." And he vanished out the front door with long swinging strides, dark hair askew and tinged with the ever-present golden grit.

Well, do as you please, sir, as long as you leave me in peace. She shook her head, then eyed the sorry collection of long desk-boards. Slates and chalk, certainly. Rubbing-cloths were in the desk. She spied a familiar shape under a fall of oilcloth and held her breath, twitching the covering aside with two gloved fingers and finding a very sorry-looking upright piano, twanging discordantly as she touched a yellowed key. Well, a tune-charmer could not be that difficult to find even here in the wilderness; if all else failed…well, she had played worse. It might do to teach some of the more promising students a little refinement.

Though they probably needed refinement here about as much as Cat needed the hair ribbons she'd brought. She had not thought much beyond gaining the town; she had expected Robbie to show his face long before now.

Well, I am possessed of a small independence, and this is not Boston. It is a start. She sighed, smoothing the covering over the wrecked hulk of the piano. How had it been hauled so far out West? she wondered. Shuttled on the railway, or bumping along on some prairie schooner, finally fetching up here? Had it been sent by dirigible from abroad, perhaps, and washed up in this inhospitable place? Flotsam of a sort, just as she may well turn out to be?

How on earth *would* she find Robbie? Even here at the edge of civilization a woman did not go wandering about a town looking for a man. Perhaps she might engage someone to take a message to him—but his last missives had been rather striking in their insistence on secrecy and that Cat must not, under any circumstances, enquire openly about him.

It was a puzzle, and one Miss Bowdler's books could not help her solve.

A faint scratching caught her attention. She frowned, glancing about. The entire barnlike structure was dead quiet, and she was abruptly conscious, again, of being miles away from anything even resembling civilization.

The back door. It rattled slightly. Perhaps Mr. Gabriel? The well was at the front of the building, a ramshackle affair but one she suspected was a mark of pride, just like the repaired gate at her own dwelling. Cat swung her closed parasol, decidedly, as she made for the back door between rows of mismatched board-desks. It was bad form to carry it inside; but there was no stand, and she did not wish it to become stained.

The door rattled again, groaning, and a fresh flurry of scratching filled the uncanny quiet. Was it an animal? Or perhaps Mr. Gabriel was playing some manner of foolish prank, seeing if the Boston miss could be frightened?

Cat's chin rose. *Robbie could hoax much better than this, sir.* The lock was a pin-and-hasp, sparking with a charter-charm; her charing, tucked under her dress, warmed dangerously. So, it was a prank involving mancy, was it?

Oh, sir, you have chosen the wrong victim. She drew the pin, her left hand closing about the knob, the parasol dangling from its strap. She jerked the door in, a small lightning-crackle charm fizzing on her fingers, for she had often dissuaded Robbie by flinging light directly at his eyes—

The rotting corpse, its jaw soundlessly working and grave-dirt sluicing from its jerking arms and legs, plowed straight through the door, its collapsed eyes runneling down its cheeks in strings of gushing decay, sparks of diseased foxfire mancy glowing in the empty holes.

She screamed once, a sharp curlew-cry that he might've taken for a girl seeing a rat if not for its ragged edge of sheer terror. Gabe couldn't remember how he got up the stairs and into the schoolhouse; he didn't even remember drawing his gun.

What he remembered ever after was the sight of Miss Barrowe, her parasol cracked clean in half from smashing at the head of an ambulatory corpse, deadly silent as she scrabbled back on her hands, her feet caught in her skirts and breath gone, her face white. And the corpse, of course, chewing on air emptily, greedily, making a rusty noise as its drying tendons struggled to work. Some of them were right quick bastards and juicy, too, but this one had been dead awhile, and his first shot near took its head clean off. It folded down in a noisome splatter, and Miss Barrowe had gained her feet with desperate, terrified almost-grace. She kept blundering back, knocking into the edges of the long three- and four-person desks on each side, and if he didn't catch her she would probably do herself an injury.

Are there any more? Dammit, Russ, the borders were solid this morning!

"*Barrowe!*" he barked, but she didn't respond, just kept going. So it was up to him to move, and she nearly bowled him over with hysterical strength. The impact jolted a hitching little cry out of her; she whooped in a breath and was fixing to scream again. He clapped his left hand over her mouth, the gun tracking the flopping corpse on the floor. Now he could smell it, dry rot and damp decay, a body left in the desert for a little while.

Someone had fallen to misadventure or murder, been buried unconsecrated, and the wild magic had seeped in to give it a twisted semblance of life.

Its naked heels drummed the raw floorboards, and Miss Barrowe tried struggling. She was probably half-mad with fear.

He didn't blame her.

"It's all right." He wished he sounded more soothing. "Ma'am, just settle down. I'm here, there ain't no need for fuss."

Amazingly, that took some of the fight out of her. She froze, her ribs heaving with breaths as light and rapid as a hummingbird's wings. Her lips moved slightly against his work-hardened palm, and he told himself to ignore it while he eyed the open door, its hinges creaking slightly as the wind teased at the slab of wood. It had been locked with a charm-pin—what the hell had happened?

Well, first things first. "Now," he said quietly, "you're perfectly safe, Miss Barrowe, I ain't about to let no creatures gnaw our schoolmarm. You can rely on that. Nod if you hear me."

She did nod, precisely once. Her breath was a hot spot in his palm, her lips still moving soundlessly. There was a scorch to the right of the door, still crawling with mancy—she must have thrown something at the corpse. Looked like her aim was put off by the thing busting through the door.

That was interesting. So she had a full-blown Practicality, did she? She could have found a decent living in one of the cities back East; why on earth would a girl with a skill like that want to come *here*?

That's a riddle for another day. "Now, I'm gonna take my hand away, and you can faint if you want, or whatever it is ladies do in this situation. But you can't go screamin' or runnin', because that will just complicate things. Nod if you agree."

Another nod. Well. He'd see if she was lying. He peeled his fingers away from her mouth, conscious of the fearsweat on his nape and the small of his back, the smell of horse and exertion that clung to every man out here. She smelled of rosewater and fresh air, sunlight and clean linen and the flesh of a clean healthy woman. Her hat was askew, and she reached up with trembling fingers, her broken parasol dangling sadly from a thin leather loop around her wrist. Her fingers moved gracefully, settling her hat, and she took one step to the side. Gabe twitched, but true to her word, she didn't run or scream. She simply swallowed very hard, lifting her chin, and that spark was back in her dark eyes.

"Good." He almost said *good girl*, as if she were a frightened horse needing soothing, stopped himself just in time. "Did you open the door?"

"I th-thought it was a p-prank." She sounded steady enough, though her color was two shades whiter than a bleached sheet. "M-my b-brother..."

So you had a brother. Maybe you'll take to the little demons we've got for children out here. He waited, but she said nothing else. He cleared his throat, and she jumped nervously. He half-turned, his back to her as soon as he judged she was unlikely to bolt, and eyed both open doors. "You heard something?"

"S-scratching." Another audible swallow. The corpse ceased its jerking, but you could never tell with wanderers like this. Even with half their head gone, they were still dangerous. "R-rattling the door."

That's interesting, too. "Charter's still solid," he muttered, more because he fancied she needed another voice to steady herself than out of any real need to say it out loud. "Was this morning, I rode the circuit myself. This place was cleaned three times before we laid the foundation. Huh."

"If you are s-suggesting *I*—"

Well, she was brighter *and* braver than he gave her credit for. "You ain't got no bad mancy on you, sweetheart." *I'd smell the twisting a mile away. It's what I do, curse me and all.* He pushed his hat farther up on his forehead, wished he could just decide which one of the two doors was the worse idea. If the corpse had gotten its teeth into her, he would have had to put her down, no matter if she had enough of a Practicality to shield her from the worst effects. "Just stay still a minute while I—"

"Sir." Dangerously calm. "You shall address me as *Miss Barrowe*, thank you."

Oh, for the love of… His hand twitched. The gun spoke again, deafening, and the shadow in the door didn't duck. *That's a bad sign.* "Stay *here*." He launched himself for the back door, worn bootheels cracking against the boards, clearing a desk in a leap he was faintly amazed to think about later, and out into the bath of dusthaze and glare that was a Damnation afternoon full of the walking dead.

Chapter 5

Crunches. Howls. Terrible sounds, and gunshots, spitting crackling mancy and thuds against the walls. Cat stood locked in place, trembling, staring at the body on the floor, her gloved fingers working against each other. *Walking dead. Here. Oh, God.*

The graveyards were well-policed in Boston, and bodies properly handled. Still, sometimes the more amenable of the wandering dead were set to work—supervised, of course, but used for brute and drudge tasks. There was a Society for Liberation of the Deceased, but Cat's mother had always sniffed at such a thing. *Liberation indeed*, she would say. *Next they shall be wanting franchise.* And her father would chime in. *Though how that would differ from the usual ballot-box stuffing, I cannot tell. Come, Frances, speak of something less unpleasant.*

She had watched as they put the true-iron nails in her father's palms, but she could not bear to see such an operation performed on her mother. Nor could she bear to witness the other appurtenances of death—the mouthful of consecrated salt, the branding of dead flesh with charter-symbols, the sealing of the casques. Thankfully, the Barrowe-Browne name, not to mention the estate's copious funding, meant her parents would not be set to drudgery but instead locked safely in leaden coffins inside a stone crypt, with chartermages making certain of their quiet, mouldering rest.

Oh, for heaven's sake, do not think on that!

Cat squeezed her eyes shut, but the darkness made the sounds worse. So she opened them wide, and counted dust motes in the air. Why she did not find a spot more conducive to cowering and hiding was beyond her, unless it was the sheriff's queer certainty.

Stay here.

Said very decisively, the gun smoking in his hand, then he had been gone, moving faster than she could credit.

If this was a prank, it was a very good one. The body on the floor was certainly none too fresh. Would someone cart a corpse all this way, and charm it, too—a dangerous occupation, to be sure—all for the sake of a laugh? Not even Robbie would go so far.

Though there had been the episode with the frogs, long ago in their childhood. And their dry-rusty dead-throat croaking. Robbie's Practicality was just barely acceptable in Society, and their father had more than once reminded him *never* to allow it rein outside the house. Especially after the poor frogs, the nursery full of the stink and…

Oh, I wish I had not thought of that.

A shadow filled the doorway. She had to swallow a scream, but it was merely Mr. Jack Gabriel, hat clamped on his dark head, his eyes narrowed and his hands occupied in reloading his pistol with quick, habitual movements. She supposed he must do so often, to be so cavalier during the operation.

"You can move now," he said, mildly. "Don't think there's more, but we should step lively back closer to town."

"Is this…" She had to cough to clear her throat. "Is this *normal*, sir? I cannot be expected to teach if—"

"Oh, no, it's not normal at all, ma'am." His eyes had darkened from their hazel, and his gaze was disturbingly direct. "Matter of fact, it's downright unnatural, and I intend to get to the bottom of it. You won't be setting foot out here, teaching or no teaching, until I'm sure it's safe."

Well. That's very kind of you, certainly. "That is a decided relief," she managed, faintly. "I am sorry for the trouble."

"No trouble at all, ma'am. You've a good head on your shoulders." A high blush of color—exertion or fear, who knew—ran along his high, wide cheekbones.

For a single lunatic instant she thought he was about to laugh and tell her it *had* all been a prank, and she was, in Robbie's terms, a blest good sport. But his mouth was drawn tight, he was covered in dust, and there was a splatter of something dark and viscous down one trouser leg.

"Thank you." She tried not to sound prim, probably failed utterly. And who wouldn't sound a little faint and withered after this manner of excitement? "I don't suppose you, ah, knew the…the deceased?"

He actually looked startled, his gaze dropping like a boy caught with his fingers in a stolen pie. "Can't say as I looked to recognize them, ma'am."

"Oh." She found the trembling in her legs would not quite recede. Her throat was distressingly dry. "I suppose you must have been…yes. Busy."

"Very. You're pale."

I feel rather pale, thank you. "I shall do well enough." She took an experimental step, and congratulated herself when she did not stagger. "Returning to town does seem the safest route. Shall we?"

There was a dewing of blood on his stubbled cheek. Where was it from? "Yes ma'am."

Cat decided she did *not* wish to know precisely what the stains on him were from, and set off for the rectangle of dusty sunlight that marked the front door, her bootheels making crisp little clicking noises. The sheriff caught her arm, his grimy fingers oddly gentle.

"Just a moment, Miss Barrowe. I'll be locking the back door, and then you'll let me go through that'un first."

Oh. "Yes. Of course." *Please let's not dally.*

"Just you stay still and don't faint. Don't want to have to carry you over my shoulder." He paused, still gazing at her in that incredibly *odd* manner. "Would be right undignified."

"That it would." She clasped her gloved hands, her heart in her throat and pounding so hard she rather thought a vessel might burst and save the undead the trouble of laying her flat.

What a charmingly gruesome idea. Use that organ of Sensibility you so pride yourself upon, Cat. Behave properly.

The trouble was, even Miss Bowdler's books, marvelous as they were, had nothing even *remotely* covering this situation. She decided this fell under Extraordinary Occurrences, and checked her hat. An Extraordinary Occurrence meant that one must take care of one's person to the proper degree, and simply avoid making the situation *worse*.

Her gloves were in good order, though her parasol was completely ruined. Her dress seemed to have suffered precious few ill effects from scurrying across the floor. A few traces of sawdust, that was all.

She found the sheriff still staring. "Sir." It was her mother's *There Is Much To Be Done* tone, used whenever something had gone quite wrong and it was Duty and Obligation both to set it right, and it was *wonderfully* bracing. "Do let's be on our way."

At least he stopped staring at her. "Yes ma'am." Another touch to the brim of his hat—and by God, *must* he wear it inside? It was insufferable.

He approached the body cautiously, grabbed it by the scruff of its rotting shirt, and hauled it outside through the back door. It went into the sunshine with a thump that unseated Cat's stomach, and despite his shouted warning, she fled the barnlike schoolhouse. She leaned over the porch stair railing, and she retched until nothing but bile could be produced.

He wished the wagon wouldn't jolt so much. She was paper-pale, trembling, and had lost damn near everything she'd probably ever *thought* of eating. She clutched at the broken stick of the parasol like a drowning woman holding on to driftwood. Damp with sweat, a few stray strands of her hair had come free, and now they lay plastered to her fair flawless skin. He wished, too, that he could say something comforting, but he settled for hurrying the horse as much as he dared.

He'd lied, of course. There hadn't been just a few undead. He'd stopped counting at a half-dozen, and there was no way a single man could put down that many.

Not if he was normal. And Jack Gabriel had no intention of letting anyone think he was otherwise. Not only would it cause undue fuss among the townsfolk, but it might also reach certain quarters.

The Order did not often give up its own, and he suspected they would be right glad to know his whereabouts.

Her charing-charm glittered uneasily. His own was ice cold, and it should have warned him long before the undead came close enough to sense a living heartbeat. Which was...troubling.

Not just troubling. It was downright terrifying, and he was man enough to admit as much.

Had it happened, then? Had he lost his baptism? Did grace no longer answer him?

Loss of faith was one thing. Loss of grace was quite another.

She swayed again as the wagon jolted, her shoulder bumping his. Did a small sound escape her? He racked his brains, trying to think of something calming to say. Or should he just keep his fool mouth shut?

"Mr. Gabriel?" A colorless little ghost of a voice. Did she need to heave again? It was unlikely she had anything left in her. And she was such a bitty thing.

"Yes ma'am." The reins were steady. He stared ahead, most of his attention taken up with flickers in his peripheral vision. If there were more of them, they would cluster instead of attacking one by one, and that was a prospect to give anyone the chills.

Even a man who had nothing to lose.

They won't get you. He decided it wouldn't be comforting at all to say that to her, and meant to keep his lip buttoned tightly.

"Thank you. For saving my life." She stared straight ahead as well. The tiny veil attached to her hat was slightly torn, waving in the fitful breeze. The heat of the day shimmered down the track, and the good clean pungency of sage filled his nose.

It was a relief. At least he didn't smell like walking corpse.

"My pleasure, ma'am." As soon as the words left his mouth he could have cussed himself sideways. He could have said, *It weren't nothin'*, or even, *You're welcome.* But no. *My pleasure?* Really?

They'd be lucky if she wasn't on the next coach to the train station in Poscola Flats, retreating to Boston. And that thought wasn't pleasant, if only because of how that bat Granger would complain, and the rest of the fool Committee of old biddies as well.

No, it wouldn't be pleasant at all.

His stupid mouth opened right back up. "What I mean to say, it's no trouble. No trouble at all. Wasn't about to let no corpses get their teeth in our schoolmarm."

Well. That was from bad to worse. Plus, he noticed as he glanced down, there was muck on his pants from the last corpse he'd put down, steel blurring into its throat and its head blasted off with a bullet and a muttered Word. It was rubbing against her pretty skirt, and there was nothing he could do about it.

Oh, hell.

"I am very grateful." Her gloved fingers interlaced, pulled *hard* against each other, and she did not wait for him to help her down when the wagon halted outside her trim little cottage. Instead, she hopped down, almost catching her dress in her hurry, and was gone inside the house before he could say *boo*.

Not that he'd want to say boo. Or anything else. Dull heat stained Gabe's cheeks, and he swallowed several times before turning his attention to the next problem presenting itself.

Which was getting the horse squared away, and then finding out just what in hell the walking dead were doing inside the town charter.

He palmed the workroom door open, and Russ jumped about a foot. The mancy he was working spit dull red sparks, and Gabe's charing-charm scorched for a brief second. He ignored it—anything Russ was likely to fling could be countered handily. "Russell Overton, what the hell?"

"What the *hell* the hell?" Russ spluttered. His office was dark, heavy shades pulled in his inner workroom because, like most professional mancers, he preferred the gloom where he could see the sparks. His shirtsleeves, rolled up, showed the pale twisting veined scars of a professional chartermage, raised and ropy on coffee-cream skin dusted with sparse coarse hair.

Even his arms were bandy and tense. Jack was struck with the idea that perhaps the man's color had made him accustomed to taking fighting the world as a given, much as Jack's natural stubbornness had.

Such thoughts occurred to a man out West, he supposed. "Just got jumped by the walkin' dead, Russ. Charter was solid this morning; what the *hell*?"

Russ's palms clapped together, shorting the mancy. It died in a cascade of heatless iridescence, and he was already rolling his sleeves down and reaching for his coat. "Where?"

At least the man didn't drag his feet. "The schoolhouse. They're not rising again, but we need to find the breach. God *damn* it, Russ."

"There *is* no breach. We rode this morning." Russ's eyes closed, briefly. "All the compass markers are in place. I can feel them. Gabe..." He licked his lips, a quick nervous flicker of a dry-leaf tongue. "The schoolhouse, you said. Did any of them—"

"She's safe." Gabe folded his arms, glaring. "Goddamn good thing *I* was there, instead of a passel of kids."

Russ paled further at the thought. It *was* nightmarish, and Gabe normally wouldn't have said such a thing. But *damn* it, if that first undead had sunk its teeth into Miss Barrowe...

Well, it didn't bear thinking of. And he didn't like the sinking, empty sensation in his gut when he thought about it. So he wouldn't, would he? There were plenty of other things to think about at the moment.

He could ignore that sinking sensation. Sure he could.

Russ grabbed his gunbelt, hung over a sturdy wooden chair. Papers stirred on a stray breeze, ruffling as the mancy-laden atmosphere twitched inside the narrow office at Gabe's back, full of shelves of bits and herbs and other things, charmer's books stacked haphazardly on a taboret near the desk. He buckled the belt with quick habitual movements. "I meant to ask if any of them looked familiar."

Oh, for the love of… He could have cheerfully throttled the man. "I didn't stop to ask their names. But no, none of 'em looked familiar. Bunch of strangers around here anyway."

"Gabe." Russ halted, his black Gladstone clutched in one hand. His hat was askew, and his blue eyes were shadowed. "What if it's…*that?*"

A cool fingertip touched Gabe's nape. "We sealed that claim up solid. And nobody's been showing up with marked bars recently. Dust and nuggets, but no bars."

"But what if—"

"*It's* gone. And that stupid kid, too." *What was his name? Face like a blank slate, you could forget it in a heartbeat.* The eyes had just slid right over him, and sometimes Gabe wondered if it was a type of mancy that had made the kid so forgettable.

"Well, the markers are all in place, and the charterstone's solid." Russ shook his head, straightened his hat. "Let's go."

Gabe held the door. Russ stamped, his bow-legged gait just like a clockwork toy's. He was through the office and out onto the porch in a heartbeat.

Sweeping the workroom door closed, the sheriff had to shake

his head, thinking of Miss Barrowe's wide dark eyes, swimming with tears and terror. The unsteady feeling hit him again, like a fist to the gut.

Then he remembered the kid's name.

"Robert Browne." He actually said it out loud, but Russ was outside already and didn't hear. It was a damn good thing, too.

Because a chartermage wouldn't take kindly to having a dead man's name breathed in his office. Jack Gabriel shook his head, ran his fingers over the butt of a gun, and hurried to catch up.

Chapter 6

Cat stared at her front door. She had her gloves on, and carried her second-best parasol, the one with fringe that quivered as she walked. Her yellow silk was quite cheerful, and had the not-inconsiderable advantage of being almost comfortable. Her hair was perfection itself, and she had clasped her mother's pearls about her neck. Her boots were buttoned firmly, and there was just a breath of rosewater remaining from her *toilette*.

But there was the front door, and here she stood, unwilling to open it.

"Ridiculous," she muttered. "You're being ridiculous." *How Robbie would laugh.*

But that was just it. No Robbie. Her plans had come to fruition; she was here, hundreds of miles from civilization, and she had not the faintest clue of how to go about *finding* him. She had thought it a dead certainty he would find *her*.

If he had moved on…but how likely was that, given what he'd written? No, there was another possibility, one she did not wish to think upon, but which must be faced nonetheless.

Foul play.

And here she stood, stupid as a toadstool, afraid to open her front door because of an irruption of undead. Quite reasonable, actually, given what a bite could do to one even if one had enough mancy to inoculate oneself against the worst effects. But there had been no harm done, because of Mr. Gabriel.

Who had called at the back door during breakfast, *again*, to express his hope that she was not *too* upset by recent events. She had reassured him with brittle calm that she did not intend to return to Boston with her tail tucked like a cur's just yet. Maddeningly, the man had simply smiled, tipped his hat, and vanished.

Li Ang had said something in her native tongue that sounded like a curse, and Cat was forced to agree. The man was a nuisance, and entirely too sharp under that slow, sleepy drawl of his. She was even beginning to believe him of a quality, though he sought to hide it.

Yet he had been practical and helpful enough, when the situation required.

Catherine, you are being worse than ridiculous. You are, as a matter of fact, being a coward.

Which, for a Barrowe-Browne, could not be borne. That forced her to move another three steps toward the door. From the kitchen came the sound of splashing water and Li Ang's odd atonal humming. The Chinoise girl was quiet, efficient, and discreet; there would be no trouble there.

You are being a coward—and Robbie needs you. If he has met with foul play, you are his only hope.

So much of life was merely doing what one was required to. It smoothed the way wonderfully to have no *choice*.

Another two steps, and her gloved hand played with the locks. The knob turned smoothly, easily, and a fresh morning breeze filled the hall behind her. Her reticule dangled. Her eyes opened, cautiously, and she saw the sun-drenched garden. It would, in all likelihood, be another incredibly, mind-numbingly hot day. She would have to be home before luncheon.

Then it's best to get started, isn't it? If the undead were in the town streets there would be more noise, one fancies.

While eminently logical, the thought was not as comforting as it could have been.

Chin raised, eyes flashing, palms sweating, and her dress rustling, Cat stepped over her threshold.

Damnation. A main street with others branching away at right angles, buildings sprawled in the dust and the heat, blowsy and blinking. Horses clopping along; men lounging in doorways, raising their hats automatically when the infrequent woman passed them. The men moved slowly in the heat; ragged children darted between hooves and ran before carts, and the few women in homespun or dark drab walked with chin-high determination.

In her bright yellow, Cat stood out far more than she'd thought possible. The men hurried to raise their hats, and she was greeted on all sides, hailed with an intensity that was a touch embarrassing. Had they never seen a schoolteacher before? Of course, she was a bright bird in a sea of dusty pigeons, and she would have been writhing with embarrassment had she not been so occupied in making polite gestures. Her mother's Greet the Peasants smile had rarely been so useful.

She had not passed more than a few sun-bleached building fronts before Mr. Gabriel appeared, falling into step beside her with a tip of his hat. "Ma'am."

"Mr. Gabriel." She stared straight ahead. "You look well."

"You haven't looked at me enough to see, Miss Barrowe. But yes, I'm well. Pleasure to see you out and about."

My, isn't he chatty this morning. "Thank you."

"It ain't much, but it strikes me you might want a guide. To show you, that is. Around town."

If this were a civilized town, I could perhaps purchase a street map. Or hire a carriage, or…dear God, do you really think me so dim I cannot find my way about this collection of dingy little alleys? "A very kind offer."

"Not to presume, but…it could be risky around here. For a woman."

Indeed? "More hazardous than the walking dead?" She sounded archly amused, and congratulated herself upon as much.

He had the grace to cough slightly. "There's some what might be worse."

What an unprepossessing little phrase. Was it even grammatical? "I beg your pardon?"

"Well, look. You passed words with Tils, right? Short little man in a bowler hat, moustaches he waxes up? Red flannel?"

She frowned slightly, her parasol swaying. None of the other women here carried them, and she was beginning to feel a trifle ridiculous. Again. And yet, she was very glad of the shade. "Mr. Tilson? I don't see what that has to do with—"

"He runs one of the three fancyhouses we have in town. The Lucky Star, and that's more saloon than…the other. Though the two are the same. Mostly." Did he sound uncomfortable? His stride didn't alter, a long loping gait that meant a single step for every two of hers. "I'd warn you not to have too many words with him. Man's outright dangerous. To women, that is."

Her throat was suddenly, suspiciously dry. "I see."

He didn't sound convinced. "Then I don't need to tell you to be careful where you step. People come out here for two reasons: They're looking for trouble, or running away from it."

"Really." It was her turn to sound unconvinced. "I must disprove your theory, sir. I did not travel to this lovely town for either reason." *Robbie, I am going to pinch you. Twice.*

Was it amusement in his tone? "Well now, that exercises my curiosity something fierce. I've been wondering why such a gentle miss came all the way out here."

Why on earth did she feel menaced? A glitter caught her eye. Cat turned aside, finding herself before a window. How, in the name of charter, did they bring *glass* out here? Did it rattle by stagecoach, wrapped and shivering?

Shabby velvet and twinkling metal—it was a store of some kind, its brightest wares displayed prominently. Two silver-chased pistols, a fine set of them by the looks of it, with bone on their handles and carvings crawling with true-aim mancy, just as in novels of the Wild Westron. Pocketwatches, a fan of folded silk handkerchiefs. A few rings, tucked on tiny, moth-eaten purple pillows.

"This is Freedman Salt's." Mr. Gabriel's tone was very even. "I'd tell you not to go in here, ma'am. It's a pawnshop."

I hardly think I shall faint at the news. "Indeed," she murmured. "I am not blind, Mr. Gabriel. I can see as much."

"Well, then I'll tell you something you can't see. Russ Overton's our chartermage. People want respectable mancy, they go to him. But there's people what want something different, and they come *here*. Haven't quite figured what Salt ran away from back East." He stood beside her, thumbs hooked in his belt, his chin up, staring through the window as if he wished to shatter it with the force of his gaze alone. "When I do, it might be time for a Federal Marshal to come this way. But until then, I just watch."

Well, he certainly received no points for grace or finesse. "I do believe that's the most I've heard you speak so far, Mr. Gabriel." *And now I believe it's time for this conversation to take a different course.* "Your theory, I presume, must hold true for yourself. What trouble did you come Westron-ward to escape?"

He was silent for a long moment. Sweat collected under Cat's arms, her lower back was soaked, and a thin trickle slid down from her hair. Even under the parasol's shade and the awnings and porches extending from almost every building on this main thoroughfare, the entire town was oppressive. The dust was rising in creeping veils, too.

Still, she was cold all through, and a taste of bitter brass filled her mouth. A wave of shivering rippled down her back, and the fringe on her parasol trembled cheerily. She could not cease staring at the gleam that had caught her gaze.

There, on a pad of threadbare red velvet, lay a square locket. It was small, a golden shimmer, and the *tau* etched on its surface held a single tiny garnet in its center. The chain was a mellifluous spill, but it was broken, and as she gazed at it, another finger of sweat sliding down her neck, the ends of the break twitched as if the metal felt her nearness.

"Well now." When the sheriff spoke, she almost started violently. She had all but forgotten him. "You start asking that question, and people are likely to get itchy."

What question? She remembered, and had to swallow twice before she could speak. "I see."

"Good." He touched his hatbrim. "I'll be around, should you want a guide. Or need help. Ma'am."

And with that he was gone, those unhurried strides of his

carrying him neatly across the crowded street and between the swinging doors of the Lucky Star Saloon. Even at this early hour there was tinny piano music coming from the ramshackle building's depths. His shoulders were broad and his dun-colored coat blended with the dust; he did not precisely dodge the traffic. Rather, it seemed that it parted for him, and he waltzed through the chaos like a...she could not think of what, for a roaring noise had filled her head.

Cat turned back to the window. Her stays dug in, and she had to force herself to breathe. The glass was streaked with dust, humming with carnivorous mancy. Her charing-charm had gone chill against her throat, again.

Danger, Catherine.

Robbie's locket winked knowingly at her. He would never have pawned it, would he? The chain was broken. How had *that* happened? He wore his charing on the same chain—*double the safety*, he had always joked. *For if Mother found out bad mancy had been lodged near an heirloom, there would be an Incident of Temper.*

His charing was not in evidence—of course, if some dire fate had befallen him, it would be broken. Or perhaps he had found another means of securing his charing to his person, and had been forced to sell the locket? And yet that was ridiculous; he had left with plenty of money. What would make him give up an heirloom, especially one he had worn since childhood?

If she could hold the locket in her bare hand, perhaps she could find Robbie. Her Practicality would certainly stretch that far. Further, indeed, if she pricked her finger, for blood always told—though blood-work was *bad* mancy, and not something a respectable lady would dare.

I have already done something no respectable young lady would do, coming here. She sought to collect her wits, failed, tried again.

There were too many people about. She was hardly discreet, and who was to say Mr. Gabriel was not still watching her?

The pawnshop's door had a bell attached. It tinkled, and a man stumbled out onto the raw-lumber walkway. He was unshaven, bleary-eyed, and smelled powerfully of rancid liquor. His hat was askew, and he held guns in both callused, dirty hands.

Cat turned and walked briskly away. Her skirts snapped, her parasol fluttered, and she hardly remembered retracing her steps to the tiny cottage behind its freshly painted gate.

She was, as Robbie would have no doubt recognized were he present, far too occupied with scheming.

Chapter 7

Those with true business didn't visit the shop by day.

Every once in a while, Gabe would settle in a patch of shadow near the mouth of a dusty alley, and watch the charter-shadow's back door. It was useful to see who was visiting Salt. It was also useful to see how they approached—swaggering or creeping, desperate or slinking.

Very rarely, Gabe found himself collaring one of the desperate and telling them to go elsewhere. It wasn't his business, and Salt didn't need to know how closely he was watched. In fact, the less Salt knew about anything involving the sheriff, the better.

But sometimes, some nights, he couldn't stop himself.

Tonight was not one of those nights. He watched, noting who came creeping down the alley. And while he waited, he thought things over.

Here came thin, dried-up Mandy Carrick, keeping to the shadows and paying who knew what for protection when he decided to jump another claim out in the hills, stealing some other man's rightful work. That was outside Gabe's jurisdiction, certainly, but he still took note of it. Struthers slithered down the alley, a blur of fawn coat and stickpin flashing, looking for cheat-card mancy. A Chinois man was closeted inside the back of the pawnshop for quite a while, and Gabe didn't like the looks of that. Their mancy was different, even if it lived comfortably within charter, and he wondered just what one of *them* would want with Salt.

It was late by the time the trickle to the chartershadow's door dried up. The saloons would be rollicking, and there had been a few crackling gunshots. Nothing out of the ordinary here in Damnation. He'd made sure the schoolteacher's house was in a quieter part of town. Respectable, almost.

As respectable as you could get, out here.

Will you stop? Irritated with himself, he took a deep breath and slid out of concealment. *She's just a Boston miss a long way from home, and you're a goddamn idiot.*

He smacked the unlocked door open without even a courtesy knock, almost allowing himself to grin with satisfaction when it banged and Freedman Salt, his lean scarecrow body seeming put together from spare parts and his thick white wooly hair shocking atop such a wasted face, actually jumped.

This back room was low and indifferently lit, and the chalked charter-symbols on the floor were all subtly skewed. Some were scuffed and others redrawn—Salt had been a busy little boy tonight. He wasn't quite a sorcerer, or a chartermage; the man didn't have the discipline. Instead, the twisted drained bodies of small furry things lay at certain points within the diagram, false-iron nails driven through skulls, paws, tails. It stank of spoiled mancy and clotted-thick rust.

"Well now." Gabe rested a hand on a pistol butt. If he had been back East, it would have been a knife instead. He restrained the urge to shake the memory away. "What have we here?"

"Sheriff Gabriel." Salt's thin lip curled. "Pleasure, as always."

"Not fixin' to be. Dead bodies inside the charter this morning, Salt. Start explainin.'"

"Since when do dead bodies have shit-all to do with *me*?" As if butter wouldn't melt in his lying mouth.

"These were walkin' around." Gabe eyed the walls, rough boards covered with an intaglio of twisted, slurred charter-symbols. Even the dust in here reeked of blood. "Ridin' the circuit again put me in a bad mood, and the charter was solid. Which means I'm lookin' real hard at you, Salt."

A mockery of innocent shock twisted the chartershadow's lean face. "Me? Maybe you need a better chartermage. That one you got is all tarbrush and no talent."

"So are you, *Freedman*." It was a sure way to nettle the man, and Gabe almost regretted it as soon as Salt's face suffused with ugly maroon.

"I ain't no—"

Gabe's free hand flicked forward, the charm biting and fizzing in midair. Salt backpedaled, his boots smearing unfixed charter-symbols. A twinge of satisfaction burned Gabe's chest just as the choking chartershadow managed to get about half a syllable out. The curse went wide, splashing against the wall and punching a fist-sized hole.

Then Gabe had the man down on the floor, the gun cocked and pressed right behind Salt's ear. This close, he could see the dark roots of the man's charm-bleached hair, and also smell the faint smoke and slippery wetroot rot of the lean lanky body as the bad mancy kept twisting him, one slow increment at a time. Salt's hair frayed, chalked charter-symbols on the flooring writhing as Gabe scrubbed the shadow's face across them.

There was, he reflected, almost too much enjoyment to be had in terrorizing the wicked. The Order did not precisely *frown* on such enjoyment…but it was dangerous.

"Settle down." *Or so help me, I will settle you. That curse could have taken my face off.*

The only problem was, Salt's replacement was likely to be worse. Every town, no matter how small, had at least one char-tershadow. Even when there wasn't a respectable mage to be found, the shadows crept in.

Harsh breathing. The tips of Salt's boots scrabbled against the planking before he went still. Gabe knew better than to think he'd given up.

But for right now, it was enough. "Now." He didn't relax. "You been doing something that brings walkin' corpses into Damnation, this'n your chance to tell me."

"Would I be so stupid?" The words were muffled by the floor. At least he wasn't writhing anymore. "I got a nice li'l nest here, *Sheriff*. Except'n you, it's a bed of fucking roses."

There's always a thorn somewhere, isn't there. "Well now. Mighty suspicious, then, that I'm the one who ran across walkin' dead."

Still, if Salt had brought the corpses in or charmed them, he would have been ready for Gabe to come through his door, and would have had a lot worse than a half-measure of curse wait-ing.

"I don't know. It warn't me." Half-hysterical now, with the edge of a whine underneath the words. Salt could have been a reasonably employable chartermage with enough application and discipline, but he was both lazy and a coward.

And mancy—or grace—didn't forgive cowardice easily.

Am I a coward now? How would I know? "You sure, Salt? You don't sound too convinced."

"It warn't me, dammit!"

He eased up a little. "And of course you wouldn't know anything about it, would you."

The chartershadow began to struggle again, heaving under him. "First time I've heard, now *leggo!*"

Gabe did. He was on his feet and observing a cautious distance by the time Salt heaved himself up, his face choked with dust and bright beads of blood from several scrapes. The gun was back in Gabe's holster—but his hand still itched for it.

"Evenin', then, Mr. Salt." He touched the brim of his hat.

"What, you ain't gonna shoot me? Threaten me some more?"

"No point. I discover you ain't been honest, it's easy to find you. You havin' such a nice little nest and all."

Salt actually paled, his wasted frame visibly trembling. Whether it was rage or fear was an open question. He wore no guns, but Gabe was sure there was a knife or two handy. It would be just like the little bastard to slit someone in a dark alley.

He would have to be more careful now. Why had he drawn a gun, for God's sake? Salt wasn't enough of a threat to justify that.

Sir, your head is none too organized right now. He imagined Miss Barrowe's clipped, cultured tones, how a single eyebrow would lift fractionally, but those dark eyes would hold a different message. She likely thought she was hard to read, the schoolmarm, but those eyes were windows straight down to the bottom of a clear pond.

Windows to the soul, Jack? Just like Annie's.

The door was still open, a night breeze redolent of horse,

dust, and Damnation breathing into the chartershadow's room.

"Sheriff?" Salt wiped away the blood around his thin lips. "I saw a new face out my window today. Dressed in yellow, and pretty as a picture."

A cold hand clenched in Jack's guts.

"Wonder if she saw anything she liked," Salt continued.

He kept his expression a mask. "Not likely." And with that he was gone, but the sweat on the back of his neck and the tension in his fists were unwelcome symptoms.

It's nothing. People love to gossip, and they'll stop talking if you don't give them anything to talk about. Just leave it alone, Jack.

Unfortunately, he wasn't sure he could. And that was almost as worrying as a Chinois sneaking into a chartershadow's workroom late at night and asking for mancy. Jack headed for Russ Overton's lodgings for the fourth time that day, the shapes of the twisted charter-symbols he'd seen in Salt's back room fresh in his memory.

It was maybe time to do a little book-learning.

Chapter 8

Miss Bowdler's books had said nothing about *this*.

It was hot as Hades, dusty as another underworld, and Cat's stays were digging into her flesh with the vigor of bony clutching fingers as her temper frayed and she assayed, once more, a calm but authoritative tone.

There were too many of them to count, and she still had not managed a semblance of a roll call. More than half the tiny savages had no shoes, and could not sit still for more than a moment or two. Less than a quarter had seen some version of soap and water in the last fortnight, and she had the suspicion none of them were literate or numerate even in the most basic sense. The older savages bullied the younger unmercifully until Cat lost her temper and her Practicality sparked. The novelty of an adult throwing mancy in a classroom bought her precious moments to compose herself, and she thought grimly that her mother's experiences with Charity Work and the Noblesse Oblige of a Lady were going to stand her in better stead than *any* d—ned book, as Robbie would say.

At least while she was corralling a group of tiny uncivilized animals, she did not think of Robbie's locket in the pawnshop window, and how to obtain such an item without the entire town remarking upon her movements.

"That is *quite* enough," she informed the group of boys who had been tormenting a younger child. "You are to sit *there*, sir, and you *there*." She pointed, despite it being unmannerly.

"What if I don't?" the largest of them—an oafish blond lump who bore a startling resemblance to the small pug-nosed dogs she had seen in quite a few fashionable drawing-rooms last year—actually *sneered*, and Cat's temper almost frayed. Stray mancy crackled on her fingertip, and she drew herself up. A shadow slid over the room, and each tiny savage she was responsible for civilizing drew a deep breath.

"Then I haul you down to the jail and tell your mother you're sassin' the marm, Dwight Caffrey," a deep voice drawled from the propped-open door. "Afternoon, Miss Barrowe."

The mancy on her fingers died. *What is he doing here?* "Mr. Gabriel." She managed a nod, tucking a stray dark curl up and back. *Have you come to laugh at me?* "What a pleasant surprise."

The spark in his gaze told her the lie was perhaps audible. However, he merely shouldered the door aside and swept his hat from his dusty dark head, and his presence had the most astonishing effect.

Every little savage in the room quieted. The girls grinned and whispered; the boys stared with round eyes. The sheriff moved easily to the last row of benches, and loomed a trifle awkwardly over their occupants. "Thought I'd come out and visit." He halted, gazing at her most curiously. "First day of school and all."

And good heavens, but did the man sound *nervous*? Surely not. Catherine gathered the shreds of her temper and found herself standing at her desk, the attendance book lying open and the pen beside it. "Yes. Well, we have been having a most interesting time all seeking to speak at once and determining whether or not I am serious when I demand a certain measure of decorum."

"I see." Was that a faint smile playing around the corners of his mouth? She decided that it was, indeed. "I could tell 'em you're serious, ma'am, but I doubt they'd listen."

They're listening now. "I have not yet had the opportunity to inform them that any of their number who misbehaves shall be visiting *you.*"

"Well now, that would fill the jail right up, wouldn't it? I might be forced to keep a few in the pigsty." And yes, that was a gleam in his gaze she had seen before in Robbie's.

He looked, now that she thought about it, downright *mischievous.*

One of the younger boys—it was the small blond miscreant who had been responsible for so much excitement on the occasion of her arrival, little Tommy Hammis—let out a small sound approximating a whimper. Jack Gabriel tucked his thumbs in his belt and stood, looming in a manner that suggested practice at using his size to enforce some manners upon the unruly.

Take note of that, Catherine. Perhaps you can do likewise, even though you are not nearly as tall.

"I certainly hope we may avoid that." Cat settled herself in the rickety, uncomfortable chair behind her desk, sweeping her skirts underneath her with a practiced motion. This brown stuff was the dowdiest and most severe dress she owned, but it was still of painfully higher quality than any rag the children possessed. She uncapped the ink, dipped her pen, and glanced up to find every eye in the schoolhouse upon her and the entire room disturbingly silent. "Now, let us be about our business. Mr. Gabriel, if you would be so good as to pause for a short while? When I have given my students their first small lesson, I should be glad of the opportunity to converse with you." *Please tell me you have business elsewhere, and merely came to make certain there are no corpses lurking under the floorboards.*

"I'm here all afternoon, ma'am."

She hoped the children could not sense the amusement loitering beneath Mr. Gabriel's straight mouth and dusty brow. Her own mouth twitched, traitorously, until she steeled herself and fixed the far-left student in the first row—a thin girl of no more than six with messily braided wheat-gold hair, the lone girl on the boys' side of the schoolhouse—with a steady, stern, but kind (she hoped) glance. "State your name please, young lady."

"M-M-M-M—" The child, blushing, stuttered, and a sudden swift guilt pierced Cat's chest.

"That's Mercy Gibbons, ma'am." Jack Gabriel's tone had gentled. "Right next to her is her brother Patrick. The Gibbonses are a mite shy."

"Very good." Catherine wrote, swiftly but neatly. "We shall continue down the row, and should you find it difficult to say your name, Mr. Gabriel will help." She did *not* bite her lip, though the urge was almost overwhelming. She did, however, glance at the girl and hazard a small smile. "The first day of school is always trying, I daresay."

"Reckon so, ma'am." The sheriff's tone still held that queer gentleness.

"Jordie Crane!" a gangly redhead next to Patrick Gibbons almost-shouted, fidgeting. "This is Sammy next to me. Samuel, I mean. Sam Thibodeau."

Oh, dear God, how do I spell that? She decided to merely approximate, for the moment. "Thank you, Mr. Crane. You will allow Mr. Thibodeau the chance to speak for himself next time."

All through that long syrup-slow afternoon, Jack Gabriel loomed in the back of the classroom, and even though Cat was heartily sick of him, she could not help but admit that his presence had a most sedative effect upon the most troublesome of her students.

Unfortunately, her nerves were a frayed mass by the time she consulted her mother's watch, securely fastened to the chain at her waist, and informed the willowy, dark-eyed young Zechariah Alfstrache that he had, by dint of being the least troublesome today, earned the right to ring the true-iron bell bolted next to the front door. Near to expiring with satisfaction, he did so, and even the awe of the sheriff could not keep the little savages from exploding into action. Ten long minutes later the schoolhouse was echoingly empty, and Cat sagged in her chair, one hand at her eyes.

Jack Gabriel's steps were measured and slow. "Well. Schoolin' seems as difficult as law-work."

I rather doubt that, sir. For one thing, there are no flying bullets. Or undead. "They are quite energetic," she managed, faintly. "Good heavens." *Still, it is very kind of you to say so.*

"Fetch you some water, ma'am?"

How chivalrous. "No, thank you. You are quite free to go, I simply wished you to frighten some of the savages into behaving."

"Had business, ma'am."

Oh? "And what would that be?"

"Makin' sure the schoolhouse is safe."

Of course. "Your diligence does you credit." Her eyes opened, and the outside world was an assault of color and light. "I think we may rest assured the environs are *quite* safe."

"Maybe, ma'am. You look…pale." The odd gentleness again. What on earth possessed him to speak so?

Cat straightened. *Come now, Catherine. You can certainly present a better form than this.* "It is very warm today." She checked the ink on the pages of her ledger—dry by now, certainly, but she breathed across the paper anyway, a slight charm to make certain sparking in the charged air. She closed the book with a decisive snap of binding and pages, and glanced up to find Mr. Gabriel looming over her desk instead of over the last row of benches, the star on his chest glinting sharply. Her stays were *most* uncomfortable, but she set her chin and glared at him. "I am *quite* well, sir. I am about to close the schoolhouse and go home, and—"

"I brought the wagon. You walked this morning." Flat statement of fact, and his pale gaze was most certainly amused, but also…what?

As a matter of fact, she had enjoyed a brisk walk in the morning crispness. She had also entirely misjudged the weather—why, it was not entirely clear, since it had been unbecomingly torrid every afternoon since her arrival in this benighted burg. "I am not certain it is quite *fitting*," she hedged, capping the ink with deft fingers and beginning the process of setting her desk to rights. "After all, Mr. Gabriel, I am—"

"About to faint." His hat dangled from his very capable left hand, leaving his right free to touch her desktop with its fingertips, in a manner that seemed most improper. She could not think just why. "You're *very* pale, ma'am. I'll fetch you some water."

Cat summoned every inch of briskness she possessed. "Not necessary, thank you." But it was no use—the man was already halfway to the door, jamming his hat on his head as if he suspected something within the schoolhouse would dump ordure upon his thick skull.

Sighing, Cat set herself to closing up her desk. Each student's slate hung neatly at the back of their bench-seat on a special hook, and tonight she would make paper nameplates for each section of desk. Pride in their desks, Miss Bowdler was fond of saying, would lead to pride in their *persons*, and that would make them neat and respectable.

Catherine had a notion Miss Bowdler had perhaps not reckoned on Damnation.

In any case, the environs were tolerably tidy by the time the sheriff stamped back up the steps and into the schoolhouse. She was taking note of a slate that had disappeared—one of the Dalrymple sisters no doubt, who all seemed more interested in simpering and sneering than giving their names or possibly learning their letters—and a suspicious stain on the floor behind the third row of benches when he appeared, holding a dripping dipper and biting his lip with concentration as he negotiated the rough plank flooring.

Cat's own lips compressed, but not with disdain. He looked very much like one of her young students, especially since he was holding his hat as well as the dipper, and his dark hair had fallen forward across his forehead.

"Very kind of you." She accepted it, and the few swallows of mineral-tasting well water made her suddenly aware of just how thirsty she was. Her lower back had collected a small pond of sweat, and her stays dug so hard she had longing thoughts of them snapping and freeing her enough to take a decent breath.

"Pleasure to be of service, ma'am." His tone belied the words. In fact, Jack Gabriel looked...was it anger, sparking in those hazel eyes? His mouth was a thin line, and that odd gentle tone had vanished as if it never existed. "You should take more care."

With what? But she was far too grateful for the water, no matter that her stomach was uneasy at containing it. "If you have made certain the grounds hold no undead, *sir*, perhaps we may be on our way?"

It was, she reflected, a trifle unjustified. Still, the disapproval—for that, she had decided, was his expression—nettled her. It was unearned, and though she knew such was the lot of every woman, she certainly did not have to enjoy it—or give it shrift.

It didn't seem to make much impression on the man. "Best we lock up then, ma'am."

"Indeed." She handed the dipper back and set about putting on her gloves. The thought of loading her tired, sweat-soaked body with more cloth did not appeal, but a lady did not go outside without gloves, even in this benighted portion of the world. "If you would be so kind as to return that to the well, sir, I shall accomplish the rest."

His footsteps were very definite against the raw flooring, and Cat closed her eyes again for a moment. The problem that had been nipping and gnawing at her all day, even while she sought to retain some decorum and control in the face of what was apparently the Lost Tribe of Almanache, returned.

The locket. How on earth am I going to...

It was quite simple. She merely had to find a way to enter the pawnshop unremarked.

Or, she merely had to not care what people would think if

they saw her entering such a place. It was not as if she had a Reputation to maintain, here at the end of the world. But still.

"Ma'am?" D—n the man. Would he grant her *no* relief from his presence?

"Very well," Cat said, as if he had sought to argue with her. She gathered her necessaries and swept down the central aisle, chin held high and her mother's Greet The Peasants smile frozen onto her features. "Thank you, sir."

Chapter 9

He began to get the idea the marm didn't like him.

Oh, she was perfectly polite. It was *Mr. Gabriel* this and *Sir* that and *Sheriff* the other. But a woman had a hundred little ways to let a man know he was not welcome, and the damn Boston miss had a hundred and one. There was freezing him with a single glance when he showed up at the kitchen door, and Li Ang's sly little smile. Not to mention Miss Barrowe shooing him out of the damn building the second day of school. Nevermind that she obviously had precious little in the way of experience for keeping the little 'uns from mischief; she was bound and determined to do things according to her own fancy. She didn't even ask him about the gate in front of her house, just engaged Carter, that damnfool, to repaint it and take care of a squeak in the hinges.

It was a *perfectly* good gate. He'd hung it himself.

After two weeks of being snubbed by the miss, as well as riding the circuit not just before dawn and after dusk but at high noon in the heat, his temper was none too smooth. He just grunted when Russ Overton asked him if it was *really* necessary to ride the circuit when the chartermage could simply *feel* the charter was intact, and there hadn't been another irruption since.

The card games above the Lucky Star were no good, either. For the life of him, Gabe could not stop losing, and *that* was enough to make him wish he had never seen this town. Dr. Howard had even asked him, with a sly chuckle, if he needed a charming to repair his luck.

The old coot.

So when the woman came sashaying into the jail early Sunday morn, he was already in a bad mood. It didn't help that it was Mercy Tiergale, tarted up in what might've been her Sunday best sprigged muslin.

That is, if a whore ever went to church. On the other hand, there wasn't much of a preacher in Damnation. Maybe the Boston miss was scandalized by the lack of a man of God around here. Some of the men read from the Book, some of the women organized hymns, and that was about it. Letitia Granger often professed herself absolutely horrified and trumpeted her intention to bring a holy man from a city somewhere.

He wished her luck. As long as it wasn't a Papist who might recognize what Jack was—what he *had* been.

If it is, I'll just move on. Gabe reached to touch his hatbrim, but the hat was on the peg by the door. His boots were caked with Damnation's yellow dust, but he had them propped on the desk anyway. There were two jail cells; one held a snoring drunk—Rob Gaiterling, who needed a bender about once a month and went crazy when he got it—and the other stood open and empty, its walls scratched with unfinished charter-symbols and finished graffiti, the iron of the doors glowing dully with imbued mancy. "Miz Tiergale."

Daylight showed the beginning of ravages to her sweet round face, but her chin was high and her dark hair was elaborately curled under an imitation of a fashionable bonnet. He'd been seeing them more and more about town this last week, maybe in response to the schoolmarm.

An inward wince. Maybe there was a charm to get the image of Miss Barrowe, terrified and pale, breaking her pretty parasol over a walking corpse's head, out of his brain. If one didn't exist, maybe he should *make* one. He could turn in some more hours laboring over Russ's charter-dictionaries; unfortunately, whatever black mancy Salt had been working, there was nothing in Russ's small collection that could shed light on it.

"Morning, Sheriff." Mercy's shoulders were rigid, her hands clasped together as if she was six again, repeating her charter-chism. "I have business."

No doubt. "Yes ma'am?" Was Tilson beating his girls again? Or was there a deeper trouble to add to the mess inside Gabe's head?

He might almost welcome some more trouble, if only to keep him occupied and away from brooding over a silly nose-high Boston miss.

"I aim to visit the schoolmarm before the churching." Mercy took a deep breath, and high color flushed her round cheeks. She was popular among the Lucky Star's patrons, most of whom liked a woman with a little heft. "I aim to have you go with me, to keep it all respectable-like. None of the gossip-ies in town are like to go, and I aim to have the marm listen to what I have to say."

That's a lot of aimin' you're fixed on. "She seems the listenin' type." Gabe got his feet under him. "What kind of business, if I may inquire?"

"*Personal* business, Sheriff." Mercy nodded once, sharply, and that was that. "Not saloon business."

In other words, Tilson didn't need to know. Gabe thought it over. Well, what could it hurt? Besides, there was his curiosity, which had perked its ears something awful. "Yes ma'am."

The saloon girl's face eased, and her earrings—bits of paste glass, with tiny charms flashing in their depths, probably to keep the dye in her hair—danced. Her eyebrows were coppery, and there was a fading set of bruises ringing her neck. She'd curled some of her hair over to hide them, but there was no hiding some things. "Much obliged, Sheriff. If you want…"

There were times when he was mighty tempted, true. "No ma'am, thank you ma'am," he said, maybe a little *too* quickly. The saloon girl's face brightened with an honest smile, and Gabe dropped his gaze as he stepped past her to rescue his hat.

Women. How could a man ever figure? He'd visited one or two of the Star's girls, when it got to be too much. They were uncomplicated. They didn't twist a man up inside.

And they were welcoming, too. What more did a man need?

His mood had just turned a little blacker, and Gabe scowled. He offered the girl his arm as they stepped outside, and at least she accepted.

Mercy was silent the entire way, her steps light and delicate. They kept to the back row running parallel to the main street, their only witnesses some chickens and stray dogs, as well as wet washing flapping on lines, crackling with dust-shake charms. And they reached Miss Barrowe's trim little cottage just as the marm herself, smartly dressed in a soft peach frock that made her glow in the morning sunshine, stepped out her front door with yet another parasol, this one bearing a ruff of soft scalloped lace.

She was obviously bound for church.

His throat tightened. His face was a mask. The gate didn't squeak, but the painting on it was a little slapdash.

Served her right.

Miss Barrowe didn't seem surprised in the least. "Sheriff. How pleasant. Are you attending church today?"

He had to clear his windpipe before he could say "No ma'am," with anything resembling his usual tone. "Miss Barrowe, may I present Miss Mercy Tiergale? She's some words for you."

"I see. How do you do?" And the marm, pretty as you please, offered her hand with a smile that, for some reason, made Gabe's chest even tighter.

"Ma'am." Mercy was back to flour-pale, and she shook the marm's hand once, limply. A tense silence rose, dust whisking along the street on a brisk fresh breeze. It would be hot later. Finally, Mercy swallowed visibly. "How do."

Miss Barrowe glanced quickly at Gabe, her expression unreadable. "Where are my manners? Do come in. May I offer you some tea? I know Mr. Gabriel prefers coffee—"

"No ma'am." Mercy's fingers tightened on his arm. A spate of words came out in a rush, like a flash flood up in the hills. "I aim to have you listen. We—some of the girls and me—we wants our letters. I mean, we want to do some larnin'. *Book* larnin', and figures." The saloon girl freed one hand, digging in her skirt pocket. "We can pay you. We want it all respectable-like." A handful of rolled-together bills came up, and Gabe noticed a stain on Mercy's gloved wrist. Looked like whiskey.

Maybe she'd needed it to brace her. He kept his mouth shut, and winced again when he thought of Tils's likely reaction to this. And the money—often, saloon girls didn't see actual cash. More of Mercy's nervousness seemed downright reasonable, now.

Miss Barrowe did not even bat one sweet little eyelash. "I see. Please, Miss Tiergale, put that away and come inside. As I am engaged to teach in this town and my salary is paid by the town itself, I see no need for you to—"

"We're saloon girls, ma'am." Flung like a challenge. "Six of us. In the afternoons before the real drinkin' starts, that's when we have time."

Miss Barrowe nodded briskly. "Then after I finish with my other pupils, I shall be glad to help you and your fellow…ladies educate yourselves. Are you quite certain you won't come in and have some tea while we discuss this?"

"No ma'am." Mercy's arm came up, rigid, and she proffered the bills. "Wouldn't want you to miss church. Do you take our money, and I'll be on my way."

Miss Barrowe's glance flickered to Gabe's face again. Her curls were expertly arranged, and that dress looked soft enough for angels to nest in. A faint breath of rosewater reached him, under the tang of cigar smoke and spilled drink, sawdust and sweat from Mercy. He was suddenly very aware that Mercy had his arm, and that Miss Barrowe might draw a conclusion or two from that.

I don't care. But it had a hollow ring, and it was maybe the wrong time for Jack Gabriel to start lying to himself.

"I believe it might be best for Sheriff Gabriel to hold your money." Miss Barrowe straightened slightly, her shoulders going back. A touch of lace around the neckline of her dress was incredibly distracting; he found he couldn't look away. "You shall engage my services as a teacher for a certain length of time—a month, perhaps? Then we shall again address the question of payment, if you are satisfied with my methods and your progress." A slight curve of her lips. "That would make every aspect of this eminently respectable, since Mr. Gabriel is a representative of the town that engaged me."

Well, now. "Seems a right fair idea," he offered, but neither woman appeared to pay much heed. Mercy's lips moved slightly as she worked this around in her head, and Miss Barrowe held the saloon girl's gaze. Invisible woman-signals flashed between them like charmgraph dots and dashes, and finally Mercy relaxed a trifle.

"I b'lieve that'll do." She let loose of Gabe's arm long enough to roll the wad of bills more tightly, and offered it to him. "Will you hold this, Gabe?"

"Be right pleased to," he mumbled. Why were his cheeks hot?

"Very well." Miss Barrowe closed her front door with a small, definite *snick*. "Are you accompanying me to church, Miss Tiergale?"

"No ma'am." Mercy stared at the ground now, Miss Barrowe's dainty boots clicking on the steps as she picked her way down to the garden path. The marm opened her parasol with an expert flicker and flutter, and—surprisingly enough—offered her own arm to the saloon girl. "It ain't proper. Leastways—"

"That," the schoolmarm said decisively, "is a great shame. Would you care to walk with me at least as far as the Lucky Star? I believe it is upon my route."

Mercy almost flinched. "No ma'am. There'd just be trouble if…well."

"Don't you worry." Gabe's cheeks would *not* cool down. He had the attention of both women, now, and he hadn't the faintest idea why he'd spoken up. "Tils gives you trouble, you come right on over to me."

Mercy actually laughed, cupping one gloved hand over her mouth. There was, however, little of merriment in the sound. She knew as well as he did that he couldn't settle down in the Star and stare Tils into keeping his temper permanently. "Mighty kind of you, Gabe. I'd best be on my way. Thank you, ma'am. When are we fixing to start?"

"Tomorrow is Monday." Miss Barrowe now looked faintly perplexed, a small line between her eyebrows. "If that suits you, and the other ladies."

"Suits us fine, ma'am. Mornin'." And with that, Mercy Tiergale turned on one worn-down bootheel and strode off, her skirt snapping a bit as the morning breeze freshened.

He searched for something to say. The parasol had dipped, so Miss Barrowe's face was shadowed. He doubted her expression would be anything but polite and cool. "Right kind of you, ma'am."

She was silent for a long moment. He could have kicked himself. Should have followed Mercy and not given the miss a chance to snub him.

"Is there likely to be trouble arising from this, Mr. Gabriel?" The lacy stuff shivered as she adjusted her parasol, and the honest worry in her clear dark eyes pinched at him.

Just why, though, he couldn't say.

"Not if I can help it." His jaw set. "You just settle your mind, Miss Barrowe."

"I don't mean for me," she persisted. "For Miss Tiergale. She seemed…concerned."

"I said to settle your mind." He half-turned, offered his arm without much hope. "Walk you to church, ma'am?"

Her gloved hand stole forward, crept into the crook of his elbow like it belonged there. "Does that mean I shouldn't worry for Miss Tiergale, as you will assist her and her…compatriots?"

"It means I can handle one whorehouse manager, ma'am." As soon as it left his lips he regretted himself. "Beg pardon."

Her lips had pressed together. Her free hand hovered near her mouth, but her eyes were wide and sparkling. She composed herself, and her smile was almost as bright as Damnation's morning sun as she turned slightly, her skirt brushing his knee as she leaned ever so slightly on him. "Indeed. I have faith in your ability, sir. Forgive my repeating myself, but will you be attending church today?"

He thought of saying he had pressing business, but it seemed all good sense had deserted him. The pressure of her fingers inside his elbow was a popcharm, jolting up all the way to his shoulder. "Yes ma'am."

Oh, Hell.

Chapter 10

Cat rubbed delicately at the skin about her eyes. It was drowsy-hot, especially in the schoolroom, and the scratching on the board was enough to set even a saint's teeth on edge. Cecily Dalrymple was writing out *I will not throw ink*, her fair blonde face set in mutinous agony. The rest of the children, temporarily chastened, bent over their slates, and Cat took a deep breath. "Once more," she said, patiently, and little Patrick Gibbons almost stuttered as he recited.

"A…B…C…"

"Very good," she encouraged, ignoring the fidgets. The youngest students chorused with Patrick, raggedly but enthusiastically. They made their way through the alphabet, and Cat's warm glow of entirely justified (in her opinion) satisfaction was marred only by the back row's restlessness.

Miss Bowdler's books were very useful, but Cat had learned more applicable skills following her mother about on the endless round of charity work a Barrowe-Browne was obliged to undertake. Not to mention the example of one of her governesses—a certain Miss Ayre, quiet and plain but with a steely tone that had made even Robbie sit up and take notice on those few occasions her patience had worn thin.

It was Miss Ayre's example she found herself drawing on most frequently, especially as every child in the schoolroom was dismally untaught. Ignorance and undirected energy conspired to make them fractious, but they were on the whole more than willing to work, and work *hard*, once she gave them a direction. Perhaps it was the novelty of her presence.

Still, there were troubles. The Dalrymple girls, for one. Turning those two hoydens into respectable damsels was perhaps beyond Cat's power, but she had an inkling of a plan. The older girl's longing glances at the sad, shrouded pianoforte had not passed unnoticed, and Cat suspected that with the offer of lessons she would have a valuable carrot to dangle before the haughty creature.

"That is *quite* enough," she said sternly. Mancy sparked on her fingers, and there was a crackle. Little Tommy Beaufort let out a garbled sound and thumped back into his seat. "Mr. Beaufort, since you are so eager, stand and recite your alphabet instead of tossing rubbish at your classmates. Begin."

"A…B…C…"

Hoofbeats outside. *That* explained the restlessness of the back rows—they had heard the noise before she did. Was it Mr. Gabriel again? Whoever it was seemed in quite a hurry, but she held Tommy to his recitation, nodding slightly.

The horse did not pass the schoolhouse. *Who could that be?* But she stayed where she was, standing beside her desk, and when Tommy finished she gave him a tight smile. "Very good. Now, first form, take your slates out and begin copying from the top line on the board—*A fox is quick.* Second form—"

Thundering bootsteps, and the door was flung open. Cat blinked.

It was Mr. Tilson, the owner of the Lucky Star. She had seen him in church just yesterday, nodding along to Mr. Vancey the cartwright's stumbling reading of the Book. Mr. Gabriel had sat next to her, his hands on his knees and his face as dull and unresponsive as she had ever seen it.

Mr. Tilson was sweating, and had obviously ridden hard. Foam and dust hung on him in spatters, and his suit coat was sadly rumpled. He was red-faced, too, and Cat stared at him curiously. His hat was cocked sideways, and the slicked-down strands of his dark hair were dangerously disarranged.

"*You!*" He pointed at Cat, and spat the word. "*You. I've words for you, Miss.*"

What on earth? She drew herself up. The children had frozen, including Cecily Dalrymple at the board. Their eyes were wide and round, and quite justifiable irritation flashed under Cat's skin. "Mr. Tilson. You shall not shout indoors, sir. It sets a bad example."

That brought him up short. The redness of his cheeks and the ugly flush on his neck was not merely from the heat. It was also, Cat suspected, pure choler.

He actually spluttered a little, and her fingers found the yardstick laid across her desk. "Step outside, sir. I shall deal with you in a moment, once I have finished giving the second and third forms their lessons. Miss Dalrymple, you may return to your seat; that is quite enough."

"I ain't gonna be put off—" Mr. Tilson started, and Cat searched for her mother's voice. It came easily, for once.

"*Sir.*" Every speck of dust in the room flashed under her tone. "You *shall not* disturb my students further. Step outside. And do close the door properly, the wind and heat are very bad today."

His jaw worked, but he seemed to finally realize the eyes of every child in the room were upon him. He backed up a single step, his gaze purely venomous, and whirled, banging the door shut.

Cat's knuckles ached, gripping the wooden yardstick. Her heart pounded. She tilted her chin slightly, an ache beginning between her shoulder blades.

I can handle a whorehouse manager, Mr. Gabriel had said. Surely a Barrowe-Browne could do no less. At least it was not a shambling corpse at the door.

That was an entirely unwelcome thought, and she did her best to put it away. "Second form, take your slates and solve the row of sums under first form's line. Third form—" *All three of you, who can puzzle out a word or two.* "Take out your primers and occupy yourselves with page six."

"Yes ma'am," no few of them chorused, and Cecily Dalrymple actually sat down without flouncing, for once. Cat suspected she might regret showing leniency, but there was nothing for it.

She passed down the aisle, stepping over the cleansed patch where the corpse had landed—there was no evidence of it on the floorboards, but she still disliked setting her feet in that vicinity—and braced herself for whatever unpleasantness was about to ensue.

"*You.*" Tilson pointed a stubby finger at her. "What are you playing at? Them whores don't need to read!"

So that's it. Her mother's voice still served her well—the exact tone Frances Barrowe-Browne would use in dealing with an overeager gentleman, or a brute of a salesman who sought to engage her custom. "You will adopt a civilized tone in speaking to me, sir." Cat drew in a sharp soundless breath. Dust whirled along the dry track serving as a road, and the horse Tilson had arrived on hung its head near the trough, its sides lathered. "And your horse requires some care."

"God*damn* the horse, and God damn you, too! Civilized tone my *ass*. What'n hell you think you're doing, teaching whores to read? I won't have it!"

She still held the yardstick, and the image of cracking him across the knuckles with it was satisfying in its own way. Cat gazed at him for a few long moments, her face set, one eyebrow arched in imitation of her mother's fearsome You Are Not In Good Form expression.

When she was certain she had his attention, and further certain that he was beginning to feel faintly ridiculous, she tapped the yardstick against the schoolhouse's ramshackle porch. The shade here was most welcome, though she quailed a bit inwardly at the thought of the afternoon walk back to her little cottage. "The next moment you use such language, sir, this conversation is over. Now, am I to understand you have an objection to some of my students?"

"Your—" He visibly checked himself. "They ain't gonna read! You just tell them that!"

"I was engaged to see to the education of those in this town." Dangerously quiet, and Cat's back ached. "Those in your employ are not heathen slaves, sir; they are members of this town and, as such, are entitled to my services. Additionally"—she overrode the beginning of his bluster, and it was Miss Ayre's example she drew upon now—"I am a charter-free Christian woman, *sir*, and you do not have any leave or right to speak to me in this manner. You may remove yourself from my schoolhouse immediately. If you do not, I shall be forced to seek a remedy against you by applying to the forces of law and justice in this town."

"What, Gabe? He ain't mixed up in this. You mark my word, you little bitch—"

"Good day, sir." She turned on her heel.

Tilson took a step forward, and his broad, callused hand closed around her arm, squeezing brutally. "I am *talkin'* to you, you little—"

The yardstick snapped up, its tip crackling and spitting sparks. She meant to merely startle him into dropping her arm, and heard Robbie's voice inside her head. *Don't let them manhandle you, little sister. That's what a Practicality's for.*

Instead, it cracked across Mr. Tilson's face as he sought to shake her, pulling her toward the three rude stairs leading off the porch. The mancy popped, and blood spattered. She recoiled, his hand falling away from her aching arm, and it was as if Robbie were next to her. The image of the locket in the pawnshop window rose, glittering coldly, and she realized that in this town, she could perhaps sally into such a place without worrying overmuch about such a thing as Reputation.

Still, she was alone with this man, with only a group of children inside, and Reputation was thin tissue indeed to shield her from violence.

Perhaps she should have been more…discreet? Passive? What was the proper word?

The saloon owner tripped, tumbled down the steps, and landed sprawled in the dust. Cat found words, harsh and rude as a lady's must never be. Still, they fell out of her mouth before she could halt them.

"Do not *dare* to lay hands upon me in such a manner, you foulmouthed *brute!*" She hit a pitch just under "fishwife's scream" and for once, did not wish to writhe in embarrassment. The yardstick fizzed with sparks, and she held it in both hands, much in the manner of a sword.

He scrambled to his feet, dust rising in puffs and golden veils. Cat's heart thundered, her palms sweating, and a curl had fallen in her face. The children had probably heard her. Gossip would run through the town, and—

You're here to find Robbie. Or find what has happened to him. This brute does not matter one whit.

And yet Miss Tiergale had been very frightened. Almost trembling. If she lived with *this* man, Cat could see why.

And the knowledge made her sick all the way through. Another session of heaving off the school's porch could not be borne either, so she merely set her jaw and swallowed the bitterness.

Mr. Tilson pointed one thick, trembling finger. "I'll get you. So help me, I'll *get* you."

"Your threats are as ugly as your character." She pointed the yardstick, a single star of light hurtfully bright at its tip. The wood was scorched, and Tilson's face was bleeding, one eye already puffed shut. The blood was shockingly bright in all the dun and dust. "Do not *ever* come near me again, sir. Or I shall hand you more of the same."

He blundered back for his horse, and Cat stood watching as he spurred the beast unmercifully. She tried to tell herself it was because she wished to make certain he would not return and possibly make another scene in front of her students.

In reality, however, it was because she was trembling, and her stomach cramped. She watched the man on the horse recede into the distance toward the smoke-smudge of the bulk of Damnation, and her mouth was full of thick, foul fear.

If I were not such a lady, I would spit. A lady did not smash a man in the face with mancy and a yardstick, however.

I would do it again, she realized. *Most assuredly I would.*

I would even enjoy it.

Chapter 11

As soon as he stepped into the Lucky Star, Gabe knew something was amiss. The hush was instant, and he didn't need to see Mercy Tiergale's badly bruised cheek to tell Tils was unhappy. It wasn't like him to tap a popular girl in the face where it would show, either.

It was midafternoon, so the serious drinking hadn't started yet, and wouldn't for hours. The card games were going full-force though, and Mo Jackson was banging on the tinny little piano, waltzing his way through "She Was A Charming Filly" and humming off-key. Mercy made a beeline for Gabe, and he barely had time to lay his littlebit on the counter and accept a shot of something passing for whiskey before she was at his elbow.

"He left an hour ago," she said, and the bruise was fresh red-purple, glaring and still puffing up. Her breasts swelled almost out of the dress—well, *dress* wasn't quite the word, it was just a scrap of corset and lace, and low. "Gabe…"

"Tils?" He nodded as the 'tender, weedy Tass Coy, slapped his hand over the bit and made it vanish. Coy's jaw was a mess;

you could clearly see where the horse's hoof had dug in and shattered bone. Not even the doctor could do much for it, and Russ Overton's mancy didn't extend to fleshstitching.

"He said he was gonna talk to *her*." It was a strained whisper. "I sent Billy to the jail, but you warn't there."

Coy watched this, his brown eyes neutral. He plucked at one of his braces with long sensitive fingers, and turned away very slowly. There was nothing wrong with his ears.

No, I was ridin' the circuit, dammit. Gabe's chest knew before the rest of him. A cold, hard lump settled right behind his breastbone. "Tilson's visiting the marm?"

"He said he was gonna ride right out to that schoolhouse and teach her not to interfere." Mercy's hands clutched into fists. "Gabe...now don't be hasty."

Hasty is one thing I'm not. "Tilson. Visiting the schoolhouse." He repeated it slowly, just to make certain he hadn't misheard. "When did he leave, now?"

"An hour, maybe more—Gabe, I—"

He bolted the shot. No use in wasting liquor, even if it was terrible. When he cracked the glass back down on the sloping counter, Mercy cringed like a whipped dog. Did she think *he* was going to tap her, too?

"God*damn*." He headed for the swinging doors, but he didn't have to take more than two steps before they whipped open as if disgorging a flood. Emmet Tilson stamped through, looking halfway to Hell. Blood and dust crusted his face, and one eye was swollen shut. It looked much worse than what he'd inflicted on Mercy, and Gabe stopped dead.

What the Hell? His jaw felt suspiciously loose, and the way his hands were tense and tight-knotted, Gabe was suddenly afraid he was going to break a finger or two.

Tils saw him a bare half-second later, and stopped dead as well. He wasn't wearing a gun, which was a piece of good fortune, because Gabe saw the saloon owner's hand twitch, and almost drew himself.

Now, don't lose your temper, something inside him was trying to say. Oddly, it sounded a little like Annie, and a little like an archly amused schoolmarm.

There was a general shuffle as everyone in the saloon noticed the two of them eyeing each other like rattlesnakes, and moved out of the way.

Gabe decided to be mannerly. Why not? "Afternoon, Tilson."

The man twitched again, and Gabe was mighty glad there was no gun on Tils's hip. On the other hand, the saloon owner had gone out to the schoolhouse without an iron? That was very unlike him.

Maybe he thought Miss Barrowe wasn't worth shooting. 'Course, Tilson preferred to talk to a woman with his fists.

A spike of heat went through Gabe. He realized, miserably, that he was not about to keep his temper. Especially if the whorehouse manager said one, small, *wrong* word.

"Sheriff." Brittle, but at least Tilson wasn't shouting. "My office. *Now.*"

Since when do you order me around like one of your whores? "Beg your pardon?" He drawled it nice and slow, as if he didn't understand. Give the man some time to reconsider his tone, as it were.

The garish blood and dust all over Tils was thought-provoking. The cold was all through Gabe now, except for that hot spike of rage in his chest, beating like a heart. He hadn't felt that heat in so long, it was almost comforting.

Whatever was in his expression made the saloon owner back up a step, his spurs jangling a discordant note against the worn wooden floor. If Gabe were still of the Faith, now would have been the moment for him to punish the man for a transgression real or imagined.

But that part of him was long gone, wasn't it? And thinking about its loss was not guaranteed to keep his temper, either.

"I mean, ah…" Tilson coughed, rubbed at his swollen lips with one hand. But slowly. "I mean, Gabe, we've got business. Care to step into my office?"

That's better. But you're still likely to bite. Cowards always are. "I ain't aware of any business between us, Tilson. Unless you *want* there to be." It was hard, but he glanced aside at Mercy Tiergale, whose hands were clutched at her mouth. "Miss Mercy. Don't you and the girls have an appointment?"

The silence was so thick you could pour it into a cup. Tils stiffened as if Gabe had just slapped him. The doors squeaked on their hinges, and the wind on Damnation's main street was a low moan as wheels rumbled and horses neighed outside.

A susurrus behind him as he returned his gaze to Tilson. "You look like hell, Emmet."

"Tangled with a she-cat." Tils straightened. The tension leached out of the air, and Mo brought his hands down on the keys again. The tinny crash almost made him jump.

"Is that so." *Looks like she tangled you but good.*

"Gabe…" Mercy sounded as if she'd been punched. Maybe she had. Or maybe she found it difficult to breathe. Mo noodled through the first few bars of "My Old Mother Is Watching," and Gabe wondered if it was the man's comment on proceedings, so to speak.

"You just run along now." Gabe said it evenly, slowly. "Take

the girls with you. I'll be along to see all's right."

Tils seemed to have a bit of a problem with this. "You can't—"

"You want to think right careful before you finish that sentence, Tilson." *And so help me God, if you hurt her, I'm going to make you pay.*

It was an uncomfortable thought. He didn't even *like* the marm; she was a prissy little miss, and he had no need to be involving himself in this trouble. It was too late, though. He was well and truly involved, because he had opened his fool mouth.

And besides, he was lying to himself again. *A knight of the Order must never commit that sin, of untruth in his own soul.* The smell of incense rose in his memory, the moment of struggle before the altar before he had turned away, leaving his brothers praying in their plainsong chant, his hands fists as they were now and a single thought burning in his brain.

Annie.

Except it wasn't her he was thinking of now, was it.

The saloon owner subsided. But the ratty little gleam in his eye told Gabe there would be trouble later.

Oh, damn.

The news had spread like wildfire. By the time Gabe arrived at the schoolhouse the Granger wagon was there too, and he winced again.

Maybe this would all blow over. Tils might not use his fists too much on the girls now that Gabe was involved, but there were a hundred other ways he could make their lives even more miserable. And the miss might find that teaching a bunch of saloon girls was not as easy as the little 'uns—though Gabe didn't know how *easy* the little 'uns were, rightly. About all he knew

was that *he* wouldn't care to be trapped in a schoolroom with them all day.

He took his time pumping fresh water for the horses. The sun beat down unmercifully, and even though the water was brown and the bottom of the trough none too clean, he still thought longingly of just sinking into it and letting the entire damn situation play itself out with no help from one tired, head-buzzing Jack Gabriel.

He had just finished pumping and settled his hat more firmly when Letitia Granger sailed out of the schoolhouse door, her bosom—the only soft thing on that big bony body—lifted high with indignation and plump with starched ruffles. The rest of her was in severe dark stuff, and she looked so rigid with disapproval he was surprised her skirts didn't creak.

She sallied down the stairs, head held high and the poor feathers on her hat hanging on for dear life. "*Sheriff!*" she crowed, her lips so pinched the word was a hoarse croak.

Oh, Lord. He tried his best not to wince yet again. "Afternoon, Mrs. Granger."

"*Do you know what she's done?*" Granger was fairly apoplectic. Her color was a deep brick-red, and strings of her graying hair stuck to her forehead, wet with sweat. She looked fit to expire right there on the steps. "*Do you?*"

He decided a measure of strategic befuddlement might work. "Last I heard, she was teachin'."

"There are *unrespectable women* in there, Sheriff! On the very seats our children...the seats..." Letitia Granger's jaw worked.

He tipped his hat back a little, scratched at the creased band of sweat on his forehead. He took his time with it, as if he was stupid-puzzled. "Well, where else should she teach 'em? At the church?"

That was probably the wrong thing to say, for Mrs. Granger's eyes flashed and she sailed across the yard, dust sparking and crackling in her wake. She was so het up she was throwing mancy even though she had no Practicality, and Gabe at least had the comfort of knowing he wasn't the only one the Boston miss had tied up in a tangle there was no working free of.

"It's *unchristian!*" The woman stopped, her hands fisting at her sides. She probably packed a punch like a donkey's kick under all that starch.

"Well, they ain't no Magdala nuns, I'll allow that." He nodded, slowly. "But they paid her fair and square, and I can't find no law against it."

"Law? *Law?* It ain't a question of law, Sheriff, and—"

"It ain't?" He hoped she couldn't tell the surprise on his face was a mockery. "Why are you all het up, then? And squawkin' at *me?*"

She looked about ready to have a fit right there. "*The town shall hear of this!*" she hissed. "Do you know what she told me? That teaching was *her* business, and she thanked me kindly to keep myself out of it. Why, *I am on the Committee! We'll see her out!*"

That collection of biddies can't even decide what color the Town Hall should be painted, let alone where it should be built and who's going to pay for it. But they had put together the subscription to pay Miss Barrowe.

He'd thought about that on the ride here. If the miss didn't watch her step, she could be sent back to Boston without a Reference.

Somehow, he thought Miss Barrowe might not mind as much as Granger thought. She'd obviously come from money and manners, which was just another puzzle about the girl. What was she doing *here?*

What did you come here to escape, Mr. Gabriel?

"Now, how would we get another marm out here?" he wondered, openly. "Was hard enough to get this 'un. Been weeks now, and she's at least kept some of the little 'uns out of trouble." He scratched at his forehead some more. "Why not just let her be?"

Granger's lips trembled. For a moment he thought the woman might actually weep. Instead, she stuck her nose in the air and sashayed past him. He hurried to help her up into her wagon, and she snatched her hand back as soon as she had hefted her bulk up as if his heathen fingers singed. The horses weren't happy to leave the trough, but they obeyed. Her wagon set off down the road for town, raising a roostertail of golden dust, and Gabe let out a sigh that threatened to blow his hat off his head.

I should have just never gotten out of bed this dawnin'.

The steps creaked under him, and he gave the door a mannerly tap. He opened it to find six women sitting straight-backed and uncomfortable in long desks just slightly too small, the bottom of the tabletops actually hitting their knees. Miss Barrowe, smoothing back a dark curl that looked bent on escaping, stood tense by the slate board, her fingers almost white-knuckled around a yardstick that vibrated with hurtful mancy discharged not too long ago.

Bet that's what she hit Tils with. The sudden certainty made him want to smile, but he banished the notion, reaching up to take his hat off. No reason not to act proper. Besides, it gave him a chance to compose his expression, so to speak.

"Sheriff Gabriel." Low, and clear. "What is it?"

Given the day she'd had, he was probably lucky she didn't say anything worse. "Just checkin' to see all's well, ma'am."

"You may sit quietly." She pointed with the stick, at the very back row. "We are rather busy."

"Yes ma'am." He settled himself into a seat.

Mercy Tiergale hunched her shoulders as she bent over a slate she shared with Anna Dayne. Dark-eyed Belle and sharp-nosed blonde Trixie sat shoulder to shoulder, and the youngest of Tils's girls, Anamarie, hunched next to tall rangy Carlota like she expected Tils to come thundering in any minute. Lace shawls more fit for the saloon than for walking around town, the comb in Carlota's hair glimmering mellow in the late-afternoon light, Mercy's cheap paste earrings swinging gaudily. They were a sorry picture indeed, and as out of place as a sheep in a pulpit.

But Miss Barrowe continued, in the same clear tone, patiently tracing each letter on the board. By the end of the session, the women could write their names on the slates, which Miss Barrowe collected and locked in her desk. "To keep them from misadventure at a man's hands," she said grimly, and the ripple that went through the saloon girls, barely controlled, reminded Gabe of a flock of minnows in a clear stream.

"Very good," she said, standing before them with her hands clasped. "You are all quick, and docile. You are capable of being educated. I shall see you tomorrow, then. You are dismissed, ladies."

They sat and blinked at her for a few moments. The silence was thick, and Miss Barrowe's gaze flickered to Gabe in the back of the room. He should have been in town, looking after whatever mayhem the end of the afternoon would bring, or watching Freedman Salt's door, or any of a hundred other tasks. But here he sat, cramped in a desk the likes of which he hadn't seen since seminary after the orphanage, and he stared at the schoolmarm hungrily.

Mercy let out a disbelieving half-laugh. Carlota breathed a profane term Miss Barrowe pretended not to hear.

Gabe unfolded himself slowly, and he found himself the object of every gaze instead of just the marm's. "Take you back to town, ladies," he said, and wondered why Belle and Anamarie blushed, and Mercy's laugh seemed more genuine this time. Miss Barrowe's smile was like sunlight, but she suddenly looked very...fragile.

"Thank you, Sheriff." Prim as always, but high color in her cheeks. The pulse in her throat leapt, and found an answer in his own chest.

It was at that moment Jack Gabriel admitted to himself that he was in deep water, and sinking fast. He couldn't say he minded.

But Miss Barrowe might.

Chapter 12

Her mother would be scandalized. Her father would be amused, but perhaps also scandalized. If either of them were alive, instead of dead of Spanish flu, she would not *be* here.

But Cat could not find it in her heart to set her course differently.

The charm-hot water in the bathing-tub rippled as she stretched a foot up, her toes spreading as she relieved them of the pressure of being crammed into a point-toe boot all day. Her charing-charm was skinwarm, resting quiescent against her breastbone.

I struck a man in the face today. Mother would simply die.

Rather too late for that, though. Her face scrunched up, and she slid down farther in the rude copper tub.

Robbie was all she had left, other than her sufficiency. There was his inheritance, the bulk of their parents' estate; but she had been left quite enough to do as she pleased for the rest of her life, or to make a fine marriage if she wished. Her father's arrangements, as befitted a practical man of the Barrowe-Browne clans, had been most thorough.

She could perhaps wish Robbie were as practical. He might not have gone haring off into the Westron Wastes seeking adventure, if…

She moved again, restlessly. It would simply spoil her bath if she continued in this manner, and after today's events she rather thought she deserved a small bit of relaxation.

A globe of heat from the stove downstairs drifted into the narrow, closet-sized water-room. It hesitated, but Cat's fingers flicked, and she brought it down to meld with the bathwater's trembling surface, sighing with pleasure as it hissed. The water sent up trails and curls of steam as she shifted carefully again.

Think of something useful. Or if you cannot, Catherine, think on something pleasing.

There was little pleasure to be had in her reflections, however. Mr. Tilson was a brute, but he was also a figure of some importance in the town. Mrs. Granger, almost apoplectic at the thought of Ladies Of A Certain Class sitting at desks reserved for the children of the hame, was a far greater worry. It was such women who were the keepers of Reputation, and Cat's had perhaps taken rather a beating.

Still, what was she to do? Allowing Mr. Tilson's threats to set her course was unworthy of a Barrowe-Browne. And Cat could not hie herself into the saloon and hold reading classes *there*. Nor was there a space in town likely to grant her leave to do so, now that Mrs. Granger was involved. Her own parlour might have sufficed, but…that would not *do*. Teaching such ladies to read and figure was a Charitable Act; inviting them into one's home for more than a cup of tea was out of the question.

At least the sheriff had not made any trouble. Rather, he seemed to have quite an interest in the literacy of the saloon girls. Perhaps he was…involved? Miss Tiergale had clung to his arm, certainly. This was the Wild Westron; perhaps such things were not frowned upon.

In any case, he was a man, and could do as he pleased.

May I not do as I please, too?

No, she could not. Yet certain things that were impossible in Boston—for example, smashing a brute in his pig face with a stick—were possible here. Not only possible, but unavoidable.

What else was unavoidable?

A chartershadow, in a pawnshop. She imagined a fading, balding man, his body twisted by misuse of mancy. In novels, the chartershadow was always a villain, and those who went to him paid a price far greater than mere mancy or Reputation. Of course, one could not take novels as a foundation for one's actions.

Oh, but wouldn't it be pleasant if one could. For one thing, all ends well in novels.

Chartershadows were dangerous. Her fingers rested against her charing-charm, and its delicate ridges and whorls were as familiar as her own breathing. A shadow could perhaps break a charing, and where would she be then? Vulnerable to any stray mancy, at the mercy of whoever wished to ill-charm her…

Think logically. Imagine Robbie is asking you to plan some mischief that must be delicately accomplished in Society. Item one: I must acquire his locket. Item two: It is in a place none should see me enter, if possible. And nobody must connect me with Robbie. Item three: I am not in Boston; I am on the edge of civilization, in a town where the graveyards are, by all appearances, not well-cleansed. Night is likely to be especially dangerous outside a charm-locked door. Her fingertip tapped one fluted edge.

She must merely plan carefully. And take measures to defend herself, should she wish to go gallivanting about after dark here in the wilderness.

Cat cocked her head. Slippered feet in the hallway, brushing oddly as if the person attached to them staggered. She smoothed away the frown rising to her face and gathered herself, rising gingerly from the tub's depths and sighing a little as cool air hit her wet skin.

She had just barely wrapped a drying-cloth about herself when Li Ang appeared. The Chinoise girl's face was contorted, and her fingers sank into the doorframe as a shudder wracked her. Great pearls of sweat stood out on her caramel skin, and her dress held large sweat stains under her arms. Her belly, held before her like a fruit, suddenly looked…odd. Flattened, almost.

The girl gabbled something in Chinoisie. She bent forward, her face contorting even further, a mask of suffering.

"Good God," Cat breathed, just as there was a gushing patter. The fluid hit the floor, and Li Ang made a small, hopeless noise as her feet were bathed in the hot flood.

Oh, dear Heaven. She is…is she? It's the only possible explanation.

The Chinoise girl was having her baby.

And just at that moment, a series of knocks thundered against the front door.

It was certainly not respectable to throw open the door while clad only in a flannel wrapper, her hair soaked and clinging. Li Ang made another long groaning noise overhead, and the cottage answered with a groan of its own.

She had managed to get the girl onto the bed in Cat's own room and bolted downstairs, her bare feet slapping the floor so hard it stung. *Please don't go, whoever you are, we need help. Please don't go,* she prayed. *Please.*

"Help!" she choked, as she flung the door open and saw the garden, dipped in dusky purple. And there, at the gate, was a familiar hat and broad shoulders in a dun coat.

A sharp prickle of annoyance—what business did he have here after today? She quickly strangled it, and cleared her throat. "I say, Mr. Gabriel! *Sheriff!* Please. It's Li Ang, we—"

He was suddenly right in front of her, and Cat almost stumbled back. He caught her arm, work-roughened fingers sinking in, grinding on the fresh bruise of Mr. Tilson's grasp. She flinched, and his hand loosened. Would men never tire of shaking her about so?

"Slow down." His pale gaze flicked behind her. "All's well, miss. I'm here."

It was odd, but instead of improper, the words were…comforting. Certainly he was dependable, in his own rather rude fashion. "It's Li Ang," she managed. "She's having her…I mean, she is with…She is in labor, sir. Fetch a midwife. A doctor!" *I don't care who, as long as they know what to do.*

"Hm." He nodded. "I see. I'd get Doc Howard, but he don't hold with no Chinee. Listen to me." He tipped his hat back with two fingers, looking down at her. "I'll fetch help. You bar this door and the kitchen door, too. Make her as comfortable as you can. Boil water, and get clean cloths. We'll need a lot of linen, and a lot of boiled water. Or at least, so I've heard midwives say. Don't you open this door until I come back. You'll know it's me; I'll shout fit to raise the dead. *Avert.*" He let go of her completely now. "Mind you lock up, and don't you open to anyone but me. Understand?"

"Y-yes." *Do you think I would invite the entire town in for a social while* this *is happening?* "Lock the door, make her comfortable. Boil water. Cloths. Of course. I shall, of course, take responsibility for the midwife's fee—"

"Don't you worry about that now. For right now, go on up and tell Li Ang that nobody's going to take her baby." With that, he backed up, reaching for the door. "*Bar* this door, ma'am. As soon as I'm gone."

"Nobody is going to take her—" *What a curious thing to say to a woman abed.* But he swung the door closed, and Cat lost no time in dropping the bar into its brackets. The kitchen door was barred as well—had Li Ang done so?

Another long groan from overhead, spiraling up into a hoarse cry. *Oh, God.* Cat's palms were slippery with sweat, and the wrapper stuck to her most unbecomingly. Her heart pounded so hard she was half-afraid she would collapse.

The girl was up there alone, and in pain. Cat bit her lip, working the pump handle to fill the huge black kettle. She set it on the stove, stammered a boiling-charm—it took her two tries to remember an applicable one from Miss Bowdler's first book—and ran for the hall.

She halted, staring at the exact spot where Jack Gabriel had stood. He hadn't looked surprised or ruffled in the least. Come to think of it, he hadn't looked ruffled since she'd met him. Such phlegm might be maddening, but it was also strangely consoling. If he said he was going to bring help, then help he would bring, and as soon as possible too.

Cat climbed the stairs on trembling legs. Clammy and damp—she should find more appropriate attire before Mr. Gabriel returned.

Li Ang's next groan spiraled into a scream, and Cat put aside the shaking…and ran.

Chapter 13

Ma Ripp was a mean-faced hag with hard claws and a widow's sour black weeds. But inside the birthing room she was efficient and strangely gentle. She took one look at the schoolmarm's preparations and barked, "Good enough. Sheriff, more water. You there, girl, set her higher on them pillows." One yellow-nailed finger jabbed at the marm, whose big dark eyes and pale cheeks threatened to turn Gabe inside out.

The poor girl looked scared to death. Li Ang was propped on pillows on what had to be the marm's bed, her knees up and her hair sticking to her cheeks in jet-black streaks. Miss Barrowe had folded the comforter under her knees, and there was another divot on the bed—where, no doubt, Miss Barrowe had sat, holding Li Ang's hand as the birthing pangs ripped through the Chinoise girl.

"What's your mancy?" Ma Ripp finished, checking Li Ang's fragile wrist for her pulse.

Li Ang moaned, cursing in Chinoisie, and Miss Barrowe flinched. But her answer came, clear as a bell. "My Practicality? It's in Light, ma'am."

Ripp nodded once, her iron-gray hair braided tightly and looped about her large head. "Well, not entirely useless. Can you charm ice?"

To her credit, the marm didn't quail further. "Yes, of course."

Ripp handed her a small, battered tin cup. "Dip some water, there, and charm little bits of ice. Enough for her to suck on. Sheriff, get *moving*. This is woman's business."

Gabe retreated, but not before he caught Miss Barrowe's gaze. She stared at him for a long bright moment, and his insides knotted up again. Her cheeks were incredibly pale, and every time Li Ang sobbed for breath, she flinched in sympathy. Her hair was pulled back into a simple braid, still dripping, and she had managed to insert herself into a dress, though the buttons were askew and she had pulled the damp wrapper back on over it.

I'm here, he wanted to say. *Don't you worry.*

She averted her gaze, hurriedly, and dipped the tin cup in a basin of water. Mancy sparked, and Gabe found himself in the hall, his breathing hitching oddly.

The doors were locked, and Li Ang was as safe as he could make her. That was the bargain, and he intended to see it through. He should warn the marm about this, though. There were dangers hanging around the Chinoise girl that would only get deeper once she birthed.

He just hadn't thought it would come so *soon*.

More water was set to boil with numb fingers; he had to try twice to get the right charm to settle into the kettle. The marm was using a powerful but volatile mancy, and it almost singed *him*, too.

He wasn't surprised.

Footsteps overhead. He closed his eyes and *listened*. At least his early training still held, and his ears were plenty sharp.

"Are you *quite* sure?" The marm, anxious.

"Walkin's best at this stage." Ripp, a good deal gentler. "That's it, girl. Good, good."

"Her legs." Miss Barrowe gasped. "And did you see…Ma'am—"

"Shh. We've enough to do now."

Of course she would notice the scars on Li Ang's legs. There were more on the Chinoise girl's back—welt and rope and burn, a crazyquilt of suffering, barbaric lines of ink forced under bleeding skin too. Gabe breathed out, slowly, through his open mouth. They wouldn't come into this part of Damnation after her. Not comfortably, at least—the Chinois stayed on their own side, and once the railroad got close enough they'd camp out to provide labor for its iron stitchery.

If word got out the baby was born, though…

Gabe, this is a hell of a tangle.

Li Ang couldn't explain much of where she'd come from, but he'd done some quiet digging. At least, as quiet as he could, being a tall-ass roundeye wandering around in the Chinois part of Damnation. He supposed he should be grateful the marm hadn't taken it into her head to explore *that* shadow-half of town. They had their own chartermage, too, a disgusting piece of dried leather with a white beard and clawlike nails.

Who just happened to be Li Ang's husband. Or, to be precise, Li Ang was one of his wives. The only one to bear him a child to term, if what he'd heard was right.

Gabe was thinking the Chinois didn't hold with divorce.

Ripp kept talking, soothing and low. Li Ang cried out again, but softly, like a bird. Maybe it helped to have other womenfolk with her.

Whereas *he* was useless. He should be out riding the circuit, too. But Russ could handle it on his lonesome this once.

Jack stared at the black kettle and kept his hand away from his gun. It looked to be a long night.

"Push!" Ma Ripp barked.

"Oh, for God's sake," the marm snapped. "She's Chinoise; she can't understand you!"

Jack tried to make himself as small as possible against the hall wall. Inside the bedroom, Li Ang's cries had taken on a despairing note. It was almost touching, to hear Miss Barrowe taking up Ma Ripp on Li Ang's behalf.

"Instead of shouting at her—*ow!*"

"That's it!" Ripp crooned. "Squeeze her hands! Almost there, duckums. I can see the head."

"Oh dear…" Suddenly the marm seemed not quite so crisp. "Is that supposed to happen?"

Li Ang's voice spiraled up into a scream, and she cursed both of them roundly. At least, so it sounded. The harsh, foreign syllables broke, agony and triumph mingling, and Gabe flinched.

"Oh…" Miss Barrowe. "Oh, my God."

"That's it! That's a good girl! Now! Now!"

Li Ang screamed again. A wet tearing sound, a gushing. Slapping, and Ma Ripp's muttered mancy. Popping, cracking, fizzing—and Miss Barrowe, softly now.

"Hush, dearie…oh, hush, all's well, yes, hold my hand…Oh, my. My goodness. My heavens."

She doesn't know what to say. I reckon I wouldn't, either.

Then, a thin protesting wail, gathering in force. "A boy," Ma Ripp announced dryly. "Breathin' now, thank the Almighty. And just as fine as can be. Missy, turn loose of her and wash this little 'un."

"I've never—"

"That don't matter. Hold his head, *so*. Just sponge him—that's right. Wrap him up good, I laid the swaddling right there. You had a doll once, dintcha? Just like a doll."

Li Ang cursed again, raggedly. Or at least, it sounded like a foul imprecation, with an edge of beseeching.

"Oh, yes, I'm bringing him. Just a moment." Miss Barrowe, half to weeping. "He's so *small*. Oh my goodness. *Oh*—he's leaking, I do believe he's…oh, good *Lord*." There was a spray and a pattering, and the baby howled with indignation.

"Healthy little cuss," Ma Ripp observed. "Use the fresh swaddlin', there. Sometimes they pee. Now comes another bit of a mess. Bleeding, too. Ho, Sheriff! Needing another pair of hands!"

What, me? But he was already palming the door open.

A squalling little bundle, wrapped tightly but inexpertly in boiled and charm-dry cloth, screwed up its tiny little face and wailed. Li Ang, wan and sagging, her knees hitched high and everything below the waist exposed, closed her eyes and clutched the bundle to her chest. It looked like a little old man, and was quickly turning purple. It produced an *amazing* amount of noise.

"Get the tit in that babe's mouth." Ma Ripp pointed at Miss Barrowe, who was braced at the side of the bed, a smear of blood on her colorless cheek. The Boston miss looked dazed. "Sheriff, my bag. Got to stanch this with mair's root and a charm."

The bed looked sadly the worse for wear, bright blood and a clot of darkness spreading from Li Ang's undersides. *That's an awful lot of blood for such a little girl.*

"I believe, ah, that she wishes you to feed the baby, Miss

Ang." The marm's fingers, clutched in Li Ang's free hand, must have been throbbing, but she merely looked pale and interested. "I, ah, think it might be best to…oh, *dear*."

"Don't you go fainting like a useless little prip." Ma Ripp accepted her capacious black Gladstone. "Or I'll step on you. Get her to put the tit in that little one's mouth; best thing for them both." Rummaging in the bag now, with bloodstained fingers, the woman looked like a graveyard hag. "And *you*, Sheriff. More cloths. Won't fix itself, and I know *you've* seen the underbits of a woman before."

"Will she be…" His head was full of rushing noise. Damn, who would have thought the little bitty Chinoise girl would have so much blood in her? Grown men couldn't stand after losing that much.

"Right as rain once we fix this. Seen worse, yes I have." Ma Ripp nodded, pushing back a lank strand of sweat-drenched gray hair knocked free of her braids. "Right fine work done tonight."

"That's it, dear. Oh, he knows what to do!" Miss Barrowe actually sounded delighted. Maybe women all loved this birthing business.

"This child yourn?" Ripp's claws were quick and deft, a charm guttering into life on the pad of fresh cloth she pressed between Li Ang's legs. "You seem mighty interested."

"She's a widow." Jack managed the familiar lie, and followed it with truth. "And it ain't mine."

"Well, her husband, God rest the heathen, has a fine son. At least he'll never have to do *this*." She licked her dry, withered lips. "Don't suppose there's no whiskey in this house."

"Madam!" The marm, genuinely shocked, blinked from Li Ang's side. The Chinoise girl had let go of Miss Barrowe's hand,

and was occupied with her new bundle, staring at the tiny little purple-faced thing as if she had never seen a baby before. For all Jack knew, she hadn't. She was awful young, and the Chinois...well. It didn't bear thinking about.

"Keep your corset on, missy. A drop's just the thing after this type of work." The midwife accepted Gabe's flask and tossed back a healthy slug. "Now, let's get this mess cleared. Dawn's coming. You should ride for the chartermage, to fetch him a charing."

"Quite." Miss Barrowe no longer sounded so pale, and the baby had quit its hollering. It was occupied with its mother's breast, in any case, and the sight gave Gabe an odd feeling in the region of his stomach.

She looks just like any of our girls. And, compelled, he glanced at Miss Barrowe. Some color had come back into her face, and she stared at the baby, rapt as Li Ang herself. The smear of blood on Miss Barrowe's soft cheek was wrong, and his fingers tingled. He could just wipe it away, couldn't he.

If he could touch her.

Don't, Jack. You know what could happen. You know what's bound to happen if you start getting ideas.

"Sheriff." A poke to his shoulder, Ma Ripp shoving the metal flask back at him. "You go fetch the mage, now. Sooner this 'un gets a proper charing, the better."

"Yes ma'am," he mumbled, and backed for the door.

Chapter 14

Tuesday was a blur of half-somnolent anxiety. There were items to be procured for a baby's care, and the midwife's fee to pay, and the news to be spread that her girl had birthed and the school was closed for the day. The Chinoise was only a servant, true, and this event should not cause her to leave her duties.

But Cat had been dead on her feet, and Jack Gabriel had, none too gently, told her to take her rest while he made sure the town knew.

She had no idea if it was quite proper or normal for Mr. Gabriel to take charge of affairs, but was grateful nonetheless. Mrs. Ripp, her terrible yellowed teeth showing in a grin, undertook to provide the things the baby would need—for a fee, of course, and Cat had paid without question. Afterward, Mr. Gabriel had words with the crone, and returned a third of Cat's money.

It was…thought-provoking.

It ain't mine, he'd said, but it was most odd, that he would take such care over a Chinoise girl's baby. It was none of Cat's concern, though, and there was plenty else to worry about on that day.

There was engaging a charmwasher for the laundry, the short coffee-colored chartermage to pay and the certificate for a fresh charing-charm to fill, a delivery of firewood to be attended to, and Cat had not eaten until Jack Gabriel had shoved a plate into her hands and told her to sit down and take a bite. Tolerable biscuits, some half-charred bacon, and there was even boiling water for tea.

She had boiled so much water she doubted she would ever forget the charm itself. It was burned into her fingers, along with its catchword. She wondered if it was the way a Continental sorcerer might feel about a certain charm or mancy, never mind that their sorcery worked differently. Mancy followed geography, as the old saying went.

She'd fallen asleep at the kitchen table, staring at the side of her teacup, and only woke when the sheriff shook her shoulder and told her briskly to get herself up to bed. It was Li Ang's pallet she slept on through the remainder of that long, terribly hot day, and so deeply she had surfaced in a panic, unable to discern who, where, or even *what* she was.

Fortunately, the feeling had passed, and she found herself in Damnation, with a baby's cry coming from downstairs and Li Ang singing to her son in an exhausted, crooning voice. The poor girl had been trying to clean the kitchen, and Cat's heart had wrung itself in a most peculiar fashion.

It had taken all Cat's skill to gently but firmly bully the Chinoise girl upstairs and tuck her in with the baby.

This cannot be so hard. And indeed the biscuits were lumpy and her gruel left a little to be desired, but it was nourishing. Or so she hoped, but then dawn was painting the hills with orange and pink, and she had to hurry to reach the schoolhouse at a reasonable hour. *Without* her parasol, no less.

Her mother would be not just annoyed, but angered. A lady did not forget such things, much less a Barrowe-Browne.

She had half-expected the schoolroom to be empty on Wednesday, Mrs. Granger having had more than enough time to spread calumny and gossip-brimstone. But the students came trooping in, some of them downcast, true, but others bright and cheery—or sullenly energetic—as usual. Now she knew their names, and a curious calm settled over her.

The children did not seem so fractious, now. Even the Dalrymple girls were no trouble, bent over their slates and newly eager to please. Amy, the elder, even elbowed Cecily once or twice when the younger girl seemed likely to bridle, and Cat rewarded the elder girl with letting her touch the pianoforte's keys during lunchtime. "There are such things as lessons," she had intimated, and the naked hope on the young blonde hoyden's face gave Cat another strange, piercing pain in the region of her chest.

Instead of savages, the children now looked oddly hopeful. Their bare feet and ragged clothing were less urchin than primitive, as if the Garden of Shoaal had been re-created here in the far West, amid the dust and the heat and the incivility. Even the freckles on young Cecily's face had their own fey beauty, tiny spots of gold on fair young skin.

It was there, sitting at her desk and staring across the bent heads as they scratched at their slates, that she realized just how far she was from Boston. Perhaps it was lack of sleep bringing a clarity all its own.

Cat drew in a deep breath, her stays digging in briefly, and wondered if she could march into a pawnshop under broad daylight.

No, night is best. But more dangerous—if you are seen, somehow…

But this was not Boston. She shook her head and attended to the third form, laboriously reciting from the eighth page of Miss Bowdler's First Primer. "Very good," she encouraged, though she would have said so if they had been reciting backward charter-cantations, or even the Magna Disputa. "You may lay that aside, and apply yourself to tracing your alphabet."

"Yes mum," they chorused, and she surprised herself by smiling.

They waited until the children were gone, then trooped silently in, faces scrubbed and mouths pulled tight. Miss Tiergale took her seat first as Cat brought out the slates.

"Good afternoon, ladies," she essayed. They were so long-faced she half-expected bad news. God and charter both knew it would be *just* the time for it.

It was Belle who spoke first, in a rush. "We don't mean to be no trouble, Miss Barrowe."

Trouble? Oh, none at all, unless you count the bruise on my arm and the loss of Reputation. It does not seem that I will miss it over-much here. Her chin rose. "Indeed you are none. In fact, on our short acquaintance I have found you all to be serious and studious."

"She means with Tils." Mercy's cheeks, one with its fading bruise, flushed uncomfortably. "He's…well, he ain't a nice man, miss. And he's been drinkin."

"That does not surprise me." She began handing out the slates, her boots tapping the raw lumber with little authoritative ticking noises. "He does not seem the temperate sort." *In any sense of the word.*

"Well, *you* ain't got to be afraid, not with Gabe looking after you." Trixie gazed at the ceiling. Today they were all dressed fairly respectably, instead of in their frail flash and feathers. "It's us what gots to watch our step."

There are so many grammaticals I could take issue with in those statements. "Mr. Gabriel is charged with the safety of everyone in this town." She handed Mercy her slate with an encouraging smile.

Anamarie giggled, elbowing the tall one, Carlota. "Not Salt's, I reckon. He hates that chartershadow."

"Wouldn't you?" Trixie was still studying the ceiling, her cheeks flushed from the heat. "Shadows ain't no good."

Let's cease this chatter. "We shall begin with—"

"She's blushing," Anamarie whispered. "I think she's sweet on him, too."

That got Trixie's attention. "Who, the shadow?"

"*Ladies.*" Cat folded her arms. Her cheeks stung, perhaps because of the bruise on Mercy's poor face. "We have much to accomplish this afternoon. I intend to earn every cent of the fee you have graciously promised me. Take up your slates."

That served to bring them to task. Her cheeks still burned, though, and it took a while for the heat to fade. It was entirely different than the dry baking outside, and Cat's head was full of a strange noise. She held grimly to her task, and by the end of the session all the women had firmly grasped not only the basic functions of the alphabet, but also the idea, if not the application, of multiplication.

"It's all groups!" Anamarie finally burst out. "Say you've a fellow buying drinks for you and him. That's two drinks. And he buys three rounds. Three groups of two, six!"

"Unless Coy waters yours so you can keep a clear head to roll the bastard," Carlota said, and their shared laughter made Cat smile before the probable meaning of "roll" occurred to her.

"Language, Carlota." Mildly enough. Cat pulled her skirts aside as she reached to wash the slate board clean in preparation for their practice at writing their names. "Very good, Anamarie. It's all groups. Multiplication and division—"

"Now hold on," Mercy finally spoke up. "Let's just stick with the multiplyin' until I get that clear inside my skull."

"I wanta read my Bible." Belle, suddenly, as she scratched lightly at the wooden frame of her slate with one broken fingernail. "That's what I want."

"I'm a-gonna move to San Frances and open up a bawdy house of my own. Be a madam, not the girl." Trixie waved one airy, plump hand. "Count the money and eat me sweet things all day."

"Where you gonna get the stake for that?" Anamarie tossed her dark head, her earrings—plain paste, like Mercy's—swinging against her curls.

"That's why I said we gotta learn numbers, so Tils can't short us none no more."

"Names, ladies." Cat began tracing them on the board. "Can you tell whose I am writing now?"

A ragged chorus: "A…N…A…M…A…"

"Why, that's me! Ah-na-mah-ree."

"*Very* good. Wait until I've written them all to copy your own name."

"It's like mancy. Like the charters."

"Except these don't glow—"

"Ladies, I know you're eager to be gone. We must finish this first, however. Please contain yourselves."

"Why you call us ladies all the time?" Carlota wanted to know. "We ain't."

Cat's patience stretched, but the clarity that had possessed her all day held. "This is the Wild Westron. Anyone can become anything here." *I can even become a schoolteacher, possessed of patience I hardly knew was possible. And helper to a midwife, and a woman who can teach fancy frails to read.*

For a long few moments, nobody spoke as Cat traced a C, an A, an R. "Which letters are these? Anyone?"

The chorus began again. "C…A…R…"

Cat Barrowe found herself smiling broadly, facing the board. Yes, indeed. *Anyone can become anything here.*

Chapter 15

Dusk was gathering, purple veils and a breath of coolness stepping down from the hills on the heels of a steadily gathering wind. Approaching autumn tiptoed around the town, but the bank of heavy gray stayed firmly in the north and didn't sweep down any farther. When it did roll over Damnation, the mud would be knee-high. He would have to teach Miss Barrowe to drive the wagon, so she could avoid getting her skirts draggled. That would mean caring for a horse close to her cottage, too, and he was involved in a long train of thought having to do with the possibility of a stall in the Armstrongs' stable when he turned the corner and saw her walking slowly, head down, from the other direction.

School was out, then, and the saloon girls were probably back at the Star. He'd had a word with Paul Turnbull about Tils. That went about as well as could be expected—Paul didn't like trouble, and Gabe gave him to understand that Tilson was fixing to have trouble with Gabe himself if he didn't leave the marm alone.

At least it was something.

She was in blue today, and her nipped-in waist was a sharply beautiful curve. Those little pointed-toe boots with all the buttons, and stray dark curls coming loose under her prettily perched hat. It was the first time he'd seen her slim shoulders anything but straight and stiff. She looked half-dead on her feet, like a sleepy horse.

Well, no wonder.

His stride lengthened. What should he say? *Evenin', ma'am?* Was that too formal? *Hello there?* Maybe something else, a little pleasantry. *Ain't you a fine sight.*

Or even, *God must be kind, because you're here.*

It had been years since he'd felt this tightness in his chest. Annie hadn't made him feel silly and stupid; or at least, maybe he'd been young enough that he hadn't cared. She had been sweet and soft, not prickly and precise as this little bit of a thing with her head down and the leather satchel swinging from her left hand pulling her to the side. She was listing like a ship limping into port, and Gabe swallowed dryly. *Oh, Hell.*

The wind picked up, and dust swirled against her skirts. She halted by the white-painted garden gate, staring at it as if she could not for the life of her figure out what such a contraption might be for.

"Don't fall asleep, now." His hand closed around her elbow, gently.

Her head tilted up, a slow movement. She blinked, weariness etched on her soft face. She searched his features, as if he were a stranger. "Mr. Gabriel?" Wondering. "Is Li Ang well?"

What? "Should think so. I just got here."

"Ah." Miss Barrowe nodded. "I see. Well, you may come in briefly to see her, but I warn you, she is still very tired."

What about you? "Didn't come to see *her*, ma'am."

"Then what are you...oh, *never* mind." She took her elbow from him, very decidedly, and he reached to open the gate. "Is it a disaster, or some new variety of excitement?"

What do you expect? "Neither. Just came to visit before I rode the circuit."

"I hope I am not keeping you."

"You treat all your visitors this way, sweetheart?"

"Sir." Frosty and sharp, now. "You shall address me as *Miss Barrowe.*"

Well, now he had her measure. And braving that prickliness was worth what was behind it. "Sometimes, yep. Other times, not so much."

At least the irritation had given her a little energy. She sashayed up the walk at a good clip, and he watched the swing and sway of her skirts. How did women move with all that material tied on? No doubt it weighed like panniers stuffed with gold dust.

Something bothered him, but he couldn't rightly figure it out. Something about gold, and Miss Barrowe.

She reached the steps, gathering her pretty blue skirts with her free hand. "I hope she hasn't barred the door. That would be simply terr—*oh!*"

Her hurt little cry pierced the moan of the freshening dust-laden wind, and he had no memory of the intervening space. He was simply *there* as she stumbled back, her skirts dropping free because she had clamped her hand over her mouth. She turned, blindly, and the thump of her leather satchel hitting the wooden bottom step barely covered his hissed, indrawn breath.

He found himself with a shivering woman in his arms, staring at the shadowy writhing thing nailed to the porch. It had probably been a rabbit once, but bad mancy was all that was left, corkscrewing and flapping the dying tissues. An unholy spark flashed inside the thing's half-peeled skull, and whatever tortured bit of soul still remaining in its tiny bone cage let out a piercing little moan.

She shuddered again, and his fingers were in her hair, cupping the back of her skull, a hatpin's prick against his wrist. "Shhhh," he soothed, only half-aware of speaking. "Shh, don't look. God*damn*. Easy there."

The wind crested, and he had limited daylight to take care of this thing and get to the circuit. Russ wouldn't take kindly to riding alone at twilight. Dawn was one thing, but dark was another, and Gabe didn't blame him.

"L-l-l—" She gulped, tensed, and tried to pull away. "Li Ang! She's inside—what if—"

He found his other hand was pressed against the small of her back, and the fading whiff of rosewater mixed with clean linen and a spice-tang of healthy female to make something utterly unique. She didn't have any idea how good she smelled. "Then I'll find out. Now come along." He didn't have to work to sound grim. "Back door. Step quiet, and stay behind me."

"What...who would..."

"Don't know." *But I aim to find out. That's bad mancy for sure, and what if I hadn't been here?* "Now you be a good girl and stay behind me, you hear?"

A nod. He was all but crushing her, he realized, and loosened up just a little. Then a little more. She might scream, or faint—no, this miss wasn't the fainting type. Even if she had swooned a little when she arrived. Who wouldn't have?

He trawled through memory and found what he wanted. "Catherine."

"Wh-what?"

"Just sayin' your charing-name. Makin' sure I've got your attention, like."

"I believe you do, sir." With nowhere near her usual snap.

"You can call me Jack."

"Thank you." A little prim, now, which cheered him immensely. She was nice and steady, and she didn't try to struggle away. Instead, she just stood there, and he let her. "Jack?"

"Hm." He kept his gaze on the twisting, flopping thing. It was nailed in solid with what was probably false-iron, and it let out another agonized little sound. *A warning, maybe. God damn whoever did this.*

"It's screaming. Could…could you possibly…"

I'd prefer to clear the house first, but since you're asking… "Stay right here, then. *Right* here. This very spot."

"I shall." Her eyes were tightly closed, and she flinched when the no-longer-rabbit thing screeched. Jack's chest cracked a little, and he found, to his not-quite surprise, that everything in him still remembered what came next, as if the intervening years had fallen away and he was still the orphan boy sold to the Ordo Templis and the man who had left the knights behind for a woman's arms.

This, he knew how to do.

It was a moment's work to mount the steps, a trifle more to take a long considering look at the mancy pinning the thing. No use rushing.

It looked odd, and his mouth thinned. He shook out his left hand, keeping his right away from a gun with an effort. A bullet wouldn't end this misery.

He closed away the moaning wind and the falling dark. The sun was a bloody clot in the west, its light dipping and painting

Damnation in vermilion. The thought of the schoolmarm at the foot of the stairs wouldn't go away, so he breathed into it. Let it fill his head, and relaxed.

I release you.

His left-hand fingers made a curious, complex motion. It was not quite charter-mancy; nor was it sorcery. A trace-map of golden veins lit the flesh of his fingers, and he *saw* the knot holding the tiny soul into violated flesh. Sometimes the best response was to unpick the strands carefully, loosening one a fraction, then another.

Then there were times like these.

I release you.

His fingers tensed, the golden light casting dappled water-shadows on the roof and floor of the porch. He had a moment to hope she had her eyes closed—this would create all manner of fuss and undue questions if she saw grace upon him instead of plain mancy—before he jabbed his hand forward, a softly spoken Word resonating with hurtful edges as it sliced the knot of bad mancy clean through.

I release you.

False-iron popped blue sparks, and the sodden little rag of fur and meat and splintered bone sagged. His left hand, a fist now, flicked down as if he were casting salt. Fine golden grains of pure light showered over the thing, and the blot was cleansed. A brief burst of fresh green scent, like new-mown hay, washed away on the breeze.

For others, I may do, by Grace. Amen.

Grace was never in short supply. Faith, though, was far rarer than the gold they dug and panned for. And he was—was he?—oddly relieved that grace had not left him.

It ain't grace, Gabe. It's...her.

His spurs rang on the steps, and found Catherine, her eyes tightly shut, hugging herself and cupping her elbows in her hands. Tears welled between her lashes. He had to try twice before his throat would unloose enough to let him speak. "It's done." Gabe's chest clenched around something solid and fiery, thrust under his ribs. "Aw, no. Don't *cry*."

"I am very sorry," she whispered. "I am *trying* not to. Li Ang." She opened her eyes, blinking rapidly and dashing away a tear on her cheek with one gloved hand. "We must find her."

I didn't mean…oh, Hell. He bent to grab her satchel, but she was quicker, and straightened with it clutched in tense fingers. "Catherine—"

"Please don't. *Don't*." She brushed past him for the corner of the house, obviously intending to sashay around to the back door in defiance of all good sense.

"Stay *behind* me, you idiot," he barked, and could have slapped himself on the forehead.

"Then hurry." Like a whipcrack, her pert little reply.

But he was already past her, checking the corner and drawing his right-hand gun. His left hand tingled, the odd pins-and-needles sensation he remembered from his Last Baptism right before his vows. Funny how it never went away.

Some things pursue a man, Jack. You know that. "More haste, less speed." The side of the house was as innocent as a newborn babe. He cursed inwardly at the thought. Russ hadn't caviled at giving a Chinois child a charing, so at least *that* was all right. But still.

"The baby." As if she'd read his mind. "Dear God."

"Probably fine. Li Ang ain't no fool. Bet she's got the house locked up tight." *But there might be another little present waiting at your back door, pretty girl, and that is not a happy thought.*

"Sir?" Breathless. At least if she fainted now it would save him the trouble of explaining himself.

"Shh."

She stayed silent, then. There was a rattling, and the back door opened, the stoop dust-scoured and charm-cleaned.

Li Ang peered at them, her son clutched to her chest. She was shaking, and gabbling in her heathen tongue, and Gabe was right glad to hear it. Catherine actually flung her arms about the Chinoise girl, and the baby squalled between them.

He took the opportunity to get them both inside and the door shut tight, then went straight to the house to the front to take care of the carcass.

His hands shook, but not with fear.

Oh, no. Not fear at all.

Chapter 16

Bad," Li Ang said. "*Baaaad.*" She clutched at little Jonathan—she called him Jin, but there had to be *something* written on the charing certificate, so he was now Jonathan Liang Barrowe, may God have mercy on them all. Mother would die, and Father might even lose his hallowed temper, but Cat was past caring. It was a proud name, and might do even a Chinoise a fair service.

"Yes, but all's well." Cat sought for a patient, soothing tone. The kettle chirruped, heating water for tea, and she forced herself to keep her eyes wide open, staring at charm-sparking against the metal. "Mr. Gabriel is here."

Odd, wasn't it, how such a sentence could be so comforting. As if she were a child, and this a nightmare banished by a parent's sudden presence.

Except Jack Gabriel was not in the least parental. He was something else. She was far too exhausted to find the proper word.

Little Jonathan burbled a bit, but he had ceased wailing. Which was very nice, now that she thought about it.

It seemed she only blinked, but then the kettle was boiling and she set about making tea. If she focused on the pot and the leaves, the water at precisely the right temperature and the cups arranged just *so*, perhaps she would not think of the little thing on the porch, screaming as some variety of dark mancy robbed it of death's comfort.

Who would do such a thing? My God.

The back door squeaked as it ghosted open, and Li Ang inhaled sharply, as if to scream. But it was merely Jack Gabriel, his eyes incandescent under the shadow of his hatbrim.

That was like saying it was *merely* a hurricane, or *merely* an earthquake. Something about him filled up the entire kitchen, made it difficult to breathe. Maybe it was the feel of his fingers in her hair, or his broad chest against her cheek, or the way he'd stood, solid and steady.

She kept her eyes down, and noted with some relief that her hands were steady as well. Her gloves lay neatly on the counter, and one of them was stained near the wrist. Ink, and she should attend to that soon before it set so deeply even a charm wouldn't remove it.

Shh. Don't look. Easy there. And a curious comfort in the midst of her fear.

Perhaps she should ask the sheriff about Robbie. But *trust no one*, her brother had written more than once.

And, *the law in this town is worse than the lack of it.*

The sheriff was saying something. She concentrated on pouring. Tea would brace her. Tea solved quite *everything*, or at least, so Miss Ayre had firmly believed. Cat was shaken with a sudden irrational urge to write to her old governess and ask *her* help. Miss Ayre would set all this to rights.

Miss Ayre had gone her quiet way years ago, once Cat was

too old to need a governess, and their correspondence had stopped after news of Miss Ayre's marriage to a man in Europa. *Quite a rich man, too,* her mother had sniffed, and there was no more said.

No, there was nobody left to solve this quandary but Cat herself, and she was rather doubting her own resources at the moment.

"Put that baby to bed," he finished, and Li Ang shuffled away. "What are you doing there, Catherine?"

A jolt all through her, as if a whip of stray mancy had bit her fingers. *I should not let him address me so.* "I am making tea," she replied, dully. "I had a governess, once." *And she would have this set to rights in a trice.*

He was silent for a long moment. "I think you should sit down."

"I am *making tea*. Such an operation cannot be performed satisfactorily while seated." She took a deep breath. *Now I must ask questions.* "Who would do such a terrible thing, Mr. Gabriel?"

"You may as well call me Jack."

For the love of… The irritation was welcome, a tonic for her nerves. It even managed to give her a burst of fresh wakefulness. "In other words, you do not know, or will not venture a guess."

"In other words, you may as well use my charing-name. And I have an idea or two. Don't trouble yourself over it no further."

Why ever not? It was nailed to my porch and began screaming as I approached. "I am quite troubled, and I intend to continue to be. Whoever did that—"

"—is gonna reckon with *me* soon enough, Miss Porquepine. You don't need to worry. And I don't think Li Ang wants no tea."

"We should be civilized, even here. And tea is a tonic. It does very well for nerves, and—"

"I think you should sit down."

"I think, sir, that you may go to Hell." What had possessed her? She was trembling. Well, who wouldn't, faced with this? And why did the man have to be so outright *infuriating*?

Boiling water splashed. She let out a shaky breath, and finished filling the pot. Thank God one could find tea in this benighted place, even though it was *not* of the quality her mother would have found acceptable.

"I intend to, if you get yourself into trouble down there."

What does that mean? "You're refusing an invitation to tea, then? I shall be pouring momentarily."

"Sit *down*." He had her shoulders, big work-roughened hands that had probably touched the thing out front, and she let out a tiny piping sound, rather like baby Jonathan's satisfied little noise when Li Ang set him high on her shoulder and patted his back. "I ain't gonna hurt you, but I am gonna make you listen. We need to have a talk."

There was no use in fighting, so she let him push her toward the kitchen table and her usual seat. She sank down, her corset stays digging in abominably, and glared at him from under her knocked-askew hatbrim. Her hair was too loose, as well, curls falling in her eyes and brushing her shoulders.

Hazel eyes, bleached to a gold-green shine most odd, shadow of stubble on his jaw, his own dark hair mussed. At least he'd taken his hat off. He pulled out Li Ang's chair and dropped down, heavily, and she had the sudden gratifying vision of wood cracking and the chair spilling him to the floor. He rubbed at his face, scratching his cheek, and let out a long sigh.

He was too big for the chair, too big for the *room*. The

dun-colored coat, the guns at his belt, everything about him was too big and dusty and foreign. Her heart hammered, because he smelled of healthy horse and heat and healthy male, leather and *tabac* and a verdant green note of mancy. An overpowering aroma, but not at all an unpleasant one.

Shh. Easy there. And his fingers in her hair. His hand at the small of her back, and the sense of being enclosed, held safely away from something howling and snapping. Quite comforting, and not at all proper, now that she considered it.

The cottage was deathly silent, except for the stealthy creaks of Li Ang moving upstairs. Had the new crib arrived today? Cat really should have arranged for that beforehand, but it had all happened so *quickly*. And there was still the question of other items that should have been delivered, and arrangements to be made—

"I can't watch you all the time. I got other work to do."

Her annoyance mounted another notch. Her cheeks, no doubt, were scarlet; they were hot enough to boil the kettle afresh. "I do not recall asking you to do so, sir."

He refused to take offense. How could he be so d—ned *imperturbable*? "No, 'cause it'd be easier if you *did*. Simmer down."

"I am *perfectly* calm."

"No, you ain't. I ain't, either. So just simmer down, Catherine, and we'll do some plannin'."

"I do not intend to do any *planning*. I've done far too much of that, and not enough…" *Shut up, Cat.*

She did, closing her mouth with a snap.

He merely nodded, wearily. "I could put you on the next stagecoach for Poscola Flats, and you could be on a train to Boston in two shakes."

"No." *Not until I have Robbie's locket. Then I will find him, no matter what condition he may be in.*

Could that be the warning? Did someone in Damnation know, or suspect? It was very likely, and the trembling going through her mounted another notch.

Oh, Robbie. What on earth are you suffering right now? Or are you…no, you cannot be dead. You simply cannot be.

Jack Gabriel held up one callused hand, as if to halt an obedient dog. "I figure you've got a reason not to go back East. Well, no matter. If you're gonna stay in Damnation, we'll—"

Her temper almost snapped. "You have no right to order me about *or* dispose of me in any fashion, sir."

"No, I ain't got a right, yet. But I'm powerful interested in keeping that pretty neck of yours out of trouble. You could try thankin' me."

"I am sure I am very grateful." She made it as prim and unhelpful as she could, which was *quite.*

"You're a bad liar."

I hope not. Oddly enough, though, she felt better. Why? "If you have finished insulting me—"

"Are you the marryin' type, Miss Barrowe?"

"*What?*" Her shriek would probably wake little Jonathan, all the way upstairs.

Jack Gabriel leaned forward in the chair, his elbows braced on his knees. He was staring at her, and the faint smile he wore was not calming *or* humorous in the least. "I mean, are you sweet on anyone, back East or here? Some poor bastard who don't know how to handle you when you get all prickly and proper?"

I'm dreaming. There's no other explanation. This is all a nightmare. "I most certainly am *not*, not that it's any of your business—"

"Good. Because I'd hate to have to kill a man over you. Now you listen to me. From now on, you stay in sunshine. I'll get Russ Overton to bring the wagon 'round to take you to the schoolhouse, and I'll walk you home in the afternoons. Tell me you will."

What is he on about? I shall never get a chance to acquire Robbie's locket if you keep crowding me in such a manner. "I don't see the need for Mr. Overton or—"

"There's a need."

His tone was so grim she leaned back against the chair, and found her hands were not so steady now. She clasped them together—where had her gloves gone? Her head was a-whirl. If she could merely gather herself for a few moments, perhaps this would not seem so overwhelming.

It did not appear he would let her. "Now, are you gonna give me your word, Catherine? 'Cause if you ain't I'm gonna have to do something you might not like."

"Do *not* threaten me. I will observe all proper precautions. Including seeking legal redress and charter protection against whoever—"

"You just leave that to me." He sighed, rose a trifle stiffly, and settled his hat over his tousled hair. With it on, the steely glint of his eyes lost under the shadow of the brim, he was not quite so comforting. "Do I have your word?"

"Certainly." Fancy that—she had gone from being grateful for his presence to wishing she could heave him out the door with exceeding force. "I shall go with Mr. Overton in the morning, and you may be allowed to accompany from the schoolhouse to my domicile in the afternoons. When it is necessary."

"Good enough." He settled his hat, turned on his heel, and strode for the back door. "Bar this behind me. And for God's

132

sake, be careful. That wasn't a May bouquet sitting on your porch." The drawl had evaporated, and he sounded clipped and precise. "Ma'am."

With that, he was gone, the night outside breathing its dust-spice in for a brief moment. Cat pulled herself to her feet, made it across the room on unsteady legs, and settled the bar in its brackets. She turned the lock too, for good measure. The kettle hadn't even finished steaming, and the teapot sent up fragrant veils as well. Everything else, she decided, could bloody well wait for morning to be sorted.

I'd hate to have to kill a man over you.

Dear God. Did he mean there was a chance he *would*?

Chapter 17

Full dark had fallen, and Russ Overton was in a state, jamming his hat on and scrambling to his feet from his usual chair in front of Capran's Dry Goods. Across the street, the Tin House was rocking with drunken laughter, and there was the high sharp note of glass breaking. "It's *dark*, Gabe! The circuit—"

"You come with me." Gabe barely broke stride. Whoever was smashing glass inside the Tin could wait. "We ain't goin far."

"What the hell—is it an incursion? What's going on?"

The canvas bag dangling from Gabe's right hand swung a little, dripping. His spurs struck sparks, bright blue bits of uneasy mancy. "Someone left a rabbit on the schoolmarm's porch."

Russ's legs were too short, so he outright scurried to keep alongside. "That's very nice, but—"

"Twisted up with a death-charm and nailed in with false-iron." His teeth ached; he was gonna crack a few of them if he kept clenching them this hard. At least he had a charm to fix *that*.

Russ spluttered. "*What?* That's goddamn *dangerous!*"

I thought so too. Gabe plunged aside into the alley, and

Russ hurried to keep up, their boots grinding against dust and small pebbles. The wind had picked up even more, and it might be another one of the storms that made everyone crazy with a constant low moaning and rasping grit in the air.

Of course, Gabe was halfway to crazed already.

He'd probably scared the life out of the girl; the words had been out of his mouth before he'd *thought*. Now she knew, and not only that. Saying it made it real.

Maybe it was just that the schoolmarm was the first miss who wasn't a saloon girl or someone's spoken-for—but that wasn't it, either. It was *something else*, he didn't have the time or the inclination to define it further.

The important thing was, she was in harm's way. Which meant Jack Gabriel had a job to do.

What a helluva mess.

"Gabe, dammit, what the hell?" Russ was out of breath already.

"Salt's." The rage mounted another notch inside his chest, and the ice all through him was a warning. Her curls were soft, a little slippery, and she had trembled against him, soft and frightened. "That's where we start. And if the sonofabitch did this bit of work, I'm putting a bullet in him."

"Gabe, now don't get all—"

He rounded on the man, itching to shake him. Might even have, if his hand hadn't been full of rabbit carcass and false-iron nails. "It was on her *porch!* It started screaming the minute she got near it!" *Why am I shouting?*

There was a spatter of gunfire from the sinks in the southwest part of town. Either that or it was firecrackers from the Chinois parts beyond, celebrating something in their heathen way. For once, Gabe didn't care.

The chartermage was pale under his caramel coloring, and thoughtful. "That's just mighty strange. The Chinee girl was there, right? She didn't hear nothin' troublesome?" Russ had his hands up and loose, and he cautiously took a step aside. "I'm just sayin', tell me a little more about this, Gabe."

Why are you slowin' me down? "She heard, and she was feedin' her baby, Russ, and she can't speak much good Englene when she's scared out of her mind."

"It's just…normally, you know, that's not a quiet or short job, something like this. And done near dusk. Are you sure it was meant for the marm?"

Who else? It couldn't be meant for Li Ang; the Chinois just didn't come into that part of town. Which was why he'd put her there to begin with, and arranged things so she could stay relatively out of sight. "Well, it's *her* damn house. And Tils is swearing up and down that he'll fix her."

"Tils ain't gonna hire Salt to cross you. Tils'll get drunk and come up sneaky behind *you*. You know that well as I do. Sides, Salt ain't going to cross you by leavin' a death-charm at your girl's door."

"My girl?" *I've been careful, have you been opening your yap? If you have, by Hell I'll…*

He realized the ridiculousness of it just in time, and noticed Russ had stiffened. Gabe shook out his fist, lowering his hand.

I have to calm down.

Russ kept a weather eye on his hand, in case Gabe changed his mind. "There ain't anyone in town who doesn't know, dammit; don't act surprised. The betting's been a right nuisance to keep track of."

"Betting?" Some of the ice cracked, and his fingers eased up a little on the canvas bag too. Getting the thing up off the planks had been a job; whoever had nailed it in had driven the iron deep. Had Li Ang been inside, quaking, hearing that noise?

It was a hell of a time to wish he knew some Chinois.

"Odds were ten to one in her favor by the time you took her out to that schoolhouse. Laura Chapwick was locked up in her room crying for a good two days, but now she's making eyes at Beau Thibodeau."

"Chapwick? The redheaded one? Why the hell—oh, dammit, quit changing the subject." *I've got someone to beat the goddamn living hell out of, and you're not helping.*

"I never bet on her. Too docile. Now listen, I'm all for asking Salt a couple questions about this little event. But you put a bullet in him, the next shadow we get might not be so damn incompetent, and we'd *both* have to work harder. In the interests of my laziness, Gabe, let's be a little cautious here."

"God *damn* it." But Russ was right. Some of the steel-hard tightness in his shoulders receded a bit, and Gabe set his jaw. The tingling in his fingers had gone down, and so had the unsteady, explosive feeling behind his breastbone. His spurs no longer struck sparks when he moved, a single restless step. "Fine. I won't shoot the bastard." *Unless he forces me to.*

"That's the spirit." Russ brushed at his lapels, swung his hat a few times, and settled it back on his curly mane. "Then we got to ride the circuit. I got a bad feelin' tonight, with the wind up and all."

You ain't the only one. But Gabe shut up and followed Russ. He had plenty to think on, now that he *was* thinking, instead of simmering with fury.

"Just promise me you won't kill the man," the chartermage

continued. "I don't want to bury no sonofabitch unconsecrated tonight."

Riding the circuit was a good way to think. Or at least, it could have been if the rising dust-laden wind wasn't enough to choke a mule, and Russ was in a bad temper. He had to keep spitting the charm to keep some clear air around them, over and over.

It ain't my fault, Gabe told himself. How could he have known they'd find Salt that way? And he hadn't been the one to break the chartershadow's jaw. Doc was flat-out amazed that Russ's small hands could deliver such a blow.

It didn't help that Russ had been sweet on the widow Holywood for as long as he'd been in town. It further didn't help that Salt had the widow on her knees and had his hands down in his trousers, obviously intent on collecting a payment for a piece of bad mancy. Salt had made the mistake of jeering, and Russ had exploded.

Go home, Gabe told the widow. *Go to the mage if you need mancy, just don't ever come here again.*

He could pretty much tell she wasn't going to listen. Whatever she wanted, neither Salt nor the widow would tell—not like Salt could, with his jaw shattered and the rest of him pretty near pulped. Restraining Russ hadn't been easy.

This had all the earmarks of a situation that was gonna end badly. But at least Russ had, after all the excitement, verified that the death-charm wasn't Salt's work.

There'd been enough blood on the floor for *that*.

Gabe flicked a spark of blue-white off his fingers, lighting a gully to their left. Each shadow stood out sharp and clear, whirling dust specks of diamond, but all was as it should be. No shambling figures, no slithering movement. The quiet held.

The last incursion of undead had been at the schoolhouse. And Gabe still didn't have an explanation for how those corpses had ended up inside the town's charter.

He didn't like that one bit.

Russ halted for a moment, his head rising. Breathing through a charmed triangle of cloth knotted around his face, blinking, he peered ahead. Gabe eased his horse forward. If there was a gap or an erasure, Russ would mend it while Gabe stood guard.

Russ's hat shook itself, *no*. He continued, and this was the worst sector—due west, where the sun went to die every day.

There were plenty of gold claims in the hills, yes. All sorts of things out in the hills where the wild mancy roamed. And one particular claim, sealed up tight as a vicar's platebox, the ancient hungry thing inside it deep in its uneasy slumber.

It was about time to ride out and check, to make certain the seal was holding. The tribes before the white man in this part of the world had whispered of something foul in the hills before they disappeared. Those garbled legends sent a cold finger down Gabe's back the first time he heard them, because those of the Order knew how much truth there could be in such whispers.

Yes, he had to go out soon. In sunshine, though. No amount of gold could have made either man venture west in the dark. Not through those hills. Some other idiots might, though, and if they brought trouble back to town it was Gabe who would be setting it to rights.

Thinking about that claim put him in a worse mood, if that was possible. Something was nagging at him, and there was no way to tease it out when people kept misbehaving. Something to do with that claim, and the—

Russ pulled his horse up short, and Gabe's mouth went dry. Sparks flew, blue-white and the lower, duller red of the chartermage's mancy. Russ dismounted, and the rifle was in Gabe's hands, steady and comforting. He covered the hole while the chartermage crouched, teasing together the circuit-strands, binding them with knots that flashed with ancient symbols of protection against malice, ill-chance…

And evil.

The rifle was steady. Dust slipped and slithered, if the wind didn't abate by morning they were looking at a regular old simoun, and everyone who was half-crazy before would go all the way into full-blown lunatic while the wind lasted. He'd be busy keeping some semblance of order, and Catherine—who knew how she'd react? The winds were the hardest thing to take, sometimes.

Russ straightened. The border was repaired. The chartermage's shoulders relaxed a little. He turned back to his horse, and the rifle jerked in Gabe's hands. He worked the bolt again, and the shadow fled, sudden eerie phosphorescence leaving a slugtrail on flying dust. There was a flash of white shirt, braces, and a suggestion of loose, flopping hair.

Man-shaped, could be anything. Nightflyer, a skomorje—but they don't like it when it's dry—or maybe even wendigo, though there hasn't been any spoor and it's not winter. That would just cap everything off. The rifle's barrel moved slowly, covering a smooth arc. *Ain't a rotting corpse, though; they don't glow at night. It could be… but we sealed that claim. I sealed that claim up solid.*

"Gabe?" Russ called over the wind's mounting rush, and both horses were nervous. The charming on their hoods would keep the dust out of sensitive membranes, but no beast Gabe had ever ridden liked a hood.

"Not sure," he called back. "Mount up."

The chartermage swung himself into his saddle with a grunt.

He waited until Gabe kneed his horse forward to continue, both animals picking their way with finicky delicacy. The western charterstone was very near, and once they reached it the circuit was finished.

Man-shaped. Tall and skinny. Flopping hair. Couldn't see much else. The glow, though. That's troublesome.

God *damn* it. He was going to have to go visit that claim again, and sooner rather than later.

Chapter 18

Mr. Overton was a curious case. His skin was the color of coffee with cream, and his dark hair was slicked down with something that resembled wax. He was no taller than Cat herself, with a long nose, and his full lips were pulled tight as he shook some of the biscuit-colored dust from his bowler hat.

His eyes were odd, too, a variety of light almost-yellow she had never seen before. His charing—a brass ring, denoting some form of servitude in his past—was alive with a soft red glow, showing him to be a chartermage.

No wonder he had come to the West. Even in the Northern provinces a chartermage of his particular color might find it difficult to find proper work—if he did not fall foul of a coffle-gang meant to drag him into the dark South where he could be drained of his mancy and turned into a soulless automaton, living only in name.

Robbie had wanted to enter Army service, but their father had categorically forbade it. The War had been fought to settle the Abolition Question, but even after all the blood and trouble there seemed precious little *settled*. Not when there were still coffle-gangs; she had seen them on the streets of Boston the very day she had left.

It gave one the shudders to think of, although Cat's parents had been firmly of the State's Rights opinion. Now, as she eyed the man before her, she wondered if she should have perhaps paid more attention to the Question. It was an altogether uncomfortable thing to have one who would be affected so intimately by such a debate before one in the flesh.

Li Ang hurried away, her step light on the stairs, and little Jonathan's wailing ceased after a few moments. Cat straightened her gloves. "How do you do, sir."

"How do, ma'am." He moved as if to touch his hatbrim, his gaze roving everywhere but to her face. "Gabe said you'd be needing an escort to the schoolhouse."

"So he thinks." She adjusted her grip on the leather satchel and lifted her chin. "May I offer you some tea? Or coffee; I believe Li Ang knows how to make such an infusion."

"No thank you, ma'am. Best get going, there's work to be done today."

Indeed there is. "Certainly." She stepped forward, and at least he was polite—he opened her front door, sparing only a brief glance at the porch outside where the…thing…had been last night.

"I'll be fetching you too," he said over his shoulder as he stumped down the steps, his stride wide and aggressive. "Gabe left at dawn, business elsewhere."

"I see." *Left? Where on earth would one go, here? To another town, perhaps? Why?*

But she could not ask. The wind had died—which was a mercy. The blowing dust and moaning air all night had invaded Cat's dreams, and she had dreamed of Robbie as well. Terrible dreams, full of dark cavernous dripping spaces and flashes of tearing, awful blue-white brilliance.

My nerves are not steady at all.

The sky was a bruise, and the dust had scoured everything to the same dun colors as Jack Gabriel's coat. No wonder the garden looked so sad and dingy. She accepted Mr. Overton's hand and climbed into the wagon, and the patient bay horse flicked his tail. He had a curious fan-shaped burlap thing affixed to his head, glowing with mancy. "What does that do?" she wondered aloud, then answered her own question. "Ah. The dust. Are such storms usual, Mr. Overton?"

"Simoun, they call 'em." He hauled himself up on the other side with a sigh. He still did not look directly at her. "Poison wind. Sometimes it goes on for days. People can't take it. They go *back East*." He gave the last two words far more emphasis than they merited, and flicked the whip gently at the bay, who stepped to with a will.

"I found it rather soothing." Cat set her chin and adjusted her veil. *And why would you suggest I retreat to Boston, sir? This is our first real acquaintance; the difference in our station does not matter nearly so much here in the wilderness. Or does it?*

"You'd be the only one. Can I ask you something, miss?"

You just did. "Certainly, sir."

"You're an educated lady, and you've got some mighty fine cloth. So fine, in fact, it's got me wonderin' what a genteel miss like you is doin' all the way out here." Now he cast her a small sidelong glance. "And it's mighty odd you get things left on your porch, too. I just wonder."

"I was engaged as a schoolmistress after sitting for my teacher's certificate," she replied, coolly enough. *Mother had thought I would make a good marriage instead of needing an ed-*

ucation. Father thought the governesses and tutors quite enough, and I did not need to attend the Brinmawr Academy, after all was said and done. A simple certificate-course after my brother sent me the oddest letter I have ever received, and I am heartily regretting my actions now, thank you, sir. "I rather thought my gentility was seen as a benefit." *I paid the Teacher Placement Society for this post, and handsomely, too. An independence is a wonderful thing.*

"You could be in San Frances. Dodge City. A place with an opera house instead of some two-bit fancyhouse saloons. I'm just curious, miss."

You, sir, are not merely curious but fishing. "Perhaps I wished for a purer life than can be found in *some places.*"

"Never thought I'd live to hear Damnation called *pure.*" His laugh came out sideways in the middle of the sentence, as if he found the very idea too amusing to wait. Cat agreed, but she had thought long and hard about what reason she might give for her presence in this place, if pressed, ever since Jack Gabriel had stood next to her outside the pawnshop window.

And Mr. Gabriel was gone today, on some mysterious errand.

"My parents fell victim to Spanish flu." She sought just the right tone of bitter grief, found it without much difficulty. "I have no family now, and Boston was...a scene of such painful recollections with their passing, that I fled everything that reminded me of them. Perhaps I should not have."

He was silent. Did he now feel a cad? Hopefully.

The wagon shuddered along the road, its wheels bumping through flour-fine dust. It was a wonder he could find the track in all this mess. The hills in the distance were purple, but not a lovely flowerlike shade. No, it was a fresh bruise; the sky's glower was an older, fading, but still ugly contusion. The sun was a white disc above the haze, robbed of its glory, and the stifling heat was no longer dry but oddly clammy. Or perhaps it was merely the haze which made it seem so, since her lips were already cracked.

The rest of the ride passed in that thick obdurate silence, and the appearance of the schoolhouse, rising out of the haze, was extraordinarily welcome. Mr. Overton pulled the wagon to a stop, and when he helped her down she was surprised to find his fingers were cold even through her gloves.

He dropped her hand as if it had burned him. He mumbled something, and was in the wagon's seat like a jack-in-the-box. The conveyance rattled away toward town, and Cat was left staring, her mouth agape in a most unladylike manner.

"Well. I *never*," she muttered. Except it was precisely the manner of treatment she supposed she *should* expect from such a man. Chartermages were notoriously eccentric, he was not Quality, either, and he was no doubt unused to polite conversation with someone of Cat's breeding.

Still, his manners were only one of a very long list of things that troubled her. Troubles were fast and thick these days. She opened the schoolhouse and waited for her students, attending the small tasks that had quickly become habitual, and as she did, a plan began to form.

If I give myself time to think, I will no doubt find a thousand reasons not to do this. She adjusted her veil once more. It was no use; she had *plenty* of time to lose her courage on the walk into town.

Dismissing the children at the lunch-hour was a risk. Yet she could legitimately claim that so few had shown up, and the return of the storm seemed so ominous, that she had done so for their safety. And the streets were oddly deserted—or perhaps not so oddly, as the lowering yellowgreen clouds were drawing ever closer.

She could even claim to have come into town to find a means of alerting her *other* students of the school's closure for the day. *That* problem she would solve as soon as she had this other bit of business done.

The pawnshop's door stuck a little, its hinges protesting. She stepped inside quickly, unwilling to be seen lingering, and glanced out through the plate-glass window. Perhaps no one had seen her.

She could always hope.

"Hello?" Her voice fell into an empty well of silence, and the walls seemed to draw closer.

It was dark, not even a lamp lit, and chill. Strangely prosaic for a chartershadow's haunt—clothing in piles, some tied with twine and tagged with slips of yellowing paper, others merely flung onto leaning, rickety shelves. A vast heap of leather tack and metal implements, and two long counters—one at the back, one along the left side—with various items on ragged velvet and silk. Pistols, knives with dulled blades, pocketwatches, hair combs. Jewelry both cheap and fine, tangled together.

She tried again. "Hello? I have come to buy."

Perhaps he was at luncheon?

At the counter in the back, something glittered in response.

Cat glanced in the window, and the oddity caught her attention. The bed of fabric, where shiny wares would be displayed to tempt passersby, was empty.

Her throat closed. Was there no one here?

She glanced at the gleam on the back counter again. Pillows of that same moth-eaten velvet, and the locket glittered, recognizing her. Its mancy sparked faintly; a thrill ran along Cat's nerves.

Her breathing came fast and high. "Hello? Is anyone here?"

Perhaps he is at luncheon. It would be the civilized thing to be doing at this hour.

But sure instinct told her that was ridiculous. Such a businessman would not leave his door unlocked and his wares half-secured, chartershadow or no. And, strictly speaking, the locket was hers by right. Surely the need to find her brother outweighed what she was about to do?

I have sliced a man in the face with mancy and a stick; I am spending every afternoon with frail women; last night I was in the arms of a man who now calls me by my charing-name; and now I am about to steal. Mother would be very disappointed.

Would Cat's mother even *recognize* her daughter now?

She inched across the floorboards, holding her breath until darkness clouded her vision. Finally remembering to inhale, she reached out a trembling gloved finger and touched the locket's gleam. Snatched her hand back, glancing about as if she expected a reprimand.

Nothing happened. The pawnshop was silent as a crypt.

Avert, she thought, and brushed ill-luck aside with a quick motion.

A few moments later, Robbie's locket and its broken chain tucked in her reticule and her satchel swinging, Cat Barrowe closed the pawnshop door behind her with a soft *snick*. There was nobody on the street, and the wind inched its way up from a low whisper to a soft chuckle, sliding dust along the boardwalks with brisk broom-strokes. A skeletal tumbleweed rolled past, and Cat hurried along in the precarious shade of flapping awnings toward Capran's Dry Goods. She could enquire after the delivery of items for little Jonathan and engage one of the store's boys to take a message to Miss Tiergale that school was canceled for the afternoon.

Her heart refused to slow its mad pounding, her hands trembled. But she put her chin up and hurried along, hoping no one had seen her.

Dear Robbie, I am now a thief. If you are alive when I find you, I am just going to pinch *you.*

Chapter 19

Hathorn was no longer the youngest horse, but she was dependable and Gabe had ridden her out of town before. She didn't get excited easily, but when she did she was fleet and smarter than the average equine. She was also prickly-tempered, and didn't respect a rider who would put up with any foolishness.

Well now, that reminded him of a certain miss, didn't it.

Don't think about her.

There was plenty of other thinking to do, and he did it best when he was alone, scanning the horizon and eyeing the tops of ridges for any silhouette that didn't belong. It was daylight, but the sky was too clouded for his comfort.

Still, he wouldn't be able to rest until he checked that goddamn claim.

The dangers out here weren't merely wildlife or some of the miners and panners getting a bit twitchy with a stranger. There were harpies higher up in the hills, and other, fouler things in some of the deep-scored gullies and valleys. The wild mancy out here, without a chartermage or people using its flood to shape and tame it, gave birth to oddities. Even the few remaining survivors of the Red Tribes wouldn't come near this slice of the Territory, and they had coexisted with this continent and its oddities before Gabe's kind had sailed west to find the spices of the Sun.

Disease and war had all but wiped out the tribes, though there was some talk of a hole in the world they had escaped through, into a paradise without invaders. Privately, Gabe hoped they had, and wished they hadn't left any of their kind behind, given how *his* kind by and large dealt with those survivors. All the same, this was a fine land, and he'd been born on its shores. Working another country's mancy would be problematic at best.

He didn't mind. Much. The Ordo Templis was far more active across the Atlantica, and escaping to a country they didn't have their fingers in would be a trick indeed. Unless he wanted to take Chinoisie lessons from Li Ang and keep heading West until it became East.

He found the lightning-blasted tree silhouetted against the sky, and suppressed a shiver as he turned Hathorn's black head toward a thicket of spinesage. She didn't like it, but she went, and when he left her at the edge of the hidden spring with its sweet-crystal bubbling top swirling with blown dust, she was content enough.

From there it was slogging through fragrant junip and wild tabac wilting under the heat, underground water heaving the devilpine trees up to clutch at the sky with their bony fingers. He was sweating by the time he was halfway up the side of the wash, and the midges had found him.

Damn biters. He didn't risk a charm to shake them off, though. No need to announce his presence any more than he already had, or any more than the grace on him would.

The going became a little easier, but he slowed as it did. Something had come this way lately, breaking branches and scuffing the ground. Didn't take a genius to read those signs, or to see the mark of a bootheel with nails crossed to ward off bad luck. Didn't prove much, but he went cautiously, his breathing slow and even and a trickle of sweat tracing its way down his spine.

A sharp hairpin bend even a mountain goat would have trouble with, but Gabe knew its trick and leapt lightly. Landed cat-foot, and crouched, hard up against an old devilpine whose bark smelled of crushed cinnamon when he leaned into its shade. He was leaving sign too; no way to avoid it. Damn the whole thing.

It was too quiet in this little defile. No bird sang here, and even the wind was muted. The dust didn't reach too far up, the devilpines sheltering the hillsides wherever there was enough water for them to cling to. Nothing slithered in the undergrowth, nothing nested in the trees, and even the midges hung back.

That would have been a mercy, if not for the cold. His breath didn't frost when it left him, but it felt like it should. The chill wasn't physical. It was *inside*.

He crouched there near the tree, taking his time. Then he inched forward, using his shoulder on the trunk to brace himself, and took a peek.

And ducked back behind the devilpine, swearing internally, clear beads of sweat standing out on his forehead and cheeks, wetting his underarms and making his woolen stockings slippery inside his well-worn boots.

Oh God, protect a sinner, now and forever. Shine Your light on us, dear Lord, and let us be as lamps in darkness. I am a sword of the righteous and You are my shield.

Funny how the urge to pray returned, even though he'd sworn never to do it again after Annie died, screaming an undead's unholy grinding cry. Only it was a pair of dark eyes he thought of now, and curls knocked loose, and her trembling against him.

He was shaking, but his hands knew what to do. One of them touched a pistol's butt, the other drew a knife.

Another look, just to be sure. He ducked back again, and this time the fear was high and hard and sharp, bitter copper against his tongue and his heart pounding in his temples and wrists and ankles so hard he thought he might slide into unconsciousness right there on the hillside. And lie there, vulnerable and alone, with the unphysical coldness breathing over him.

That brought him up in a rush, and he stepped out into the open, facing the dark mouth of the unsealed claim. It yawned, a fracture in the hillside full of spilled-ink darkness even broad daylight wouldn't penetrate, and the cold struck him like a wall of flash-flood water in a gully.

And Jack Gabriel, who had once been a priest, went about his holy work.

He slumped in the saddle instead of riding straight. Hathorn knew her way home, but he should have been more alert. Instead he was thinking through cotton. The chill exhaling from the mouth of the seal-cracked claim got into a man's bones.

Think about something warm, then.

His thinking wouldn't listen. Instead, it hitched on the boy. What was his name?

He couldn't pull it out of his memory at first, and that was odd. More than odd, since he had a suspicion it wasn't the first time. It was downright *unnatural*, the way the boy's name kept slipping through the cracks.

Jack's fingers were strips of ice; he had long ago ceased shivering. The sky was a congested mass, dust billowing as Hathorn picked her way carefully, the fan-shaped charm-hood on her sleek head bobbing. A good horse, even if she was getting on in—

There it is again. Getting distracted.

Devilpine trees shook as the wind rattled them. Soon they'd be in the flats, heading for town, and he would see Catherine's face again. Those wide dark eyes, and the sweet way her mouth turned down at the corners when she tried to put on a prim face. The single dimple in one soft cheek when she forgot herself and smiled.

There. That's it.

"Robbie Browne." His feet were numb and his hands, too. The cold was all through him, except for the flame in his chest that was the light in a pair of dark eyes. Such a small, still spark to hold back that ice. "That was him."

Just a greenhorn, a boy with a quick tongue and deft hands at cards. An expensive charing and good cloth, but he slid around trouble like grease on a griddle. Dark eyes, a stubborn wave to his dark hair, and a jaw just begging to be set right with a fist when he smiled that easy smile.

With so much other trouble to keep in check, though, Gabe hadn't worried about him. Just another dreamer come Westron-ward without the sense God gave a mule.

Like Catherine?

Damn the woman, dancing into his thoughts all the time. But the thought of her pushed the ice back, gave him space to breathe. He lifted his head slightly, checked his surroundings. The hills were behind him, falling away like a sodden coat.

When Robbie Browne showed up with gold bars and a mysterious smile, there was a certain amount of grumbling. But there was grumbling any time a miner struck anything worthwhile out there. But then there had been the incursion, the circuit broken and something deadly lurking in the junip and wild tabac, something whose breath brought the corpses up out of sandy soil and gave both Russ and Gabe plenty of trouble.

It was the claim, of course. Just sitting there waiting for someone, and the boy had stumbled across it. Tracing the incursion of bad mancy to its source had led Gabe straight to the claim, and he and Russ had arrived just in time to see the boy vanishing into the dark crack in the hillside. Waiting for Browne to come out had been nerve-wracking, but Gabe had been sure he would.

And lo, he had. Seeing a sheriff waiting for him, though, the boy had drawn, and Gabe's gun spoke first.

At least they had buried the kid right. It had...bothered Gabe, a bit, to see Robbie Browne's charing gone. It could have been lost in the claim, true. The thing that had chased Browne out into the fading dust-choked light of that long-ago afternoon could have broken the chain of his charing-charm.

Still, he didn't like it. He didn't like it at all, so he had gone out that night and made sure the earth around the hasty grave was blessed as one of the Ordo Templis could make it. If he had enough grace to seal up that hole in the hill again, and enough to take care of the death-charm left on Catherine's porch, then Robbie Browne was sleeping safely.

Jack Gabriel's head came up. The cold receded, its fingers scraping his shoulders and trickling down his spine.

The thought of her just kept coming back. The exact sound of her steps, her point-toe boots clipping along with authority. The graceful lift of her arm as she pointed to the large slate board and helped a child along with a recitation. Her inviting Mercy Tiergale in to tea, as if it were no great shakes. And her holding Li Ang's baby, a disbelieving smile like sunlight on her wan face as she looked at Jack Gabriel.

A look like that could go straight through a man.

The smudge on the horizon was Damnation, and Hathorn picked up her pace a little as the wind's moan mounted. The simoun had just been taking a breather, not spent yet.

If he made it back to town in time, he could see her. Might even tell Russ he'd take the wagon out himself, though with Hathorn's gait that wasn't too likely. It didn't matter; Russ would see her home safe. One of the Bradford boys was riding the circuit with the chartermage tonight, so Gabe didn't have to worry about that.

And tonight was also their weekly game at the Lucky Star. Maybe his luck had changed.

Gabe set his shoulders and rode on, the cold fading even as the hot rasping wind rose.

Chapter 20

Sleep hovered just out of reach, held off by little Jonathan's fractious wailing and the wind scraping at the corners of the house. Pops and sparks of stray mancy danced in the charged air, and Cat's nerves were worn clear through.

She rolled over, pushing down the sheet. At least she had returned to her own bed; Li Ang's cot and the new crib were both in the small room down the hall. The evening was stifling, clammy-hot even though the dust sucked moisture from every blessed thing under its lash. Her hair was misbehaving as well, curls springing free instead of lying in a sleek decorous braid.

The locket was warm against her breastbone. It would rest under her dress, the mended chain longer to accommodate Robbie's larger frame, and the secret of its presence was oddly comforting. After the sun had reached a comfortable distance above the horizon, she could unleash her Practicality on the metal; a simple finding-charm would at least show her what direction to take.

If Robbie had moved on to another town, well, Damnation would be missing its new schoolmarm. She suspected the town would be relieved, and no doubt Cat herself would share that relief. This was *not* what she had expected.

Well, honestly, what *had* she expected? To come sailing into town and find Robbie in some small bit of foolish trouble, and to have everything smoothed over by teatime? An adventure from a novel, full of Virtue overcoming Vice and rescuing the Foolish? A penitent Robert Heath Edward Barrowe-Browne, ready to return home to Boston to take up the reins of the family fortune and, not so incidentally, take some of the onus of being In Society from the shoulders of his younger sister?

Cat sighed, moved restlessly again. Jonathan's cries vanished under the sound of the grit-laden moan of simoun, and she understood now what Mr. Overton had said about becoming crazed by the wind. It was certainly possible.

Poison wind. What a terrible name.

It was no use. Whether it was the locket against her skin or the baby's fussing, the wind's sliding scrape or the heat, sleep was impossible. No matter if she would need it for whatever tomorrow held.

There was a thumping rattle from downstairs, and baby Jonathan set up another thin cry. This one sounded frantic, and Cat sighed. Perhaps Li Ang had dropped something. In any case, she was awake; she might as well go downstairs.

At least the Chinoise girl was company. Cat was beginning to suspect Li Ang knew far more of Cat's own mother tongue than she employed, too. There was a steely glint in Li Ang's gaze, a certain something in the way she held her shoulders now, that seemed to say so.

Cat drew a blue silken robe over her nightgown and sighed afresh, sliding her feet into well-worn slippers. Shuffling down the stairs, she yawned hugely, and there was another thumping from the kitchen.

What on earth is she doing? Throwing the crockery? I would not be surprised.

It was, she reflected, dreadfully uncivilized here. She outright hated it. And yet, there was a certain freedom to her daily routine that would have been unthinkable in Boston. Was that not why Robbie had left? *It stifles me here, sister dear.* His wide grin as she bade him farewell at the train station—Mother would not come, and Father had not seen fit to leave his club that day. *Don't you worry. I'll send for you soon.*

But he never had.

Cat wiped at her cheek. She pushed the kitchen door open, soft lamplight filling the hall and her slippers noiseless as she stepped through.

Her greeting died on her lips.

Baby Jonathan, in his wicker basket on the table, set up a furious howling. The wind screamed. A man had Li Ang by the throat, pressed against the bar on the back door, and the Chinoise girl's face was plummy-red as she struggled. The man had a long black braid bisecting his blue-cotton-clad back, and odd slipper-shoes, and Cat Barrowe clapped her lips shut over a scream.

There was no time for reflection. Mancy crackled on her fingers, and the stinging burst of bright blue-white hit the man squarely in the back. He yelped with surprise, dropping Li Ang, and Cat had enough time to think *Why, he's Chinois too...*

...before the man was somehow right in front of her, and a stunning blow to her midsection robbed her of breath. She stumbled back, clipping her shoulder on the kitchen door, and went down in a heap, the table jolting and little Jonathan sending up a fresh wail at the indignity of being bumped about so. Stars exploded inside Cat's skull as the Chinois man struck her again, and her Practicality, uncontrolled, bit *hard*, striking through her charing-charm in self-defense.

He made no sound, but the mancy flung him back. Li Ang choked, and the baby screeched. The table waltzed dangerously as the attacker fell against it, and Cat's belly gave a flare of agonized red pain as she scrambled, her fingernails tearing against rough planks. The basket spun, the baby howled, and there was a queer meaty *thunk*ing sound.

Li Ang's scream rose, matching the poison wind's fury. Another meaty thumping, with a crack at the end. The basket was heavy, and its wicker bit Cat's fingers. She hit the ground in a useless lump, all her breath stolen, and baby Jonathan waved one tiny fist as if hurling an imprecation at Heaven. It would have been quite amusing to witness such fury, but Cat could not *breathe*; her body refused and darkness crawled over her vision, spots of unhealthy foxfire dancing in the sudden gloom. She curled around the basket, its fall to the floor arrested by her own body. Some instinct deeper than reason had forced her unwilling flesh to move, to save the tiny newborn thing.

There was a sudden, ugly stench, and Li Ang's face loomed through the dark. Cat tried to gasp, but her lungs would not obey her.

There was a creak, Li Ang's fingers striking her abused midsection in a peculiar manner, and Cat whooped in a grateful, unending breath. The air sobbed out, and she found her cheeks wet and her entire body shaking as if with palsy. Li Ang crouched, pulling the wicker basket toward her, then collapsed. The two women lay, the basket between their bellies, and the baby screamed as they stared at each other, nose-to-nose. Cat's breath mingled with the Chinoise girl's, and the spark in Li Ang's pupils found a matching flare in hers.

Her wind returned in small sips and a fit of wretched coughing. The stench did *not* fade. It was a privy stink, and the moment Cat's nose wrinkled she decided she could, indeed, push herself up on shaky arms. The locket swung free of her chest, sparks dancing on the metal as it struck against her charing, and she could not even clutch at it, being fully occupied with heaving her reluctant body upright.

As if her movement had broken a paralyzing charm, Li Ang moved too. She scooped the baby from his basket. The little thing quieted, his lips smacking a little as he fought for breath as well. Li Ang sat amid the shattered table and unbuttoned the top half of her dress. Her breast, luminous gold in the single lamp's glow, rose like a moon, and the baby latched on.

Cat surveyed the kitchen. The stove was sullenly giving forth heat, and the shelves near the washbasin were knocked askew. The table would be useless unless she could find a mending-charm for two of its four legs, and the chairs were matchwood. A bottle of dyspepsia syrup had broken on the floor, and a sticky red tide spread under the Chinois man, who lay with his head—or what was left of it—cocked at an odd angle, the stain on the seat of his threadbare blue breeches announcing where the reek originated from. The cast-iron skillet propped in the ruins of what had been his skull further announced what Li Ang had hit him with.

Cat found her shoulders against the wall. Next to her, Li Ang crooned to Jonathan, who had fallen silent, suckling and content. The Chinoise girl's hair hung in her face, strands of black ink, and she was sweating. Great pearly pale drops of water stood out on her skin. Crockery lay smashed across the floor, other implements were scattered, and the largest knife their household possessed was rammed into the barred back door, its wooden hilt still quivering from whatever violence had sunk it into thick wood.

Her head lolled a little, and she found herself staring at Li Ang, who was regarding her with narrowed, black Chinoise eyes. Cat swallowed several times, seeking to clear her throat.

"Li Ang." Husky, the name dropped into the kitchen's hush. Outside, the wind mounted another notch.

"Bad man." Perfectly reasonable pronunciation, too. "He come for baby."

Well, obviously. "And...to hurt you." *To kill you.*

Li Ang nodded, grimly. "Husband. Wants baby."

A husband? "I thought you were a widow." Her entire body was heavy as lead. Her mouth tasted of things best left unsaid.

"Husband sorcerer. *Mage.*" The girl spat the world. "I youngest wife."

Oh, dear heavens. "Ah. I see." *Except I do not. Youngest wife. Wants baby. She's hiding.*

Apparently the girl who did her washing and cooked her meals had a secret, too.

Cat coughed. Her stomach cramped, and she doubled over. The pain eased in increments.

Li Ang still watched her. "He no take baby. He want go into from baby, make him young."

Oh, God. Cat's gorge rose. She retched once, pointlessly, and only grim strength of will kept her from doing so again. That was mancy of the blackest hue, only whispered of in old faerie-stories of witches stealing breath and body from princesses. "Go into? Into...into *Jonathan*?"

Li Ang nodded. "Brass kettle and herb, and Jin. Fire and mage. Make husband young. I no want husband young. Old man. Nasty. *Bad.*"

Good heavens. Cat saw again the marks on Li Ang's legs and back, the ink rubbed under the skin making odd characters, Chinois writing. She recoiled from the memory, her own flesh twitching, and another thought took its place. "Mr....Mr. Gabriel? He's helping you?"

"Jack help hide." Li Ang's gaze was still steady, gauging Cat. "Li Ang *hide.* Hide Jin. Hide *both.*"

"I see." The cramping subsided. But the *smell*, dear God, it was terrible. How could anyone bear it? He had...the man had tried to kill Li Ang, and now he was...dead. Dead on the kitchen floor, and Cat had absolutely *no idea* how to begin dealing with this.

But Li Ang was looking at her.

I am a Barrowe-Browne. I came all the way out into the uncivilized wastes to find my brother, and since I arrived I have done things no lady should ever do. Perhaps I am not quite a lady anymore, but by God... She coughed again, and decided the pain in her midsection was retreating enough to allow her some leeway.

"By God," she muttered, "I am a Barrowe-Browne."

How would Mother handle this? Well, there is a dead body on my kitchen floor. This is not The Thing, as she would say. It must be dealt with, and quickly.

The answer occurred to her in a flash. She braced herself, wincing, and wondered if her legs would carry her.

Gingerly, Cat rose, her nightgown falling in folds of linen, marred with dust and splinters. Her legs were obedient, at least. The silk robe—a present from Robbie—had torn, and she felt a pang as she inched her shoulders up the wall and arranged her clothing afresh. The movements soothed her nerves, and by the time she was reasonably respectable she was at least also able to draw a lungful or two of cleaner air.

Li Ang gazed at her, and the girl's lips compressed into a thin grim line. Did she think Cat was going to march her baby down into the Chinois section of Damnation and get out the brass kettle?

She set her chin. "Very well. I shall dress, and I shall find Mr. Gabriel." *Jack. He'll know what to do.*

Another article of faith, but not as childish as her urge to write Miss Ayre. No, she could all but *see* Jack Gabriel pushing his hat back and surveying this scene of destruction and confusion. And glancing at her, that small reluctant half-smile turning one corner of his mouth up, before he settled into making it all right.

Li Ang examined her from top to toe, and Cat might have felt unreasonably ashamed under such scrutiny. But the Chinoise girl must have found whatever she sought in Cat's expression, for she sighed and sagged against the wall. Livid bruises were purpling on the girl's slim throat, and it seemed a wonder that she could put up such a terrible fight. A lioness protecting her cubs could hardly do better.

And, therefore, Catherine Elizabeth Barrowe-Browne could do no less.

"Very well," Cat repeated. "Can you stand? I do not think we should be apart until I leave. I shall dress myself, and I shall find Mr. Gabriel, and we shall make this right."

Though how it could be made right was beyond her.

Chapter 21

The Lucky Star was going full-tilt, rolling like a whaling ship on the North Atlantica. The tinkling pianoforte was spitting out a reel, and miners and gamblers were dancing, either with the saloon's fancy girls or the dancing girls who would cozy up to a miner through "Clementine" or "That Old Gal of Mine," as long as he paid for the drinks.

Doc was the first to arrive, in his dusty black, and he gave Jack Gabriel a narrow-eyed stare. "You look like hell, Gabe. Something been keepin' you up nights?"

"Riding the circuit." *That damn storm's too thick tonight. Wonder where Russ got himself off to, he should be back by now.* Gabe tossed back the shot of what passed for whiskey, set the bottle in the middle of the table. The thumping and jollity from downstairs was enough to give a man a headache.

"Not a pretty pair of dark eyes?" Howard's laugh was dry and rasping as the dust. "Someone should tell Laura Chapwick she's still got a chance."

Gabe stared at the amber liquid in the bottle. The old man would grow tired of baiting if the bear didn't respond.

Sure enough, Doc dropped down in his usual seat. "You *are* looking rough, Sheriff. It isn't like you to drink before the game, either."

"Might make it easier to lose." *Since my luck's been so bad.*

"Might, at that." Doc's spidery tabac-stained fingers drummed the table.

"Well, *Hell*," Paul Turnbull announced, stamping into the room and slamming the door so hard it was a wonder the whole place didn't shake. "Gabe, God *damn* it. The whores are accusin' Tils of skimming, and that goddamn man's been taking it from my cut too. He's drunk, the books are a damn mess, and that Tiergale whore says she'll fix 'em if I pay her. What in God's name is goin' on around here?"

Gabe made a noncommittal noise, and Doc's laugh scraped the corners of the room again, harsh as the grit-laden wind outside. "You're just now noticing Tils is a thief? There's a reason I won't play cards with him, Turnbull."

Paul's footsteps were like to rattle the room. He yanked out his chair, its legs screeching discordantly against the floor, and a shout went up downstairs. Gabe tensed slightly, but it was immediately followed by a flood of drunken laughter. *Seems usual enough*, he decided.

"Hell, I *knew* he was a thief." Turnbull eased his bulk into the chair and sighed, rubbing at his moustache. "I just didn't think he'd steal from the whores. Ain't good business, what with the trouble of getting more of them out here. No reason for the dancin' girls to work like that when they can get what they want for a few turns around the floor."

"Maybe Letitia Granger could take up a subscription." Doc found his own witticism hilarious, and wheezed through another laugh.

There was a tentative tap at the door, but instead of Russ Overton, a corn-gold head poked through atop a pair of massive shoulders. It was Billy, the boy who ran errands for Coy and the girls, and he shuffled into the room with his hat in his broad paws, blunt fingers working nervously at the battered thing. His dark eyes were sleepy and one of them drooped at the corner; whenever he was nervous that cheek would twitch madly like a spider-charm was trapped under the flesh. His charing was a cheap brass disc, barely sparking even when he worked a simple mending. For all that, he was good with those graceless hands, and never touched the booze.

"*Now* what?" Turnbull barked, and Billy all but cowered.

"Guh-guh-guh…" The stammer got worse when he was excited. Nobody knew where he'd come from; he'd just arrived in Damnation and slept out on the main street in the dust until Turnbull let him sweep the boardwalk in exchange for a meal. "*Gabe*. Missah Gabe."

The flash of white he was crumpling along with his hat was a piece of paper, and Billy extended his arm. He stayed where he was, trembling in the face of Paul's glower.

What the Hell? Gabe gained his feet and did his best to block Billy's view of Turnbull. "What's this now, Billy? For me?"

"L-l-lady." Billy nodded his head several times. "Lady."

The note was stained by Billy's moist palm, and Gabe clapped him gently on one meaty shoulder. The boy was built like an ox, and it was a good thing he didn't like the liquor. He'd be unrestrainable if he took a mind to go on a tear. "Good boy, Billy. Thank you." He dug in his pocket and found a half-bit, pressed it into the boy's palm. "Good boy. You done good."

"A *billet-doux*?" Doc Howard found this intensely interesting. "Oh, my."

The paper was high quality, and as soon as he touched it he knew *something* wasn't right. His heart gave a thundering leap, because when he opened it, the firm, clear handwriting was familiar.

She had a beautiful hand, that was for sure.

Jack, I need you. Yours, etc., Catherine.

He folded it up, deliberately. "She waitin' on a reply, Billy?"

The boy nodded enthusiastically, his hair flopping in his face. "Y-yuh-yussir."

"Show me." He glanced over his shoulder. "Duty calls, boys."

Doc Howard was about to make some sort of rejoinder, but it was lost in Turnbull's exasperated sigh. The silent owner of the Lucky Star threw his hands up in an almost comical gesture of disgust. "Ain't that just *great*. Get the cards out, Doc. I ain't leavin' this room until I've had a few hands."

"Russ'll be along soon." Jack followed Billy out into the hall, closing the door on Paul's curse. Doc would be the one to keep the peace between those two tonight, and it served the old buzzard right.

I need you. It was after dark, and she was outside her house. And *Yours, etc., Catherine.* As if he had a right to her charing-name.

There was something in his throat. Gabe swallowed, hard, and wished Billy would shamble faster.

Billy pointed him out the Lucky Star's front door, and Gabe had to peer into the dust-heaving dark before he saw her.

She was at the corner, a shawl wrapped over her head, blinking furiously against the grit. A charmed handkerchief was pressed over her nose and mouth, struggling to filter the air before she breathed it. Stray curls fluttered on the wind, and he stepped around her, blocking the force of it, without thinking. He leaned down to examine her—she wasn't visibly injured, but her jacket had been hastily buttoned and was slightly askew. Under the shawl her hair was braided and pinned, and she trembled so hard her skirts shook when the wind wasn't flapping them.

He tilted his head to the side and took her arm. She went willingly enough, and the wind fell off sharply as he got her into the shelter of the Skell boardinghouse—not nearly as nice as the Hammises' place, that was for sure. The day's heat had dropped off as well, and with the wind now it was too chilly for what she was wearing.

She shook the charmed handkerchief, a flash of white. "Th-thank you. You c-came."

"'Course I did." *What, you thought I wouldn't?* "What is it? Another little somethin' on your porch?" *Because if it is, I will hunt someone down tonight. I'm just in the mood to do it, too.*

"N-no. It's w-worse." The shaking was all through her, and even in this dimness he could see she was paper-pale. "I c-can't even begin to tell you how much worse."

"Are you hurt?" He had her shoulders, and she winced. Was he hurting her? He tried to make his fingers unclench. "Catherine, someone hurt you?"

"N-no. Well, my stomach, but…" She drew in a deep, shaking breath. "It's Li Ang. Someone…he broke in through the parlour window, the shutter was loose. He…he wanted the baby. He hurt…he hurt Li Ang." Another deep breath. "Jack…Sheriff…sir, he is dead."

"Dead." He repeated it, just so he could be sure he'd heard her correct-like.

"Yes, sir." Her pupils were so large her eyes looked black. "Sir…there is a corpse in my kitchen. I don't…I do not know what to do." The shaking in her threatened to infect him.

There was a fist made of cold metal in his guts, and it squeezed. Jack pulled her to him, resting his chin atop her shawl-covered head. He hunched a little, wishing he could close himself around her like an oyster's shell around the meat. "Easy," he murmured, under the wind's low moaning and hissing. "Easy there. I'm here, sweetheart. All's gonna be well. You did right coming to fetch me."

She said something he couldn't hear, muffled by his shirt. Her breath was a warm spot through the material, and perhaps she was crying. He hoped not—maybe she needed it, but the thought of tears leaking from those big dark eyes made him feel a little unsteady. Like he'd been after Annie, powder looking for a match.

He could have stood there a little longer, but she moved restlessly and he had to let her go. She wasn't so pale now, though, and there was that determination on her soft little face again. It was right cheerful to see.

"Thank you." She swallowed, hard, and he could not look away from her lips shaping the words. "I…thank you, Jack."

"Catherine." The rock was back in his throat. It was dry as the sand in the air, and he suddenly longed for another jolt of whiskey. Digging out his flask now didn't seem like a good idea, though. "No need. Give me that rag of yourn, I'll charm it to keep the dust out and we'll set this to rights."

The transparent relief on her face was worth all the gold

in the hills, so he repeated himself as she handed over her handkerchief. "Yes ma'am, we'll set it to rights. You can just rest easy now."

I sound like an idiot. But he would say it as many times as needed to reassure her. Which meant a number of things. Not least of which was that he was going to have to have a serious talk with Miss Catherine Barrowe about her future.

And his.

Chapter 22

Li Ang?" Cat called cautiously up the stairs. "Mr. Gabriel's here. It's safe now."

She had left the Chinoise girl barricaded in her own bedroom, since the door was a solid piece of oak that would stand up most admirably to some abuse. Mr. Gabriel's spurs rang as he strode down the hall, and Cat shut her eyes briefly, listening to him push the kitchen door open. He viewed the vista inside for what seemed an *exceeding* long while, then his measured tread came back as the door's hinges gave a slight creak.

"Li Ang?" Cat called again, and there was movement in the shadows upstairs.

The Chinoise girl appeared, a candle clutched in one trembling hand. Her hair was a wild mess, but Cat's was hardly better. And her other hand held the largest kitchen knife, worked free of the back door and freshly honed. She stared down at Cat with wide dark eyes, and slowly picked her way down the stairs. Her feet were bare and soundless.

"No doubt about it." Jack took his hat off, ran stiff fingers back through his dark hair. "Bastard's dead."

"Language, sir." Cat drew herself up. "What shall we do?"

One corner of his mouth twitched, but he sobered quickly. "Ain't no *we*, sweetheart. You go on up with Li Ang now. I'll take care of this. Thank God it's Chinee." He scratched at his hairline, his stubble showing charcoal against tanned and dust-polished cheeks. "If it was a white man, might've been a mite troublesome."

"Mr. *Gabriel!*" Cat's hand flew to her mouth. "What a terrible...my God, sir! He is *dead!*"

The sheriff shook his head, settling his hat afresh. "I ain't sayin' I hold with it, mind. I'm just sayin' that's how it is."

She forced her fingers away from her lips. "I...it is a body. Dead by violence, and the risk of reanimation—"

"This ain't the first murder we've had in Damnation, sweetheart. I told you to leave it to me, didn't I? Go on up and set with Li Ang. Don't think there's likely to be more of his kind tonight." But he gazed past her as he said it, pale-hazel eyes thoughtful, and Li Ang halted two stairs up.

"No more." The Chinoise girl made a short stabbing motion with the knife. The candleflame danced, a spark of mancy keeping it lit as it struggled with a sudden draught.

Why, she's trembling as much as I am. Cat forced her shoulders back. "Well, I am relieved to hear as much. Mr. Gabriel, sir, it is hardly fair of me to retire while you deal with—"

"I ain't havin' my girl haulin' no corpses. Go on up with Li Ang, or I'll drag you myself. He ain't gettin' no fresher."

Her jaw was suspiciously loose, and the irritation—dear God, must the man be so infuriating?—was nevertheless wonderfully bracing. *You most certainly will not drag me.* "Your girl? Mr. Gabriel—"

Now he looked damnably amused. "It's *Jack*, sweetheart, and yes, *my* girl. You think I'd come running like this if you weren't? We ain't got time to fix no plans now, but later we will. You can scream and stamp that pretty little foot of yours all you like." He touched his hatbrim, bidding her farewell. "Now get on up those stairs before I take a mind to *carry* you up."

Li Ang made a small noise. Almost like a smothered laugh.

Perhaps wisely, Cat decided to retreat. "Thank you, sir." She reached for the banister, and found with some relief that her legs were much steadier now. The deeper relief—that there would soon no longer be a dead body in her kitchen—did not bear mentioning. But what was that sharp piercing behind her collarbone?

I am not "your girl," sir. In fact, come tomorrow, I am not even certain I shall be remaining in this charming little hole of a town.

Somehow, it seemed the wrong thing to say. And ungrateful, too. She barely remembered writing the note. *I need you.* Three simple stark words, and he had left the Lucky Star in a hurry, following the boy's pointing finger toward her. God alone knew what he had been doing inside that place—portly balding Mr. Capran, just locking the dry goods store's door before heading home for the evening, had said that was where the sheriff would be, and lo and behold, there he was.

Tall, broad-shouldered, dust all over him and shadows under his bright piercing eyes, and he had hadn't even blanched when she informed him of the…the problem.

Oh, Cat, do not be an idiot. The body. The corpse. The man you helped murder.

She followed Li Ang back up the stairs, feeling Jack Gabriel's gaze on her like a heavy weight. Another thought occurred to her—Mr. Gabriel had hidden Li Ang here; perhaps he felt responsible in some small way for this turn of events?

After all, the Chinois man in the kitchen could have killed Cat as well. This very unwelcome thought brought her up short, and she half-turned to glance back at the sheriff, who waited patiently at the foot of the stairs, his chin tilted up as he gazed steadily at her.

Did you suspect this would happen, sir?

It was a terrible thing to think. And now the dead rabbit nailed to her porch took on an altogether more sinister hue as well. Perhaps Mr. Gabriel thought his manner of rough courtship would keep her quietly providing a safe haven for Li Ang.

Now was not the time to ask *that* question, either. And if the poor mancy-blighted thing on her front porch had been intended for Li Ang, did that mean nobody here knew of Robbie?

"Catherine," he said, quietly, under the moan and rattle-whisper of the poison wind. "If he'd hurt you, I would have killed him myself."

The drawl was gone, and the words sounded clipped, precise, and very educated. She studied his features for a moment, or what she could see of them in the light of the single trembling candle Li Ang held.

She could find no reply, so she simply turned wearily and climbed the rest of the stairs after Li Ang.

Perhaps it was the shock to her nerves. In any case, she was deeply asleep as soon as her head touched her pillow, baby Jonathan cuddled between her and Li Ang, whose warmth somehow dispelled the clamminess and overpowered the rasp of the wind. She woke to the dim dust-filtered light of dawn and the smells of bacon and coffee drifting up the stairs.

The kitchen was set to rights, although there were no chairs at the table. Mending-charms still vibrated in the wood of the table-legs, and the floor was charm-scrubbed, innocent of any stain. Cat paused in the doorway, her braid hanging over her shoulder and her bare feet protesting the treatment they received from the boards underneath.

Slippers had not seemed a worthwhile trouble this morning.

The broken crockery had been swept up and disposed of, and baby Jonathan's basket was set in the corner. He burbled a little, and Li Ang was occupied in attending to a panful of biscuits. The bacon sizzled most fetchingly.

Jack Gabriel was crouched by the table, his eyes smudged with sleeplessness and his callused hands running over the table-legs, making certain the charms had sunk in fast. His dun coat hung on a hook by the door, and his boots had traces of sandy earth clinging to them, grinding as he shifted his weight and frowned slightly. Under the worn pale fabric of his shirt, muscle moved, and his mended braces had seen much better days. The guns at his hips gleamed sullenly in the lamplight. It seemed impossible that so large a man could make himself so temporarily small. He had laid aside his hat, too, and his hair was mightily disarranged.

Cat stood there for a long moment. Li Ang turned from the stove and nodded, her face breaking into the widest smile Cat could ever recall gracing her features. "Morning!" she chirped, and Jack glanced over his shoulder.

Her hand had curled around the jamb. Cat stared at the pair of them, and a yawning emptiness opened behind her breastbone. Robbie's locket was tucked safely under her nightgown, and her charing-charm was warm.

She turned, and let the kitchen door shut itself.

I have never belonged here. She swallowed, twice, very hard.

There was no point in seeking a breakfast. Instead, she should dress herself, pack her trunk, and draw out Robbie's locket. Her Practicality would spark in the metal, and—

"Catherine?" Did he sound uncertain?

She steeled herself for what she was about to do. Halted, and stared at the front door, barely noticing the parlour opening to her right, full of fussiness and shabby chintz.

I should never have left Boston.

"Did it fail to occur to you that I might appreciate a warning, Mr. Gabriel?" It was her mother's Dismissing A Servant tone, and it hurt her throat, stung her tongue, and filled her smarting eyes afresh.

The wind filled in the spaces between each word, and rasped against the house's corners. Dust *everywhere*, and even if she retreated to the Eastron edge of this blasted continent she did not doubt she would hear the poison wind the rest of her life.

I am a fool. He is, after all, so far beneath me.

He was silent.

So she spoke, each word precisely polished. "A warning that perhaps the servant girl you had procured for me might be at risk of drawing murderers to my home? A warning that perhaps I should be on guard against evil mancy nailed to my porch? Or perhaps a warning that I was at risk of being slaughtered in my own bed by a Chinois criminal?"

"I didn't think—" Was he breathless? And well he should be.

"Precisely." *I wish I would have dressed for this.* "You may leave, Mr. Gabriel. I do not appreciate, nor will I brook, being misled in this manner. I came here in good faith, sir, and have narrowly missed being murdered for it."

"Catherine—" As if he had been struck in the belly, lost all his air. Just as she had been struck last night.

"You shall not address me, sir. You may leave." Though she rather doubted he would. The man was nothing if not stubborn, and there might be a scene.

Well, I have done nothing but behave disrespectfully since I came to this awful place; I might as well continue.

Just at that moment, there was a rather brisk knock on the front door. Cat put her head up and strode for it, not caring that she was in her nightdress. She had the bar down in a trice and wrenched the door open; dust swirled as Jack Gabriel gave a sharp warning sound.

But the locket was burning against Cat's chest, and it was merely Mrs. Grinnwald, the sturdy postmistress. She stamped inside, shaking her head as dust fell from her in rivulets. "Didn't think you'd come check for it, miss; there's a letter for you." Her bloodshot blue eyes greedily drank in the scene—Cat in her undress, the sheriff in his, and the letter in Grinnwald's horny hand was rudely snatched away. Behind the postmistress's ample bulk, the porch was a dim cave, dawn's glow eerie and muffled through the flying dirt in the air.

Cat nodded briskly. "Thank you, Mrs. Grinnwald. I am very sorry to put you to the trouble. How long has this been waiting?"

"Two days, ma'am. Bit of a wind, and—"

"Your devotion to service is no doubt to be commended." *You nasty, gossiping old hag.* Cat drew her nightdress about her as if it were a morning-dress. "Thank you very much. Li Ang is preparing breakfast; perhaps you, as Mr. Gabriel, will avail yourself of my hospitality in the face of this regrettable weather."

And with that, she sallied up the stairs. The silence was almost as satisfying as the odd, queerly breathless tone Mr. Gabriel employed as he told the postmistress to come inside and shut the damn door, if she was going to be nosy.

Chapter 23

I don't know," old Grinnwald huffed. "Some special delivery from Boston. Was paid to take it to her, that's all I know."

Wonderful. Although he didn't mind the old bat seeing Catherine in her nightdress and Jack right behind her. The news would be all over town by afternoon, and he couldn't say he had any objection.

I have narrowly missed being murdered for it. Well, he deserved that, didn't he. Here he was thinking she'd be grateful, and he could have slapped himself silly for it now. It had seemed so simple. Put Li Ang somewhere he could keep an eye on her, and then he had just hoped…or what? What exactly had he been hoping?

He wished the old woman would just go away and leave him the hell alone. Li Ang stared wide-eyed at this interloper in her kitchen, who stood and shoveled away every damn biscuit on the plate, complaining that there was no jam.

"And in this weather, too!" Grinnwald continued, querulous through a mouthful of biscuit dripping with baconfat. "I came all the way from the posthouse to deliver it. Well. La-di-*da*, the miss dismisses me!"

Jack grunted. What the hell did she want, anyway? He had work to get to. *You shall not address me, sir.*

Well, if Grinnwald gossiped, Catherine would be linked to him anyway, and he would have time to change her mind. Maybe explain. Women were convoluted creatures, and she'd had a shock last night. What Boston miss would come out in a dust storm to get someone to deal with a dead body in her kitchen? She wasn't made for this.

She was made for finer things, no doubt, and he...was not.

"She's a bit too big for herself if you ask me." Grinnwald nodded. "Carrying on so. Why, I've heard those *frails* at the Star are taking lessons from her, high and mighty as you please. You should look into that, Sheriff. They's bound to be a law agin' it."

"There ain't." The words came out sharp and hard. "And that's my girl you're talking about, missus." *She could have died last night.* "Stuff your hole with more of her biscuits if you like, but keep a civil tongue in your head when you're talking about Miss Barrowe."

Grinnwald gaped, biscuit crumbs strewing her dusty bosom, and Jack slid his arms into his coat. Li Ang made a soft smothered noise, almost like a laugh, and the baby replied with a sleepy burble.

And that made him think of Catherine, smiling disbelievingly as she held the little bundle, wan and pretty in lamplight. And her softness last night, trembling against him. *I need you.* Well, he'd shown up, hadn't he? And he'd heaved the Chinois, hands and feet pierced with true-iron and the man's dead mouth full of consecrated salt, over the charter-circuit border himself. Let him rot outside the charter, dammit. He hadn't had time to dig a grave, and the thought of consecrating more earth made him sick.

Wait just a goddamn minute… But it was gone. Something important, but Grinnwald had shaken her bustled rear, declaring she'd never *been* so insulted.

"Stay and fill your fat gullet, then," he told her, jamming his hat on his head. "I'm sure I'll have some more to say in a bit."

But he did not exit through the barred back door. No, instead his spurs rang as he climbed the stairs. Her bedroom door was firmly closed, and he would have bet it was locked, too. Which just made it worse.

What kind of man did she think he was? Good enough to deal with a dead body, but not good enough to…

Except she was right. She could have died.

And it would be Jack Gabriel's goddamn fault.

"Catherine." He knocked, twice. Nice, soft, polite raps. "I know you're listening." He caught himself, tried to fix the drawl back on his tongue. It had become a habit, to slur his words together. Just one more way to hide. "I know you're angry, and you have a right to be. I never thought you'd be in danger here. You have to believe me."

Silence. The sound of the simoun scraped at his ears. Was she leaning against the door to catch his voice? He hoped so. His hand spread itself on the smooth oak. Nice and solid. If she had to barricade herself in, it was a good choice.

He tried to think of what to say next. There wasn't a whole hell of a lot. Usually he just chose to keep his fool mouth shut. But she had a way of turning him upside down and spilling everything out onto the ground. There was only so much of that a man could take.

"You can be as mad as you want, sweetheart. You can call me

every ugly name you want. You can tell me to go to Hell, and that's fine. I deserve it. But you and I are going to come to an accounting one way or another. I'm giving you fair warning."

Which sounded like a threat. Hell, he was probably just making her even more angry. Was there a sound behind the door? Cloth moving, a woman's skirts?

"I have to go ride the circuit now. I'm going to give you some time to calm down. Think things over, like." *And I hope you don't just dig yourself in even more stubbornly. Though you probably will. Goddamn woman.*

Why was his chest aching? And he was thinking of other things too. The screaming. The gun speaking, and Annie's body, free of hellish undead jerking, falling in slow motion. He'd been careless with her safety, thinking God wouldn't repay Gabriel's service by taking such a gentle creature and making her suffer so horribly.

Except the incursion had happened, and Annie hadn't had enough mancy to shield herself from an undead's bite. Out on the sod frontier, each homestead had a ring of charterstones, and Jack had stupidly not checked them that nooning, instead sleeping under the willum tree while Annie, poor Annie, barricaded herself in the house and the sun sank toward the horizon…

And now there was this woman behind her bedroom door, terrified and angry, who could have died last night. There was just no plainer way to say it. He hadn't learned a goddamn thing. He didn't even deserve to have her spit on his shadow.

Jack's spurs made a discordant jangle as he headed down the stairs. He strode through the kitchen, where Grinnwald was still bleating at Li Ang, who probably didn't give two shits in a rabbit hole about whatever the fat woman would say. He touched his hat to the Chinoise girl and vanished out the back door, into the howling wind.

Chapter 24

Her fingers trembled. The outer envelope was from the firm of Hixton and Bowles, the solicitors she had engaged for all business pertaining to her identity as Miss Catherine Barrowe, neophyte schoolmistress. Her father's solicitor, Hiram Chillings, would have forwarded this letter to the Hixton office to be sent to Cat. Which meant it would have traveled from Damnation to Boston and back again.

It was worn and stained from the journey, but Robbie's familiar hand was on the outside of the folded inner envelope, and the charmseal tingled as she broke it. It had not been opened, and she had a flash of Robbie biting his lower lip as he sealed the outer sheet in his own peculiar manner.

Dearest Kittycat, it began, and she had to blink, furiously. "Oh, Robbie." The locket burned against her chest, so she drew it out and held it with her fingertips, spreading the letter's pages as much as she dared on the tumbled bedding.

Two knocks on her bedroom door. "Catherine?"

Dear God. She froze, staring at the unlocked barrier between herself and Jack Gabriel. Would he turn the knob and seek to come *in*? Well, should she expect any less of him?

He spoke further, but she looked away at the shuttered window, filling her head with the moan of the poison wind. When his footsteps retreated, she returned her attention to the letter.

What I have to set down will no doubt shock and frighten you, but it will also explain why I do not, under any circumstances, want you anywhere near this deadly blight masquerading as a town. I have limited time, but what I do have I will spend here in this boardinghouse, scribbling to you. Dearest Cat, best little sister, I will not be coming home. I am sorry for it—I know how Mother and Father will vex you for news of me. But dear God, Cat, do not wish for my return. The way is closed for me.

I thought I was so lucky, finding a claim. It was a black crack in the hillside, and a lightning-struck devilpine showed me the way, due west of Damnation and in those cursed hills. No wonder they call this town what they do. I should have listened.

There was something there, Cat. Something in the dark. Then, two scored-through lines, unreadable—the nib had scraped the paper cruelly.

Was the bed shaking? No, it was the sobs wracking her frame. She read through her tears, her nose filling, doing her best to weep silently. Halfway through the letter she rose and tacked drunkenly across the floor to her bedroom door, throwing the lock and retreating to the window, where dawnlight was strengthening as the wind's moaning receded.

The thing in the claim is terrible, and it has a hold on me. It lives inside me, filling my head with whispers and already I have done such things—but that's not fit for you to hear, Kittycat. I shall soon be dead, but not before I have rid the world of one more evil. It will take all the strength I have, but what will give me the will to strike is that you shall be reading this in the future, and you'll know you can be proud of me. At long last.

It's just a damn shame I had to come all the way out here to become such a beast as a brother you do not have to be shamed of.

My charing is beginning to sear the flesh underneath. It's only a matter of time before that cursed sheriff notices, or the damn chartermage. The chartershadow here—don't faint, I am bargaining with the Devil to fight the Devil, you remember that old game—will at least take payment for a weapon to fight the thing. I traded my locket since he wouldn't take the gold from the claim. Wise of him, perhaps. Mother would just die, *wouldn't she.* Avert!

In any event, Cat, keep this to yourself. Let Mother and Father think me the wastrel and the fool. I can do what I must bravely, because I know you *will know. You were always better at pleasing them than I, and this is my punishment. I should have listened when you begged me not to go. I wish to God I had.*

I love you, Kittycat. You are best and brightest. Polish your Practicality, and do well. I regret I will not ever see your dear face again.

It was signed with a simple scrawled R.

Cat read it once more, and once again. The front door slammed—perhaps Mrs. Grinnwald, perhaps Mr. Gabriel. Who knew? She rested her forehead on the windowsill, white-painted wood cool and slick against her fevered skin.

Oh, Robbie.

She cried as she had not since her mother's last breath had rattled from a wasted body. Father had succumbed the day before, and in her bitterness Cat had railed at her brother. For it was Robbie's leaving that weakened Mother so badly, and Father...he had not spoken of it, but he was not right without his son. For all Robbie did not please them, he was the heir to the Barrowe-Browne name.

They had thought he would return. So had Cat…but the silence had grown so unendurably long. Why had this letter not reached her before?

She was somehow at her bed again, her face pressed into the linens still bearing the frowsty smell of shared breath—Li Ang's, and Cat's, and little Jonathan's. "*Robbie*," she keened into the muffling, mothering darkness, and there was no answer but the poison wind slowly dying…

…and a distant rumble of thunder in the hills.

Chapter 25

T here you are!" Russ Overton looked like hell, his hat sideways and his jacket askew, stubbled and red-eyed. It wasn't a surprise—Gabe looked like hell too, he supposed. "God *damn* you, Gabe, where the *hell* have you been?"

Heaving bodies over the circuit-line and destroying a woman's faith in me. "Around." He lifted the glass, took another belt. Coy eyed him speculatively, but wisely kept himself over at the other end of the Star's bar, polishing some glasses with what passed for a white cloth in Damnation. "Time to ride the circuit, Russ." And so it was. Since the simoun had died, and the bruise-dark clouds over the hills had loomed closer. There was thunder, and the breathless sense of a storm approaching.

Approaching? No, it's damn well here.

"You're drunk." Russ halted in amazement, scooping his hat from his head and running his fingers through his waxed hair. It didn't help—the sharp tight curl in it was coming back something fierce. He was pale under his coloring, too, and his bloodshot gaze was a little too stare-wide for Gabe's comfort.

"Not yet." The Star was a dim cave this early, the dance floor empty and the upper balcony full of shadows. And Gabe had the wonderful, marvelous thought that perhaps he could well *get* drunk. "Not enough, anyway."

Everyone else in the building was asleep, including the fat, snoring Vance Huggins in the corner, who used the Star as his philosophical office every night. As long as Paul took a cut, he was welcome to, and Tils held his peace for once.

"Gabe, we have a problem. A *huge* problem." Russ stepped close, grabbed Gabe's shoulder. "It's the marm. The goddamn schoolmarm."

Jack Gabriel set the glass down very carefully, and Coy, perhaps sensing a feral current in the charged air, ducked through the low door behind the bar, into the cellar's darkness. A spark of mancy popped and fizzled to give him lee to see by, a charter-rune sketched on a small glass disc he kept chained like a pocketwatch, so he didn't have to mumble a catchphrase to light it. His ruined mouth wouldn't shape many phrases, that was for damn sure.

"You be careful, Russell Overton." Gabe enunciated each word very clearly. "Be *very* careful what you say about her."

"Gabe, for God's sake, listen. Remember that claim in the hills? And the boy? The Browne boy?"

What does that have to do with the price of tea leaves on a Chinoise whore's boat? "Russ, for God's sake—"

"Robert Barrowe-Browne. That's how he signed the register at Ma Haines's boardinghouse. *Barrowe*. And the other day, when I took her to the schoolhouse? Blood, Gabe. She's his blood." Russ drew in a deep breath, and his paleness was more marked. "I divined all *goddamn* night after riding the goddamn circuit, trying to find the connection. She's his sister."

The world spun out from underneath him. *That* was the familiarity—she had the same way of tossing her head, and the same high cheekbones. In her eyes, too—big dark eyes, similar to Robbie Browne's and thickly lashed. Why hadn't he seen the resemblance?

You weren't looking for it.

"It don't make sense," he found himself saying. "What the hell…"

"Maybe he wrote home that he had a sweet claim and then disappeared. We just assumed he had no kin; Ma Hainey never heard him speak of none and neither did any of the whores, right? And *Browne* ain't a name you would remember. He just slid by, and probably *what he woke up* helped with that. So here comes sister dear, looking for him."

He thought it over, alcohol and sleeplessness fogging him. "But she's from money, Russ. Why wouldn't they just hire someone? One of the Pinks, or a Federal Marshal?"

"Who knows? I just know she's his blood. And she's here under that name—Barrowe. What if she knows where that goddamn claim is, Gabe? What if he wrote to her? What if he was supposed to meet her here?" Russ threw his hat on the bar and scrubbed his hands over his scalp again. "What are we gonna do?"

Gabe stared at the bottle on the counter. He'd taken down far too much amber alcohol masquerading as whiskey to be entirely sure of his own ability to deal with what the chartermage was telling him.

"Do?" He sounded strange even to himself. "You're sure, Russ? You'd better be *damn* sure of what you're telling me."

"We have time, right?" The chartermage actually looked *anxious*. "She ain't been out to that claim yet, has she? *Has she?*"

"She ain't had a chance." *I'd stake my life on it.* Funny, but he would, and he was about to. "Things in town been keeping her busy. Russ, you're *sure*? They're blood, that boy and my Catherine?" He didn't even care if he was showing too many cards; it slipped out. *My Catherine.*

Even if she hated him.

"I went back to Salt's and looked in that cabinet in back. There was the boy's charing-charm, looks just like hers; I put it in my pocket, Gabe. Figured it was safest, what with you riding out to check the claim." For some reason, Russ turned even paler—some trick, with someone of his ancestry. "It lit up like a goddamn Yule tree. When I had enough time to concentrate, and handed her down from the wagon, mind."

That had better be all you handed down, Overton. "I see." He stared at the bottle. The liquid inside was trembling, for some reason. Little circles on its surface. "The claim was open. I sealed it up again, but…"

Russ swore, vilely, and Jack heartily agreed. He scrubbed at his face, stubble and dust scraping under callused skin, and the thought of just crawling under the bar and getting *real* good and drunk was tempting.

"All right." He dropped his hands. "All right. Let's go have a talk with her. May be time to tell her just what happened to her brother."

"You mean, that you killed him?" The chartermage's hands wrung together. He was probably completely unaware of the motion.

Jack took a firm hold on his temper. "He was dead the

minute he set foot in that claim, Russ." *But I don't think she'll understand that.*

Maybe it's best if she doesn't, Jack. You ever think about that? Maybe it's better if she hates the very sight of you. At least then, you won't be putting her somewhere she can end up dead.

He took his foot off the brass rail and wished he hadn't sucked down quite so much almost-whiskey. The world reeled again, but he held on, grimly, and settled his hat further on his aching head. "Let's go. The circuit can wait."

He should have known it would be too late.

The schoolmarm wasn't at home. Li Ang merely shrugged when asked where she'd gone, and they lost precious time riding out to the schoolhouse, only to find it empty for the day. Back to Damnation, then; Capran at the dry goods store had seen her dressed in a blue velvet riding-habit, walking past with her head held high. *Didn't even say hello*, he'd grumbled, and Gabe had only restrained himself from swearing by sheer force of will.

A riding-habit meant a horse, and the closest of the two liveries in town was Arnold Hayrim's, the one that *didn't* send rotgut whiskey out with the stage. Arnold was out at Brubeck's farm looking over a few prospective hacks, but his son Joe—big lumbering dolt that he was—rummaged around in his memory for a while before saying that yes, the marm had engaged a horse for the day. She had money, and she knew how to ride, so Joe had saddled a bay mare for her and she had leapt into the saddle neat as you please. *No sidesaddle, that miss*, Joe said, his blue eyes gleaming. *Right pretty seat she has, too.*

When asked which way she went, Joe spat and shook his head. He had horses to care for and the stagecoach was due in later today. He didn't give a damn where she went as long as she brought the mare back before dark.

The whiskey had burned off. Jack's head throbbed, and there was a deeper ache in his chest. Russ took his hat off, eyeing the boiling dark clouds over the hills. Thunder rumbled, growing closer. The betting on just when the rains would come would be in full swing by now.

Russ scrubbed at his forehead with his fingertips. "Today of all days," he moaned. "Do you think maybe…she couldn't know I've got her brother's charing. I was careful."

Gabe blinked. "A letter." *Curse me for a lackwit.* "She got a letter today. From Boston, the postmistress said. God*damn.*"

"Maybe it…dear God." Russ looked sick, leaning against the livery's splintery wall. The morning light had taken on the eerie greenish-yellow cast that meant the storm was coming sooner rather than later. "What kind of brother would tell his sister where that claim is? Or…do you think he did? Maybe she's got some way of knowing. She's got *some* mancy."

"Enough to have a Practicality." He wished his skull would cease squeezing itself to pieces. "Let a man *think*, Russ. Just shut your hole for a minute or two."

"We may not have a minute," the chartermage worried. "If she breaks open that claim again, she might get infected. And you know what that means."

Gabe clapped a lid on his temper. "I sealed it up, she ain't gonna break it." *Except where there's a will, there's a way, and she's got no shortage of will.* "Now just shut *up* and let me goddamn *think.*"

Russ wasn't listening. "We may have to put her down like a rabid—"

Gabe had him by the jacket-front, up against the wall, his

fists turning in the material. *How the hell did I get here?* "Shut. Up. You hear me, chartermage? *Keep your mouth shut.* That claim was *sealed* as of yesterday, and she ain't gonna break in. You are gonna go check Robbie Browne's grave and see if her mancy led her there. *I* am gonna go check that goddamn claim, and if I find her there I am going to *make* her listen to some sense. One way or another, we are bringin' her back to Damnation." *And I am not letting her out of my sight until we get a few things settled.*

Russ gaped at him. How fast had Jack moved? And it wasn't like him to hold a man up against a wall. His temper wasn't certain, and that was a bad sign.

"All right. All right, Jack, just settle down—"

"I ain't settlin' until I see my girl's safe. You just mind me, mage. That damn schoolmarm is…well, you ain't gonna make any pronouncements about her without my say-so." *And if she does break into that claim…No, she won't. She can't.*

Except he had an uneasy feeling that *can't* wasn't a word he could apply to his Miss Catherine Barrowe. She didn't know the meaning of the term. And if the thing in the claim infected her like it had her brother…

What, Jack? You'll shoot her? Another woman dead because you didn't do right.

"All right," Russ was saying, the words under a heavy counterpoint of thunder. "All right, Gabe. We'd better get started." In the distance, lightning flashed, silver stitches under ink-black billows. And that was a trifle unnatural, though it was hard to tell with the way the storms swept through at this time of year.

She *would* go out just as the rains were coming in. If there was an easy way to go about things, the damn woman would arrange it the other way 'round just to spite him.

"Reckon so." His fingers threatened to cramp as he released the chartermage. "You remember the grave, right?"

"I remember." The weird light did no good by Russ's complexion. The man was ashen, and staring at Gabe like he was a stranger. "You just be careful up at that claim, Jack. I'd hate to lose you."

"Got no intention of being lost." *And no intention of losing her, either.*

Chapter 26

After the heat, a cool breeze was welcome—until it turned chill, and she realized the clouds were *not* a good sign. She had not brought a coat—what need, when she hadn't ceased sweating since she arrived? The wind held a fragrant promise of water, too, just the thing to tamp the dust down.

The bay mare was sweet-tempered and had a good pace, but for a long while the hills due west of the town seemed to grow no closer. She'd struck out from the western charterstone, the brass compass from Father's desk tucked safely in her skirt pocket and her mother's watch securely fastened. Her veil kept the dust away, crackling with a charm she had seen Mr. Gabriel perform, and the thought of him was a thin letter-knife turning between her ribs.

Perhaps he had thought Li Ang would be in no danger. Perhaps he thought—

Who cares what he thought? I shall find Robbie, or whatever remains of him. Then…what?

The locket tugged against her fingers, its chain wound around each one. The finding-charm was simple, and as soon as she had uttered its first syllable, the locket had lit with blue-white mancy, strange knots that were not quite charter running under the surface of the metal.

The ride gave her plenty of time to think, though her entire body began to protest that she was no longer practiced in such things. She had ridden with Robbie, of course—pleasure jaunts, and sometimes a hunt when invited to a country house.

If she found a grave at the end of the locket's urging, what then?

Then I shall shake the dust of this hideous place from my person and leave at once. Perhaps I shall go to San Frances, or return to Boston.

Except the thought of returning to the city of her birth was too bitter to be borne. And there was a certain…well, the sand-dust ground, broken only by hunched figures of thorny plants and stunted junips, tumbleweeds scurrying from the lash of the wind, had a charm about it. The stifled parlours, parquet floors, endless rounds of social calls and charity work, the decisions of dress and etiquette and prestige, did not close about her so here. There was, she decided, a freedom to be had here in the Westron wilderness, but the incivility of Damnation was not the place to seek it.

And if she was quick enough, she would never have to see Jack Gabriel's face again. Embarrassment all but made her writhe in the saddle. What had she been thinking?

But the heat of him, and the quiet capability in his hands, and that damnable half-smile when he glanced at her. *Don't think on it any further.*

Except that was what he would say, wasn't it? *Don't trouble yourself.* And he would quietly go about solving a difficulty.

Like a body on her kitchen floor.

A body Mr. Gabriel probably had *not* been surprised by. But still...*My girl.*

A hot flush rose to her cheeks, and Cat muttered a highly impolite term in response. The man was a nuisance, scarcely better than Mr. Tilson and his bestial rage. He had put Cat in the path of murder—and now that she thought on it, the rabbit nailed to her porch must have been a warning to Li Ang, and therefore to Jack.

Not Jack. Mr. Gabriel. Thus he is, and thus he shall remain, world without end, smote it be, amen.

She would do well to remember that. She did not need to feel *grateful* that he had dealt with such unpleasantness. He was, after all, part of its making. It was his *duty*, and she knew of duty, did she not? One performed it with head held high and smile cheerfully set, and it was only in the privacy of one's soul—and sometimes not even there—that one railed against it.

The locket tugged, and she lifted her head. The hills were growing larger, and the sky overhead was full of ink-billows. Flashes of lightning crackled among the clouds farther into the pleated, jagged almost-mountains, and the breeze freshened, tugging at her clothing and her securely pinned hat. The bay was nervous, but Cat's knees clamped home, and she soothed the horse as best she could.

As soon as she followed the locket's urging to its source, she would be free. She could do as she pleased at that moment. Both duty and love urged her to make certain of Robbie's grave, at least. Whatever his ravings of dark things in a cave, or hints of bad mancy, she had to find him.

He was her brother, after all.

Cat clicked her tongue and kneed the bay into a canter. The

hills rose around her like teeth, and she suppressed a shiver as she rode into their jaws.

The mare grew increasingly fractious, and Cat sighed inwardly as she held the beast to her task. The locket tugged, and she followed—though finding a path grew more difficult as the sun vanished behind the heavy, ink-dark clouds and the undergrowth thickened. There was evidently some water here, for the junip and devilpine were no longer stunted but thick and clutching. The pines rose, and there was a trail leading up.

Unfortunately, the bay flatly refused to climb past a certain point, and Cat did not blame her much. The trail doubled back on itself in a series of hairpin turns, but a simple charm—one of Miss Bowdler's—found a spring close by and Cat left the bay tied near its hidden bubbling. The locket wished her to proceed in a straight line up the hillside, which Cat was *not* prepared to do. So she followed the path, reasoning that it would either lead her where she wished to go…or not.

There was a convenient set of thick-growing, fragrant junips to relieve herself behind, and she was startled into a half-laugh as thunder rattled overhead. In Boston, such a thing—relieving oneself behind a bush while bolts of lightning crackled from the heavens—would have been farce, or unthinkable. Here, it was simply what must be done.

Mother would simply die. Avert!

Oh, Robbie.

Slipping and stumbling, she worked her way up the path. Roots tripped her, and devilpine clawed at her hair and habit. When she returned to town, she would be a sorry sight indeed—at one point she fell, scraping both hands and breathing out another curse that would have made Robbie proud. The locket was safely clasped in her fingers, though a bit grimed, and she did not glance up. If she had, she would have perhaps seen a lightning-charred tree twisting against the darkened sky, and guessed where she was.

As it was, she rounded a massive spice-smelling devilpine, shook her head, brushing bits of stuff from her dress, and halted short, tucking her veil aside.

It was a clearing of sorts, a shelf of dirt and stone before a frowning hill-face glowering down at the growth upon its chin. Its mouth was a vertical crack, large enough for a carriage to pass through, but very black. Above, the eyes were full of twisted, wind-scoured junip, and the devilpines around her soughed in the wind, pronouncing sibilants that sounded eerily like laughter. The nose was a ruin, a shelf of crumbling stone, and the locket tugged insistently. But not toward the crack.

Instead, it fairly leapt, the chain biting her fingers, and a clump of junip shook itself as thunder rolled. Cat let out a faint cry, stepping back and almost catching her abused bootheel on her skirts. Spatters of rain plopped down, and the earth released a heavy fragrance, junip stretching and tossing as the wind loaded itself with fresh moisture and the promise of renewal.

The figure, a scarecrow with dark messy hair, his once-white shirt smeared with crusted filth, leapt back as well, startled. "Who the Devil—oh, damn your eyes, Kittycat, what are you doing *here*?"

Cat stumbled and sat down, *hard*. Her teeth clicked together, and she tasted copper blood. The locket went mad, its chain sinking into her flesh as it sought to escape her grasp and fly to the scarecrow.

"Robbie?" she whispered, but the word was drowned in thunder. "*Robbie?*"

"What in God's name are you *doing* here?" he hissed, and it was unmistakably Robbie. But so thin, and his eyes blazed. Their familiar darkness lit with a foxfire gleam, and another flash of lightning drenched the clearing, turning the face above into a leering skull. "You have to leave. *Now*. Before it takes over again—"

"Robbie..." Her heart pounded so hard she thought she might faint. Tears trickled, thick and hot, down her cheeks, cutting through dust and dry grit. "My God, *Robbie!*"

He beckoned, one pale hand flickering as a fresh spatter of rain fell, warm drops the size of baby Jonathan's fist steaming as they splatted into dust and hit tossing devilpine branches. "This way, dammit. I can't hold him forever...come on, Kittycat!"

She scrambled to her feet and ran for him; he caught her arm in a bruising-hard grip and yanked her aside—

—just as a searing flash lit the clearing afresh. She was tossed from her feet, a massive noise passing through her and a devilpine's trunk rearing to break her fall. Or not quite, precisely, for she hit badly and there was a brief starry flash of pain before unconsciousness.

Chapter 27

One thing about the weather in these parts: there were no halfway measures. It was either dry enough to parch you in minutes, or it was a solid wall of water fit to drown you even if you were upright and riding through it.

He had a bad moment when he found the bay tied to a tree near the hidden spring, and he barely remembered stumbling up the hill as the storm broke, the rain becoming a curtain and then, thicker. He'd thought to knot a bandanna over his mouth and nose, and the charm to repel dust could be altered easily to give him some breathing room. The rain danced in silver strings from his hatbrim, and his coat wouldn't turn this downpour aside for long.

God, just let her be alive.

As if God would listen to *his* prayers. Those of the Templis were sworn to chastity, and he'd betrayed *that*, hadn't he? Along with all the other virtues, one after another, like dominoes.

The lightning-charred tree was no longer a rarity on this hillside; nevertheless, he knew the trail and struggled up, shaking aside the clutching wet fingers of undergrowth. Out here, any scrap of moisture was to be clung to, and Damnation rested where it did because of the aquifer underneath.

Later, when Jack Gabriel thought of Hell, he thought of that battle up the hilly trail, every branch and root conspiring to clutch and hold, the lightning throwing bolts at earth and sky alike, and the sick knowledge beating under his heart that he might be too late. Wet dirt crumbling and the sick taste of failure in his mouth again, his boots slipping and grinding, the guns all but useless in their holsters and his hands prickle-numb with grace that had no outlet.

There was the large trunk of the devilpine, and he rested his back against it for a moment, his ribs heaving. If he kept this up, his heart was going to explode. He blinked several times, his hatbrim sagging under the water, and wished he'd had time to step behind a bush on his way up. Fear had a way of making a man's water want to escape.

He stepped around the devilpine, guns out, and saw nothing but the clearing before the grinning crack in the hillside, deep velvet-black and exhaling a cold draft that turned the rain to flashing ice. Another gem-bright dart of lightning, almost blinding him, and there was a shape at the claim's threshold—a woman's skirts, fluttering as she was dragged by a tall scarecrow into the gaping maw. He was running before he had time to think, a thundercrack of rage lifting him off his feet and his spurs ringing in the moment before he touched ground again, the bright white-hot flash of God's fury scorching all through him before he landed, flung through the entrance and into an ice-bath of torpid bad mancy. He collided with the scarecrow, and the thin man threw out an arm. The blow tossed Jack Gabriel aside, against the cave wall, and he slid down with red pain tearing a hole in his side.

Cath—

But the thought cut off, midstream, and a black curtain descended.

"I think he's waking up." Hushed, a woman's voice. Very soft, its cultured tones a brush of velvet against his skin.

Jack blinked, or tried to. There was something crusted in his eyes. A damp, cold, clammy touch brushed against the crust, but not hard enough. You had to scrub to get dried blood out of crevices.

"Just keep him over there." Harsh, a man's voice, but oddly familiar. "I can smell it on him."

"Ah, yes. You were saying?" Another tentative brush. She was touching him, and his head was pillowed on something soft but damp. There was a living warmth underneath it, and he tried to clear his eyelids of the crust. Sound of running water, thunder rattling above a roof of stone and earth. Hard ground under his hip, he was half on his side, and his hands were flung out, empty.

"He buried me in consecrated ground, Cat. So...here I am."

"The consecration kept you whole. So you're...dead. And...not dead."

"Well, yes. You keep *saying* that."

"Pardon me for having a tiny amount of trouble with the idea, Robbie. It is rather unholy."

"Mother would just..." A heavy sigh. "But she has, hasn't she. I'm sorry, Sis."

Catherine shifted slightly. "Well, what are we to *do*? He's a sheriff, after all, but perhaps he will see things in a reasonable light."

What's reasonable? Jack wondered. It was the longest span of time he'd been close to her, and he was loath to move. *That you're alive, or that we're inside that goddamn claim and you're talking like it's a tea party?*

"I don't know. I didn't think much beyond keeping *it* contained. Now it's getting out, and God alone knows what will happen. When does the stagecoach come?"

Tension invading her. "I am *not leaving*, Robert. I thought I would find your grave, but instead, well, here we are. In any case, we are Barrowe-Brownes, and I am not leaving you to the mercy of…whatever happens next."

Jack tried blinking again. It was no use; his eyes were crusted shut, and if he could get hold of whatever rag she was using, he could scrub the crust free. But that would tell her that he *was* awake.

And listening.

"I swear, I will carry you into town and throw you on the stagecoach myself. You should go back to Boston."

"*Do* try it, Robert. I shall take great pleasure in teaching you not to manhandle a lady so. I struck a man in the face with a yardstick recently, and was also party to a murder by skillet. I advise you not to try my temper."

A shuffling sound, and a sigh. "Have I told you lately how deadly annoying your stubbornness is? It's unladylike, Kittycat."

"I would curse you, darling brother, but I suspect you have heard worse. And he *is* awake." She shifted again, dabbing at his forehead now. "Hello, Sheriff Gabriel."

He cleared his throat, harshly, felt new tension invade the chill air. "It's *Jack*, sweetheart. And is that Robbie Browne I hear?"

"Yes sir, Sheriff sir." The same edge of mockery, the same irritating *I am of quality, sir, and you are not.*

Yes. It was most *definitely* the boy Gabe had shot. "I thought

I killed you. And you, Catherine, have been keepin' secrets."

Her stiffness now was *quite* proper, and she ceased dabbing at him with whatever rag she had been using. "No more than you. I would call you a murderer, but I suspect you would take it as a compliment."

The prickly tone cheered him immensely. At least she was well enough to bristle at him. "You're the one who asked me to get rid of a corpse, sweetheart." He found his arms would work, and his hands were clumsy but obedient. Scrubbing at his eyes rid them of crusted blood, and he blinked furiously several times before his vision cleared and he was treated to the sight of a pale, fever-cheeked Catherine Barrowe, her hat knocked most definitely askew and her curls all a-tumble, hovering above him. Her dark eyes glowed, the sleeve of her jacket was torn, and she was so beautiful it made his heart threaten to stop.

"He seems quite familiar with you, Kittycat." The boy sounded like he was enjoying himself immensely, for a dead man. "I don't know about his family, though."

"Robbie, if you do not cease irritating me, I shall *pinch* you." She sighed, and her gaze rested anxiously on Jack's face. "Mr. Gabriel, you buried my brother in consecrated ground. He is…as you see, he is not dead—you saved him from complete contamination, he tells me. I would ask you to—"

I doubt I saved him from anything. "Give me a minute." He didn't want to, but he found his body would do what he asked, and he rolled onto his side. From there it was short work to get his legs under him, and he gained his feet in an ungraceful lunge.

Unfortunately, his guns were missing. One of them was in Robert Browne's skeletal white hands. The boy was so thin his bones were working out through his dead-white flesh, but he was remarkably steady as he pointed the six-shooter steadily in Gabe's direction.

"Move away from him, Sis." Robert Barrowe grinned, his lips skinned back from very white, pearl-glowing teeth. His canines were longer than they had been, and wickedly pointed. "I think it's safest."

Catherine, her riding habit sadly torn and her curls damp with rain, still on her knees on the sandy floor, gazed steadily at her brother. "There's no need for that. If he promises to—"

"You'd *believe* a promise from the *sheriff*? That's rich. He's the enemy, Cat. We have larger vexations, too, in case you haven't noticed. *It's* loose, its attention is away from me for the moment. But Damnation is the first place he's going to visit, once he can get back in through the cracks in my head. We have to leave, and now."

"He? *It*?" Jack's fingers found the source of the blood crusting his face. Head wounds were messy. Other than that, he seemed just dandy. Except his ribs were none too happy, and his head felt like it was going to roll off his shoulders. "Just what did you wake up in here, Browne?"

"Yes." Catherine tilted her head. Two curls fell across her wan little face, and he saw how thin and tired she was. She winced as she moved, as if her ribs were paining her as well. "I was waiting to hear *these* particulars too, Robbie. What is…*he*?"

Robbie Browne's laugh was a marvel of bitterness. "Can't you *guess*? Coming into the wilderness has softened your brain, Kittycat. It's—" Thunder tried to drown his next few words, but Jack had heard enough. He went cold all over, even colder than the ice breathing from the back of the cave, where the claim spiraled down into the bowels of the earth.

God have mercy. He stared at Catherine's brother, his hands filling with the pins-and-needles of grace again. If he could close the distance between them...

The schoolmarm rose slowly, brushing off her skirts. "Then," she said briskly, as the thunder receded, "we shall have to find a priest. Come now, Robbie, don't be a dolt."

And she stepped toward her brother, whose finger tightened on the trigger.

Chapter 28

Cat was never quite sure afterward what happened. There was a flash, golden instead of blue-white like lightning, and a roar of rage. She fell, *hard*, her handkerchief—stained with Jack Gabriel's blood, and full of rainwater and dirt—knocked out of her fingers. The cave's rock wall was so cold it burned, and the crack of a gunshot was lost under another huge rumbling roll of thunder.

No, don't—

But they would not listen to her, would they? Just like her parents, or really, anyone else. The simple, sheer inability to *listen* to anything Cat said seemed to be a hallmark of the world at large. It was not ladylike to shout, but the thought occurred to her that perhaps, just perhaps, it was the only way to be heard.

"Catherine." A scorching touch on her cheek. "God in Heaven. Say something."

I fear I am quite beyond words, sir. "Robbie?" Wondering, the name slurred as if she had been at Mother's sherry a bit too much. "Oh, please, *Robbie?*"

"Gone. Think he didn't fancy hanging about once I took

my guns back." Mr. Gabriel sounded tightly amused, and as the clouding over her vision cleared, she found herself propped against cold stone, with Jack Gabriel crouched before her, his green-gold gaze disconcertingly direct and his face decked with dried blood, grit, and speckles of rainwater. "Enough time for him later. Are you hurt? Did he...tell me now, Catherine, did he hurt you?"

Robbie? "He would never," she managed, though her tongue was thick and dry. "Sir...please. *Please.* He's trying to keep the thing trapped here, so it doesn't harm the town. Please don't hurt him."

"If he is what I think he is..." But Mr. Gabriel shook his head. "Don't trouble yourself. Here. Stand up, now. We've got to get you inside the circuit before dark."

But she pushed his hands away, weakly. "Sir. *Sir.* Please don't hurt him. He didn't know what he was waking, and he has been seeking to keep it bottled—"

"Well, he didn't make a good job of it. Claim was open as recently as a couple days ago, sweetheart. Now give me your hands and let's see if you can stand up. If you can't I'm of a mind to throw you over my shoulder and carry you down that goddamn hill."

"Language," she managed, faintly. "He is my brother, sir. Please don't harm him."

"For the last goddamn time, it's *Jack.* Not sir, not Mr. Gabriel, and for God's sake don't push me, or I might do something I'll regret. Now, if you can't stand up, just lean on me."

Her head hurt most abominably, and so did the rest of her. She found herself staring at a battered, still bleeding, and incredibly sour-looking sheriff, who nevertheless helped her to her feet with remarkable gentleness. The floor of the cave was sandy—well, what was sand but dust, and this horrible portion of the world had that in awe-inspiring quantities. He steadied her when she swayed, and had even rescued her handkerchief from somewhere, for he proceeded to dab at her forehead with it while biting his lower lip, quite uselessly on both counts.

She took it from his fingers, and swallowed several times. "I suppose you are rather angry."

"I've had more pleasant days, sweetheart." But his mouth, incredibly, turned up at one corner. That same infuriating half-smile bloomed as she watched, and the sound of the deluge outside was like a gigantic animal breathing. "But not by much. Hope the horses ain't run off."

"Horses?" She seemed to be thinking through syrup. "I do think you are perhaps furious."

"I'm none too pleased, if that's what you mean. But I am damn glad to find you in one piece, and this goddamn claim empty. No wonder it sealed up so nice and easy the other day. *It's* already found—or reinhabited, is my guess—a vessel, and escaped."

Reinhabited? Oh, dear. That does not sound very nice. "Does that mean you *knew*—"

Now he looked annoyed, the smile fading. "Only thing I know is that I've got to get you back inside the circuit before dark. And it ain't gonna be easy with this storm on, but God help me, I'm gonna. You can scream at me all you like, Catherine, and you can stamp your foot and throw things at my fool head, I'll listen. And duck. But you ain't gonna go haring off into the wild after no goddamn—"

"*Language*, sir—"

She barely had time to say the words before his mouth met hers. There was a tang of whiskey and the copper note of blood, fear and pain and her teeth sinking into his lip, and the bulk of his body pressing hers against cold, cold rock. But it gentled, and she had time to be amazed and breathless as her fingers worked into his hair and his hands were at her waist, and the storm outside fell away into a great roaring silence.

It was like drowning, only not quite. It was like waking from a nightmare and finding a soothing voice, but not quite. It was as if she were alone on an isle in one of the novels of the Southron Seas, but inside her skin beat two hearts instead of one. It was as if the world had shrunk to a pinpoint, and expanded at the same moment.

And when it ceased she was left bereft, except for the fact that he leaned against her, her head against his collarbone and the weight of him against her oddly bearable. "Catherine," he whispered into her hair. "Don't leave me. Don't you leave me."

She could make no reply, other than to hold him while the thunder overhead roared its displeasure.

The bay had broken free and fled, and Jack's horse was a sweet, older black mare who did *not* like the thunder, but bore it well enough. Cat's foot found the stirrup, and she was in the saddle after a heave or two. Her ribs ached dreadfully.

"I got business here," Jack shouted, over the drumming rain. "Hathorn knows the way home. You just go on now, and bolt your door, and *don't open it* until I come back. You hear me?"

Her cheeks had to be burning. Cat nodded. "But what are you going to—" She had to scream to make herself heard.

"Don't you worry about that," he yelled back. "*Ride*, dammit, and bolt your doors!" And with that, he stepped aside, smart as you please, and slapped the mare's haunch. She took off, affronted by such treatment, and Cat bent low over the horse's neck. Branches freighted with cold water clawed at her; it took all her experience and strength to hold fast as the mare, deciding she had suffered far too much indignity, settled into a bone-rattling canter.

Damnation was a very long way away, and Cat could only pray she made it before the faint sun gleaming through the stormclouds set.

He's old and hungry, Kittycat. And there's no use killing it; he just comes back. That thrice-damned chartershadow cheated me. There's no weapon that can kill it. I thought I had it contained, but…

What was Jack going to do? Her mouth still burned, and other parts of her too. Had Mother and Father ever felt—

The black mare burst out of a tangle of junip, and the storm fell over them both with incredible fury. Lightning sizzled, the devilpines tossing their spiny green arms, and Cat was suddenly acutely aware that in a short while they would be free of the hills and the trees; she and the horse would be the tallest items on a broad chessboard dotted with loose scrub and sand probably made treacherous by this second Flood.

Chapter 29

The rain had slacked to a penetrating drizzle, but the gullies were full of flash-flood, brown foaming water like beer but without John Barleycorn's kindness. It was a mixed blessing, because Gabe had found the bay mare from the livery at the edge of one of the gullies, unhappy and shivering with fear. It was a job to catch and calm the horse, but he managed, and then the problem became getting back to the town.

As long as he thought of it that way—the next problem to be solved, and the next—he could push aside the sick fear under his throbbing ribs and the lump in his throat. The cold crawling on his skin was nothing new, and the habit of shoving it aside so he could work was nothing new either.

But the warmth of grace, pins-and-needles in his extremities but a bath of balm to the rest of him, was a new thing. For a few terrible moments, standing before the leering cave-mouth as the storm moved farther east, it had refused to answer him. He'd gone to his knees on the soft-squish ground, and instead of rage that God had failed him yet again there was instead a terrible fear that he would no longer be able to consecrate anything—and that meant his best weapon, his best way of protecting what he had to protect, was gone.

Faith doesn't leave, he had thought, staring through the falling water, at the churned-up earth and the darkness. *It just goes underground.*

And then the grace had come roaring back, because of the feel of Catherine's mouth under his, the slim curves of her described under his aching hands, and the sweet dazed look she wore when he'd finished all but kissing the breath out of her. Easy and warm, not a painful swelling to be excised because he no longer fought it. It simply *was*.

The claim mouth was sealed again, and this time, he thought it just might take.

What am I gonna do about her brother? She won't take it kindly if I put him down. But he's infected, and...but I buried him consecrated, which means he might be well-nigh unkillable. And to hear her talk, all we need to do is find a priest. It ain't that simple.

And God alone knew what she would think if she found out about *him*. The Templis were not regarded kindly in many quarters. And she was such a decorous little thing, too. Would she even consider a man who had broken his vows?

It was too dark, as if night had come early. That was worrisome as well, and the bay mare was tired and still shuddering. Still, he couldn't leave her out in the wild, with God-knew-what roaming around and the storm still heaving its way across the flats.

At the foot of the hills, he turned north instead of plunging straight to the east. It took him a mite longer than he liked, but he found the stand of crying-jessum trees, their long silvery branches flickering and tossing droplets as they shivered in the knifing wind.

The grave was there, at the foot of a once sand-crusted boulder serving as a headstone. The slightly sunken earth still resonated underfoot, meaning it was still consecrated, but Russ Overton was nowhere to be seen. The ground was a mess, not a lot of sign to be found, but Gabe thought there were two sets of hoofprints—one coming from Damnation, the other heading back.

Well, the mage could probably feel something rising to threaten his town and his charterstones. It wasn't like Russ to not come and find Gabe, though. That was…worrisome.

Just add it to the list. Jack stared at the dancing trees for a moment. The wash right next to them was full now, roaring along instead of just a trickle of sandy slugwater in its bottom. Everything in the desert was going to drink well tonight, and the mud in the town would be knee-deep before long.

Won't Catherine hate that. He stroked the bay's neck, soothing, and realized he was talking to the beast. The thunder had receded, and the horse shivered afresh. "Easy there, we're going back to town now. You'll be having a mash and a combing and some rest soon."

He hoped he wasn't lying to the poor dumb animal, and decided to walk her for a bit. She'd had a terrible day.

Ain't we all. Irritation, frustration, and the need to hurry boiled under his skin, but he breathed deep and let out a long sigh. There was no use in exhausting himself or killing the horse. He had just enough time to get back before sundown, even if it was too dark now. Even the worst evil couldn't make the sun sink faster.

But it could thicken the clouds, and do nasty work underneath them.

Your trouble, Gabriel, is that you can just imagine too goddamn much. Focus on what needs doin' instead.

Jack Gabriel set off for his town, still talking to the horse. After a while, he realized he was praying.

Old habits died hard.

Damnation seethed under a dark, rain-lashed sky. He came on the town from the northwest, and knew something was wrong the moment he stepped over where the circuit should have been, its invisible hand a weight that said *home* to a tired body. The weight was absent, and his head came up, bloodshot eyes squinting through the drizzle. The mud had begun, sucking at the bay's hooves, and the horse plodded forward thoughtlessly, past caring.

There was a sound, too. He cocked his head, listening intently. A metallic clanging, with a long reverberation. The grace in him responded, painful prickling all over, the warmth intensifying to just short of a burn. He didn't need to look to see his charing would be alive with golden light, but he did reach up and tuck it under the edge of his shirt, just in case.

It wouldn't do to have questions asked.

That's the charter-bell. The big iron thing hanging outside and above the chartermage's office, glowing dully every night as they rode the circuit, was usually silent. There was only one reason for it to be tolling.

An incursion. A bad one. The charter-circuit was broken.

He didn't even swear, just set his jaw grimly and urged the tired bay forward. She obeyed, and though he longed to put the spurs to her, it wasn't fair to ride her to death.

Catherine. Did she make it before the circuit broke?

He tried to tell himself he'd find out soon enough, that nothing would be served by riding in all a-lather. Everyone knew their duty when the bell rang—women and children locked in the safest place they could find, the men gathering to patrol in groups with any weapon that might serve against reanimated corpses, the saloons to stay open and dispense news and courage, in whatever increments they could, the jail to be manned by special deputies who were probably even now scrabbling for their tin stars and getting their folk to safety. They were good men, and steady, and hard from work.

Better hope it's enough.

Still, he was the sheriff. He rode the circuit with the chartermage; the town's defense was his concern. Keeping the peace was a matter of allowing the chaos to bubble just enough, but not overflow; keeping order during an incursion required something else.

So it was that Jack Gabriel straightened his spine, counting the tolls of the charter-bell. It kept gonging, over and over, and that was serious. It would sound until Russ stopped it, like a metronome or a heartbeat, and Gabe almost stood in the stirrups as he peered ahead, trying to guess what the hell was going on.

The town is the first place he'll go, Robbie Browne had said.

The thought of that ancient, hungry *thing* crossing the circuit-line was…well, enough to make a man's knees go weak. The town was safe enough during daylight, wasn't it? Even though it was dark under a pall of stormcloud, and the diamond stitcheries of lightning were centered directly over Damnation.

You have to face up to it, Jack. That thing could be riding inside any flesh it could find. If the thing ain't inside the town, it's just waiting for dark. Which isn't that long off. And it's no doubt sent in some troublemakers to sow chaos and contagion early.

Still, fending off the thing from the claim on home ground was better than facing it out in the hills. Damnation hadn't been here long, but charters drove deep, and every man in the town would fight. Even the Chinois would, and now Jack could hear their charter-bell ringing too, a brassier sound lifted on a flirting wind from the south, driving drizzle into his face. The rain was intensifying again.

Fighting in the mud. Again. No matter how hard and fast he ran, he always ended up in the filth with his guns to hand.

The bay mare, sensing something amiss, lifted her head. Jack blinked away falling water, his sodden hatbrim drooping, and he wasn't mistaken.

No, there were things rising from the boiling dirt. Claw-shaped things. Hands, tearing at the surface from underneath as the undead rose. He was fairly sure nobody had been buried out here, so that meant these were *gotar*—pure contagion, human-shaped and shambling, their jaws working and their teeth chips of sharp-flaked stone. And of course the thing from the claim would call them up and send them into Damnation. It would be child's play for *it*, now that *it* had found a vessel.

The fact that the vessel might be Catherine herself was enough to send an ice-knife all through him. Had she been caught outside the circuit by a fleeting shadow, holes driven through its shroud by the falling rain? It would be so easy for the *thing* in the claim to snap a saddle-strap or loosen a stirrup, and if she hit the ground wrong and her neck snapped, inhabiting the still-warm flesh would be child's play. Or, maybe Russ had felt the cold breath, and—

Don't think like that. Solve the problems right in front of you, Gabe.

Jack breathed a soft curse, the mare began to shudder, and his left hand was at its gun before he caught himself. Bullets wouldn't do anything against mud-things. Cold iron or blunt force to shatter their coherence was the only way—and the half-dozen or so who were rising were already turning blindly in his direction, making wet snuffling sounds under the lashing rain.

I'm sorry. There ain't no choice now.

He put the spurs to the mare, and she leapt. Clods of mud flew from her hooves, and he bent in the saddle, urging every ounce of speed out of her.

Joe swore at him, for the bay was covered in mud, shaking, foam-spattered, and probably near ridden to death. Gabe answered with a term that was a near anatomical impossibility, and the chaos enveloped him. Hiram Greenfarb was passing out torches, Capran's Dry Goods was alive with a crowd as he passed out scythes and other implements, and the Lucky Star was a poked anthill. The jail was open, and Gabe arrived at a dead run to find Tils and Doc Howard there already, tin stars pinned to their vests. Tils was red-eyed and smelled of rye, but his jaw was set and he appeared at least mostly sobered-up.

"What we got?" Gabe yelled, and Doc swore at him with a mixture of profound relief and irritation, bracing an ancient shotgun against his shoulder as he watched the street outside.

"Where the hell is Russ?" Paul Turnbull appeared from the back room, a bloody rag tied around his head. "We ain't seen no one from the outlying farms, even though that damn thing's been beating itself senseless. The graveyard looks like someone stirred it with a stick—Salt got us to drag him out there, and he threw down a boundary. Then he passed out, I got him upstairs with the whores. Some wounded, mostly fools hurting themselves. South end of town's a mess; the Chinee are having a time of it too. Guess their chartermage died last night."

Now that's interesting. The cabinets set along one wall were all unlocked, he found the one he wanted and shook his hat off. His eyes burned with grit and his heart galloped along far too fast for comfort. "*Shit.* South end of town?"

"South and west. Western charterstone got hit by lightning. Goddamn thing shattered. Where's Russ?"

I don't want to guess. "Don't know. Get Granger, he's the closest thing to a chartermage we've got otherwise." *The charterstone was hit? Goddamn. No wonder the boundary's broken.*

Thankfully, Tils just set his jaw and took off when Paul pointed at him. Doc nodded, once. "I'm off for the Star; the girls are making bandages and Ma Ripp's there. So far everything's holding at the south end of town, but I don't fancy the chances of the outliers."

"Serves 'em right, outside the charter!" Paul hollered, but Doc just bared his yellowing teeth and left. The door banged open, and it was Granger—a paper-thin nonentity of a man, but more solid now that his wife was probably locked in the attic of their neat little two-story house and not looming over him.

"Where's the damn chartermage?" Granger's graying hair stood up in wild tufts, he shook the water from his hat and clapped it firmly back on his head. "And Lordy, Sheriff, what the hell happened to *you*?"

"Got caught in the rain." The belt loaded with extra ammunition wrapped around his hips, and he breathed into the sudden weight. He grabbed at the canvas satchel he had checked just last week, settled the strap diagonally across his body, and jammed his own hat firmly on his wet, filthy hair. "You come with me. Paul, stay here and wait for the other deputies. They should be along any moment."

"Not so sure, they all live south of Pig Street." But Turnbull just waved at him. "Nobody's seen the schoolmarm today either, Gabe. Are you—"

I hope she's at home. "Well, then, guess I'd better go find her. Come on, Granger. Limber up your charm-throwing and let's see what the hell's happening out there."

"Always in the mud," Granger muttered. "You'd think they'd attack in the dry season. Shitfire."

A hard barking laugh surprised Gabe, and then it was outside again, the storm overhead rattling and smashing every inch of sky. He turned south, peering out from under the flapping awning over the jail's front, and a confusion of men's voices and high horse-screams broke through the rain. He wasted no more words, and behind him Granger puffed to keep up with the sheriff's long loping strides. Mud sucked and splashed, and all Gabe could think about was if Catherine had made it safely to her little cottage.

The sooner he dealt with this mess, the sooner he could find out.

Chapter 30

Her throat ached.

Cat stirred. There was something soft underneath her, but it was so *cold*. The shivering began, great waves of it passing through her, and when she sought to open her eyes and push herself up, she discovered two things.

One was that it made no difference whether her eyelids were open or closed. The dark was complete, phantom-traceries of colors she could not name bursting as she blinked. She could *feel* the lids closing and opening; her eyes were so dry they scraped. Perhaps she was blind?

Dear God, no.

The other thing was silence. She could hear her own heartbeat, and a sliding sound when she moved, her riding habit rasping across some other cloth. There was no thunder, no lightning.

What happened?

She had been riding; she remembered *that* much. Across the flats, the black mare giving a good account of herself. Then, confusion. Something had happened—a figure cut from black paper rising up, a geyser of earth spewing heavenward, concussive blasts of lightning and an immense sound tumbling her from the saddle. It bent over her, the thing, and consciousness had fled her.

Cat frowned—or at least, she thought she was frowning, her face twisting on itself. Her Practicality had flashed, blue-white to match the lightning, and the thing had hissed at her. Its breath was so cold the rain flashed into spatters of ice, a chill-fog rising like white steam from the streets of Boston on sunny winter mornings.

Then, nothing.

She patted about her with trembling hands. The softness was a pile of cloth, and the sounds of her movement fell away into the vast darkness. Her throat burned as she swallowed; her side cramped with pain as her ribs protested the treatment she had endured.

"Robbie?" she whispered, and the word vanished, swallowed by the all-encompassing dark. Then, a little louder, "Jack?"

No answer. *Am I dead? No, my heart beats, I breathe. Am I blind? Or…*

She swallowed through the dry pain, held up her fingers. Concentrated, breathing as deeply as she could. Two of her corset stays were broken, and she had to be careful lest they jab at her in a most distracting manner.

The dim glow clinging to her fingers scored her dark-sensitized eyes. Still, she blinked several times, tears of relief welling up. The simplest of light-charms, mancy responding sluggishly to her call, but still wonderfully welcome.

She gazed about her.

The softness underneath her was a pile of discarded, rotting clothing on flat sterile earth. The chamber was large, and its walls were rock. Moisture clung to the stone surfaces, and in the distance she saw a fluid glimmer—water, catching and holding the light she was producing.

At least I shall not die of thirst. I do hope it is potable.

She examined the clothing underneath her. There was no rhyme or reason to the pile—dresses, petticoats, frock coats, torn stained shirts, even some articles of children's garb. She tugged the locket free of her dress's neckline and transferred the light-charm to its metal; the shadows danced and spun as she rose on legs unsteady as a new foal's, arranging her clothing as best she could. One of her bootheels was broken, her dress was torn and damp. Still, it was comforting to see her attire was still whole; it wasn't torn *that* badly. She twitched at the fabric, gingerly, and twisted her hair up as best she could. She could find no pins, and her hat and veil were nowhere to be found.

With her person set to rights as much as possible, she stood next to the sad little pile of clothing and sought to calm herself further. Her neck twinged, and when her fingertips explored the pain they found two crusted scabs. She had bled on the front of her dress, and a cold knife went through her as her fingertips brushed the throbbing clots. She was cold, but the wound on her throat burned.

Oh, dear. But her charing-charm lay quiescent, and when she gingerly touched it there was no scorching to her skin. *This is troubling. Very troubling indeed.*

Do not be maudlin, she told herself sternly. *You have been carried into this place, there must be a means of carrying yourself out of it. Then you may decide what to do next.*

The gleam of water was a large underground lake; this place was a semicircle of sandy beach. The pile of cloth was at one tip of the crescent, and the weeping stone walls gleamed sullenly as she worked her way along the shore, finding more blank sheer stone. She found a handkerchief in her skirt pocket, and washed her face and hands as best she could in the cold, clear water. It had a faint metallic taste, but it slaked her thirst tolerably well. She would be hungry, soon.

Unless the water held something that would gripe her.

Where the crescent of sand was thickest, there was a narrow aperture, and she eyed it for some time before stepping close enough to peer through. Her nose and fingers throbbed with the cold, and she wondered if the chill would kill her before whoever placed her here returned.

The darkness yielded only grudgingly to her tiny light-charm. She pressed forward, uncertainly, one damp hand reaching out to touch the stone. There was a nasty odor, striking her chilled nose and twisting her empty stomach into knots.

She stepped just over the threshold of the door in the stone, breathing a word to strengthen the light-charm—

—and stumbled back, retching, from the twisted pile of meat and snapped bone, a pile of naked corpses pushed against the wall of the passageway like a jumble of unordered firewood. The momentary sight almost drove every scrap of wit she possessed from her, and she went to her knees, heaving as the water from the lake sought its escape.

And ch-children, there are ch-children's clothes too... The light-charm flickered as her concentration waned, and the inside of Cat's skull throbbed painfully. If the charm failed she would be here in the *dark*, with that pile of bodies, and oh *God* she could not, *would not*, bear it.

She found herself huddled on the pile of discarded clothing again, hugging her knees, rocking back and forth and moaning softly. The broken stays scraped her most painfully, but she didn't care.

"Oh God," she kept saying. "Oh, God. Please. Dear God. Oh, please. *Please.*"

The light-charm did not fail, but it took a long time for Cat to raise her head, her hair falling forward in a distinctly hoydenish manner and the wounds in her throat finally ceasing their infernal throbbing. The stain of bile-laced water she had vomited had stopped steaming, and was only a dark spot in the sand.

Now she could see that the pocked surface of the beach was the result of footsteps. Had others been brought here, and left? How was their clothing removed? And the…the bodies…

A faint scratching sound. Cat scrambled to her feet, stumbling over the mound of clothing, catching her broken heel on a dress of gray linsey-woolsey that looked just large enough for a girl of eleven or so.

A rushing noise filled her head. She found her back to the stone wall, the light-charm's glimmering dying to a low glow as fear threatened to overwhelm her reason. She gripped her charing-charm tightly, the locket's glow full of shadows now, and the scratching became movement.

Rats, perhaps? What would live down here in the dark?

The shadows leapt and spun, crazily. A figure melded out of the dark mouth at the back of the crescent, and Cat made a small inarticulate noise.

It stopped dead. A long, shuffling sound, as if something was sniffing. A sharp exhale. Was it a dog? If it was, perhaps the animal could be persuaded to—

"Cat?" A familiar voice. "Are you awake?"

"*Robbie!*" She ran forward, blindly, stumbling through the pile of clutching cloth, and when her brother's stick-thin arms closed around her, Catherine Barrowe-Browne gave herself up to sobs.

"Don't breathe," he told her. "And don't look. Come, we haven't much time. I lost my wits, then I thought I'd come see if…well, never mind. *It* must have caught you on your way back to town, dear Sis. Bad luck, no doubt."

"Robbie…*Robbie*…" *I am not making a good show of this, no, not at all.* She sought to restore her nerves. "What is this? The clothes, and those…those *bodies*."

"*He's* been calling people here." Robbie's face was graven. He was so dreadfully thin. "For a long, long time. Sometimes, if they were able to go past the corpses, he would hunt them in the dark. There's passages down here, all sorts of tunnels. Do not ask me further questions, Cat, I do *not* want you thinking on it. Come this way, and for God's sake do not…wait." He touched her chin, pushing her hair aside, and gazed at the scabbed marks on her throat. "Dear God. I…Cat…"

It was a shocked whisper, and Cat swallowed, hard. "I do not know what happened. One moment I was riding for the town, the next…I woke here. It was cold." The shudders would not cease, shaking her so hard her skirts made whispering little noises.

"Damn him." Robbie's dark eyes, phosphorescence glowing on the surface of his irises, narrowed. "Damn him to *Hell*. He probably thought this would make me behave."

If he knew you, Robbie, he would not have thought any inducement could work such a miracle. She immediately felt much more like *herself* again, and took in a sharp breath. "Behave?"

"No more questions. Come quickly. Do you trust me, Kittycat?" His fingers in hers, and her skin was far warmer than his even though she shivered. His fingers were thin flexible marble, and she had never felt such terrible strength in her brother's hand.

"Oh, Robbie, how can you ask? Do not be ridiculous." She found, much to her surprise, that she could summon a crisp, authoritative tone. "What are we to do now? I am not sorry I came to find you."

"I am. I'd have preferred you safe in Boston." He half-turned, and she did not demur as he led her for the grisly doorway. "Will you faint, do you think? If you have to see…that…again?"

"I do not think so." But she was not entirely certain. "Robbie…will my charing start to burn me, do you think?"

"Not until daylight. Look." He faced her again, his jaw working and the mud and dirt on his face not hiding the incandescent fury. His free hand worked at his shirt collar, and he drew forth a leather thong. It was a charing, but not the silver and crystal confection that matched her own. Instead, this was a plain brass disc with a charter-symbol stamped upon it, lit with the same soft glow that sheened his eyes, and as she peered at the skin underneath she saw only a faint shadow and a dusting of wiry hair. Yet it was indisputably a charing-charm, and she found herself unwilling to question its appearance. "The damn chartershadow owed me. Anyway, consecrated ground, you know. It doesn't burn me now. You have to trust me, though, Cat. We have somewhere to reach before dawn, and then…"

"Then what?"

He turned back to the doorway. "Then we will be cursed and outcast, but at least we'll be together."

"Oh." She shut her eyes as he pulled her forward, and stumbled on her broken heel. *Cursed and outcast, but his new charing doesn't scorch him. This makes no sense. Who could consecrate a patch of this wilderness so thoroughly?* "What must we reach before dawn?" The smell filled her nose, and she held back a retch by sheer force of will, trembling so hard Robbie actually drew her forward, sliding his arm over her shoulders. He was as cold as the stone walls, and his flesh was as hard…but he was her brother, and he had found her in the dark.

"A place by some pretty jessum trees, Kittycat. Keep your eyes closed."

Chapter 31

The *gotar* shambled forward. *Why are they attacking from the south?* "Give 'em Hell!" Gabe yelled, and the men of Damnation went to work with flails and scythes. The mud-creatures were falling apart; Granger had actually thrown a charm-blessing that spread and sparkled between drops of rain, turning the water fair-holy. He stood upright behind the defense-line, holding the mancy active for as long as he could.

It was bad, but there was hope. Russ Overton had limped into town, madder than a wet cat and all over mud, his clothes scorched from the shattering of the west charterstone. A group of men were hauling a chunk of granite from behind Ma Hainey's boardinghouse—she'd braced two boards on it and used it to chop off chicken heads, so it was already blooded—to the west border in Cam Salthenry's rickety wagon, with Russ perched atop the chunk of stone muttering charter-charms to prepare it. The instant they heaved it upright among the shattered ruins of the other stone, he could repair the boundary—and that same group of men would go with him to ride the circuit and keep any undead off the chartermage.

It was now a question of how long they could hold. They still had the *gotar* bottlenecked south of Pig Street, but there were more of them every time thunder rumbled overhead. At least the rain had slowed.

Jack wasn't sanguine, though. The sun was sinking, and if Russ and the stone didn't get to the west in time, it could get ugly. Underneath the stormclouds, a furnace of gold was turning orange and red, giving the entire town a coat of wet gilding. The *gotar* gleamed like seals, too, but the sunlight raised steaming welts on their dirt-skins.

Where are all the other undead? Salt put a boundary around the graveyard, but—

"Sheriff!" A boy's voice, high and piping. "*Sheriff! Sheriff! They're here! Help us, they're here!*"

It was Zachary Corcoran, and he was running down the street as fast as his thick little legs could pump, throwing up clods of mud and dirt. He gabbled, pointing to the northwest, and the pins-and-needles all over Gabe's body were almost driven back by cold fear.

The dead from outside the boundary shambled, their jaws working, and Gabe finally had an answer for a question that had bothered him a long while. It had to do with the undead in the schoolhouse, and why they'd gone after Catherine.

It was Jack's fault, actually. He'd buried Robert Browne in consecrated ground; Robbie would find charter-boundaries no bar to his passage. The thing in the claim had probably forced the boy to carry corpses over the line, to see if it could be done. Once over, those dead could spread contagion and break the charter-circuit from the *inside*.

They clustered in shadows, some of them freshly dead—he recognized Amelia Gerhardt from one of the outlying farms, her head stuck at a strange angle and her eyes blazing with unholy red pinpricks as she shuffled toward him on bare, flayed feet. The sun flashed, clouds scudding and tearing as the wind rose, and the thing that had been Rich Gerhardt's wife squealed and fell, its flesh smoking.

Zach Corcoran was sobbing with fright. The *gotar* set up a chilling rumble-noise—their version of a battle cry, maybe.

I have had enough. Gabe drew in an endless breath. "*Keep them back!*" he roared, and pointed at Granger. "*Protect him!*"

"What are you *doing?*" Emmet Tilson screeched at him.

What I should have done a long time ago. He faced north, and walked toward the approaching undead, his boots sinking in squelching mud. Zach Corcoran wailed, and the hiss-rasp of dead throats working as they tried to eat clean air was fit to drive a man mad.

Jack Gabriel spread his arms. The pins-and-needles of grace rose through him, and he stilled the fruitless inner thrashing.

The surprise was how easy it was. He'd spent so long hiding it, avoiding the questions, like a hooded horse, just plodding ahead and refusing to look. But the space inside him that had opened at his Last Baptism dilated, and inside it, the still small voice spoke.

Not for myself, but for others I may ask. Underneath the words was a single thought.

A pair of dark eyes and a sweet little face, dark curls and the feel of her against him. Her teeth sinking into his lip before the startlement passed, and then the sweetness and the thunder-crack inside him as her name rose like the charter-bell's clanging.

Catherine.

Grace burst free, a point of golden brilliance that shrank before it exploded outward. Time halted, and the wetness on his cheeks was not mud or blood or rain.

It was, after all, so easy. The Word spoke itself in silence, and the undead cringed from the sound. Their faces smoothed, the corpseglow leaving them in puffs of gold-laced steam, and Jack struggled to hold the place inside him open.

One question nagged him, though. *From the north. Catherine. Dear God, Catherine. Please, if I have ever served You, let her be safe.*

The golden light winked out, and he fell heavily to his knees with a splash of liquid dirt. The silence was immense, broken only by little Zach's sobbing for air and Emmet Tilson's wondering, breathless curse.

The charter-bell had stopped ringing. And now everyone in town would know what he was.

Gabe shut his eyes. *I don't care. Catherine. I have to see her.*

But when his group of Damnation's citizens reached the schoolmarm's house, they found it afire like half the northern part of town, smoke rising into a rapidly clearing sky.

He stood before the burning cottage, and the whispers rose in a tide behind him. The sun finished dying in the west, the stars peeping through torn clouds as the storm moved away.

Man of God. Turned the undead back.

But we all saw him kill Parse Means that one time, and he drank and visited the whores—

Sweet on the schoolmarm too.

Maybe one of those Papists. Maybe he's a spy for the Vaticana Arcane.

Naw, it's just Gabe. His reasons are bound to be good.

Where's the marm? And that Chinee girl?

Gone. Nobody can find hide nor hair.

Well, maybe there'll be a body in the house…

The cold closed about him, and the pins-and-needles of grace left him, cold ash after a fire. His face froze, and the flames crackling through the snug little cottage mocked him.

Perhaps she had not reached the town after all. Or if she had, was she inside the flame and the…

"Gabe?" It was Russ Overton. Mud cracked on his face and his bloodshot eyes blinked furiously, a muscle in his stubbled cheek twitching. "The charterstone's solid, it'll hold. What now?"

Why the hell you askin' me? he wanted to howl. But it wasn't a fair question. He was the one they looked to. The responsibility was his. "Contain the fires. Go house to house. Deal with every corpse we find." Who was using his voice? He sounded harsh, and savage-sullen. "Get the wounded to Doc Howard and Ma Ripp, and ride the circuit in groups all night. And give Freedman Salt a goddamn tin star; if he hadn't put a boundary over the graveyard we would've been in a world of hurt." He stared at the flames. It was an inferno, and he thought he knew why.

The thing from the claim was not going to be happy with this turn of events.

"Gabe—" Russ's hand on his shoulder, fingers digging in. "Did you find her?"

He shook his head. *Don't ask me, Russ. You don't want to know.* "Later. We need to deal with the dead."

"You…" This was Emmet Tilson, and he was pale under the mud and the blood, his moustache a limp caterpillar clinging to his upper lip. "You're a goddamn priest, Jack Gabriel. Don't you try to deny it, we all saw you. You're a goddamn Papist!"

He didn't think he could explain the history of the

Order of the Templis to this jackass whorehouse dandy. Even if he had the urge, he doubted he had the patience. "I was something, once. Then I got married to a nice sweet girl who showed up dead one day." The words tasted like wormwood. "I had to shoot my own wife, the woman I'd broken my vows for. Do you want to give me some grief, Tilson, you're welcome to. And I'll answer." *By God, will I ever answer.*

"That's enough." Russ was between them, for Gabe had turned to face Tils, and the firelight played over both of them as the drenched wind cut through sodden clothing and laid a knife to the skin. "We have *other problems* right now, God damn you both! Tils, take a group of men and start ridin' the circuit."

"I don't take orders from no tarbrush son of a bi—" Tils began, but Gabe stepped forward.

The punch hit clean, with a high cracking sound. It threw Emmet Tilson to the mud, and Gabe had his gun out. It was a damn good thing too, because Tils had drawn, and pointed his own iron up at the sheriff. The skin on Tils's cheek bled, laid open, and his eye was already puffing.

The cold all through Gabe didn't alter one whit. "One more body to put iron and salt in won't be no trouble tonight." He stared at the man, realizing just how small Tilson really was. "You want to meet me, Emmet, you do it at high noon. Say so now, or shut your goddamn mouth and get to work. I ain't havin' no more of this from you."

It was, he realized, all the same to him. He could kill this man now or later; it didn't make a goddamn bit of difference. He'd sent Catherine to her death.

Told her to go home and bolt her doors, and they would probably find her corpse in the flames. Iron and salt in that body he had held, filling the mouth he had kissed; the kiss that still burned all the way through him.

How could the kiss be in him if she was gone? How was it possible? Was the God who had spun the world into motion that brutal? That...that *unrighteous*?

Tilson lowered his gun. Gabe's finger tightened. It would take so little to solve the problem of this irritating jackass once and for all.

In the end, though, he holstered his own gun, and offered Tilson his hand. "Get up. Let's get the town cleaned out, dammit."

But Tilson scrambled to his feet without help, and glared at Gabe. He shoved off through the crowd, and Gabe ended up having wide blond Paul Barberyus gather a group to ride the circuit with a hollow-cheeked, glaze-eyed Russ. Who, thank God, asked him no more questions.

Maybe Russ knew there were no more answers to be had. In any case, Gabe had enough work organizing the shattered town back into some semblance of order.

Then, he told himself as he cast one last glance at the burning wreckage of the schoolmarm's house, it was time to go hunting.

Chapter 32

Perched on the wagon's swaying front seat, Cat peered through the rain. Each time it jolted, her side ached; her bottom was *never* going to forgive her. She clung to his thin, stone-hard arm, and blinked away falling water. Her hair was an absolute sodden *mess*. Neither of them were respectable at this point, and the heaviness of the trunks in the back of the wagon probably kept the entire contraption from flying away in this dreadful storm. "Does it…hurt?"

"No more than living." Robbie's laugh was a marvel of bitterness. "Neither of us will be carrying on the Barrowe-Browne name, I fancy."

Of course not. The undead do not procreate, even the conscious ones. "Don't be nasty, Robbie." She sighed, exhaustion swamping her. "But please do answer me honestly: Does it *hurt*?"

"What's pain? For God's sake, would you rather be one of *its* corpses?"

She jabbed her fingers in just under his ribs, and *pinched* him. The skin gave a fraction, resilient stone. He actually laughed, and it was Robbie's old carefree, surprised merriment. "Ow!

Very well. It stings, Kittycat. I won't lie, it stings a bit. But that's only until you fall asleep. I'll do it as gently as possible."

"And you're...you're certain I'll wake up?" She suddenly felt very small, and as the rain intensified and the wagon's wheels cut into a sludge of mud, she huddled closer to her brother and wished Jack Gabriel were here too.

But he won't take very kindly to what Robbie is, and what I'm going to be. She shuddered a trifle, but her brother was right. The...the *it*, the master, or *him*, as Robbie inevitably referred to it as, had contaminated her brother. A man of Jack Gabriel's stripe would not allow such a contaminated thing to live. He was a *sheriff*, for God's sake. And so irritatingly...well, he was so *irritatingly* Jack. It was the only word she could find.

"I'm absolutely certain." Her brother's tone was so grim she dared not question further.

Now that Cat's throat was throbbing with pain, *she* was contaminated, too. The *thing* had not outright killed her, perhaps because it still needed Robbie's aid. But it had put her in that ghastly underground cave...and the *bodies*, dear God, the corpses piled up, waiting to serve the master's bidding at some future moment—perhaps when it was certain it could overwhelm the town and add to their number in one great mass.

Some of them were merely bones, and older ones, slowly mouldering in the labyrinth's depths, were dressed in strange and primitive costumes. The removal of the clothes was a newer tradition, it seemed, and Cat's shudders were coming regularly now, in great gripping waves.

"I don't feel quite right," she murmured.

"Try to rest. You lost a lot of blood."

"How *gruesome.*"

He shook a spatter of rain away, the familiar forelock falling over his pale forehead. "Well, that's what it is. Cattle are good, other animals—but you won't have to bite anything. You can just take from me; I'll hunt for the both of us."

This was a highly indelicate conversation, and her stomach was none too steady. "Robbie..."

"You shouldn't have come."

Well, you shouldn't have left in the first place. "I *had* to."

"I know. I just wish..." Mercifully, he stopped. "Should be around here. Why this patch is consecrated, I can't tell you. You'll feel it as soon as we get there. It's actually pleasant. And then, after dusk tomorrow, we'll set out. We'll go to San Frances. If we're careful, we may actually pass unnoticed."

"We won't for long. Or do you think our presence will not spread the contamination, and cause a great deal of suffering?"

"Well, I haven't turned anyone into a slavering undead yet. I believe the consecrated burial is what saved me from..." Robbie trailed off, lifting his head. The rain was coming down harder now, and Cat discovered she was *quite* sick of frontier living, no matter how Miss Bowdler rhapsodized about its purity.

I will never see my students again. Or the ladies from the Lucky Star. She found, much to her surprise, that she quite missed them already. And Li Ang's round, now-familiar face, and little baby Jonathan's piping cries. She even missed the heat and the dust. *Any* heat would have been welcome now.

Is Jack well? He stayed behind at the cave, to do...what? He said he had business there. Oddly enough, the thought of him—dirty, stubbled, and comforting—hurt somewhere in the region of her chest. A piercing pain, as if she had been stabbed.

Her head ached quite dreadfully, too. "I truly do not feel well." Her voice was high and rather young, as if she were nine and afraid of the shadows on the nursery wall again.

"Don't worry." Her brother tautened the reins, and the horses—thin nags, but tough as bootleather—halted, switching their tails. "We have arrived. Straighten your fan, dearest."

The words—just what he would say before a ball, in the carriage as they braced themselves for another night In Society—made a small, forlorn giggle escape her. How far they were from Boston. Here, in the middle of a wet night in the cold, and her throat throbbing terribly... but still, she clung to his arm until he fastened the reins and hopped down from the wagon.

It was dark, and the rain came down in sheets. She could just make out a roaring river, its curve reminding her terribly of the crescent of sandy beach and the soul-eating blackness on its other shore. But there were white-trunked jessum trees, shaking their jangling bracelet-leaves under the wind, and as Robbie lifted her down she felt a tingle along her skin. It was a comforting warmth, and even though her breath came in puffs of white cloud as the wind veered and cut through her sodden riding habit, she felt it like a blanket about her shoulders.

"Oh," she said, a thin breath of wonder, and her brother laughed again.

"I *told* you that you would feel it. Now, step this way, sister."

She did, holding fast to his arm, and the rain was a curtain of jewels. The jessum trees waved their long fluttering finials in greeting, and there was a patch of sunken earth with a stone at its head.

Robbie drove the shovel in at the foot of the grave, his booted foot stamping it cleanly home. It would wait until needed.

She clung to his arm with all her remaining strength, and when he turned to face her, there was a break in the heavy clouds, and starshine played over his pale, ravaged face.

"Are you quite sure?" he asked her, pointlessly.

"Don't be ridiculous." Her throat really did hurt most awfully, and her head was full of rushing noise. She stepped away, her hands falling to her sides, fisting inside the ruins of her gloves. "We shall go to San Frances. The opera there is quite fine, I've been told." There was a gleam in his hands. The rain slackened. The gleam was a pistol, and the fear was suddenly very large, and she was lost in it. "Robbie…" Breathless, and she lifted her chin. *I am a Barrowe-Browne. I shall not cry.* "Do it, for God's sake. Do not let me become a mindless slave to that thing. I would rather…well." *I would rather die, but I will, won't I? Either way. It is six of one, a half-dozen of another. At least this way I shall not become a slavering hag.*

"I…" His throat worked, and the warmth enveloping her skin was familiar. Where had she felt it before? "I am sorry, Kittycat."

She nodded, strings of wet hair falling in her face. If she ever reached a dry warm place after this, she would stay there for a *month*, she promised herself. Thick woolen socks, and a wrapper, and some of Li Ang's harsh black tea would do very well right at the moment.

The pistol's mouth looked very large as he pointed it at her. Where had he acquired such a thing, she wondered, and decided not to ask if it had been bought in a pawnshop on Damnation's dusty main street.

What else had Robbie bought from a chartershadow, she wondered?

"If this hurts," she managed in a queerly husky, ruined voice, "I shall simply *pinch* you, Robert. *Twice.*"

He squeezed the trigger, and squeezed his eyes shut at the same time, and there was a terrific blow to her chest.

How odd, it doesn't hurt. The warmth spilled through her, and there was a rivulet of something hot on her chin. She reached up to dab it away, but her limbs would not obey her. A swimming weakness took her, and Robbie cried her name, over and over.

It is all well, she wanted to tell him, but the bubble of warmth burst on her lips and she fell. She did not feel it, spilled sideways onto the cold ground…

…and Catherine Elizabeth Barrowe-Browne died.

Chapter 33

I ain't giving you a horse." Joe glowered, the bandage around his head glare-white in the livery's lamplight. "You rode Bessie near into her grave, dammit, and that school-marm—"

"It warn't her fault." Gabe's eyes burned, and he was sure his temper was none too steady. "And I ain't *asking*, Joe. I need a horse, Hathorn's missing, and after the night we've had, you'd do well not to question me."

"Give him a goddamn horse." Russ coughed rackingly, leaning against a stall door. "He's got business."

Gabe pulled his hand away from the gun-butt. "How long you been standin' there?"

"Long enough." The chartermage fixed him with a piercing glare. Russ looked about ready to fall down and sleep right there against the stall door, but his gaze was clear and his hands were loose, leftover mancy popping and sparking about him. "She might not have been in her house, Gabe. And that thing in the claim…"

"It can't have her." The words had to work their way

around a wet rock lodged in his throat. "By God, if I have to, I will put her in a quiet grave. But *it won't have her.*" *And if it killed her, I will return the favor. I have grace enough for that.*

I have to.

Russ nodded, wearily. His hair, free of the wax and grimed with mud, stood up anyhow. He'd lost his bowler hat somewhere, and the guck smeared all over him was thick enough to turn aside a curse. "You want some help?"

As if you could give me any. "I ain't askin'."

"But I am."

Joe set about saddling a big white cob-headed beast of a horse, mutiny evident in his every line. He cast both Russ and Gabe reproachful little glances, but neither of them paid attention.

"Damnation needs you more." Gabe considered the chartermage for a long moment. "I'll take the ammunition you're carrying, though."

For a moment there was silence, as Russ unbuckled the belt full of cartridges and leather boxes of stacked bullets. He handed it over, and Gabe weighed it. Almost full; Russ's battle had not involved gunplay.

"I was of the Templis." The words surprised him, and the fact that he could say it so calmly surprised him as well. "I was a Knight, full-made and Baptized. I left them to marry Annie, but it follows a man, don't it."

"Fate tends to do that." Russ leaned back against the stall door. The exhaustion had turned him gray, even in the warm lamplight. "I didn't think the *Ordo Templis* still existed."

Oh, they do. "My...my wife. She...died." Why had he not told the man before? *I had my reasons.*

But were they good ones? Was it too late to offer an explanation, or even ask for...what? Forgiveness?

My way is to cleanse, not to forgive.

"So I gathered." Russ coughed again. "I ain't gonna see you again, am I."

"Maybe not." But Gabe paused, taking the reins from Joe as the big pale animal snorted and eyed him nervously. "You're a good friend, Russ Overton. I wish to God I'd told you what I was."

"Shitfire, Gabe, you think I didn't *guess*?" The laugh was worn and threadbare, but it still made the chartermage look years younger. "Go on now. Do what you got to."

That's all I ever do. What I got to. Some days I wish it weren't. His foot found the stirrup, and he heaved himself up with a grunt, his entire body protesting. "This ain't, by any chance, that man-eating bastard of a horse your dad was swearing to put down, was it?"

Joe's gaptooth smile was pure malice. "*Hyah!*" he yelled, and slapped the pale beast's flank.

The horse lunged for the livery doors, and Gabe cursed.

The sun had long since set, and riding outside the circuit at night was a fool's game. Just like everything else in Damnation. The rain had become an intermittent mist and drizzle, and the roaring of water in the desert mixed with the rolls of receding thunder.

He set his course west-northwest. The thing from the claim would likely return to its hole to lick its wounds, but Gabe wanted to check Robbie Browne's grave first. If the consecration still held, he wanted to know.

What are you thinking, Jack?

Not much, he admitted. You didn't need to think when you had a job to do, or so he had always told himself. When he started thinking, that was when the trouble happened. It was thinking that got him tangled up with Annie, because he couldn't get her out of his damn head. It was thinking that had gotten him all the way across the goddamn continent to this Godforsaken place, and thinking that had landed him the sheriff's badge. Nobody else would take it, and Jack didn't care, so why the hell not? And it was thinking about Catherine that had led to…what? Being silly and stupid, and costing another woman her life.

She might be alive. She might not have been in that house.

Then she was wandering out in the wilderness during a storm, with the thing from the claim wandering loose, too. And nobody had seen hide nor hair of Li Ang and her baby; he could add that to the list on his conscience.

Yes, if the ground was still consecrated, Jack wanted to know. He would need somewhere to rest after killing the thing.

Especially if the battle ended badly.

There was a swelling of cold light on the horizon, and as a waning moon shouldered its way clear of the hills and began peeking through the tatters of flying cloud, Jack Gabriel began to sing.

It was an old tune, one he had heard over and over in the dimness of his orphanage youth. A hymn to the Templis Redeemer, its notes full of sonorous dolor, meant to be chanted plainly by plain men whose task was to cleanse and revenge.

If the thing from the claim was anywhere near, it would be

maddened by the syllables. And it heartened a man to sing a bit before the battle began.

Come find me, he thought, and felt the prickles rise all over his skin again. His charing flashed gold, a challenge he didn't bother to hide under his shirt anymore. *God damn you, come and find me.*

If you don't, I will find you.

Chapter 34

It was cold.

She could not *breathe*, there was a weight atop her, and she clawed at wet dirt. *Out, get out—*

The intent to rise ran through her bones like dark wine, and she found herself exploding from the ground in a shower of wet dirt and small pebbles. Coughing, retching, she fell and lay full-length on cold soaked ground, and the sky was so *bright*, dear God, it burned along every inch of her, smoking through rips and rents in the riding habit, driving needles in.

Something landed atop her. It was a blanket, followed by a warm living weight. A thundering filled her ears, and she went still.

There was a voice, too. Familiar, and piercing the thundering thudding beat like a golden needle, a queer atonal screeching. There was another thump-thump, a very small one, some distance away.

What on earth...I am not dead. I am...oh, no. No. But yes. Robbie, where is he?

"Quiet," Li Ang said, finally. "You quiet."

Chapter 35

The moon's cheese-rotten grimace rose through spilled clouds; its sullen light turned the flats into a treacherous chiaroscuro. The plainsong had burned its way through Jack's throat, and he coughed and spat once, breaking the monotony of its rise and fall.

When he did, the shadows pressed close, and he hurriedly took up the thread again, despite the scraping to his voice and the vicious nips of pain all over his body as weary flesh told him just how thoroughly he had abused it. His head tipped forward, and when he glanced up he saw with no real surprise gleams of paired eyes in the ink-black shiftings, oddly colored like beasts' eyes.

He was not merely being watched, for when the massive, ill-tempered white horse pranced restively, some of the shadows would dart in, nipping at the gelding and making him difficult to control. Only the song kept them back, and he heard the sliding sound of mud-beasts rising from the wet earth. By tomorrow, the flats would be a carpet of wildflowers, seeds that had lain dormant springing into brief, gloriously colored life.

Another set of racking coughs. Her throat was dry paper, and she suspected that very soon, she would be very thirsty. "Yes." She blinked and recognized the blanket—it was the quilt from her very own bed, and it stopped the terrible burning all over her. She could *sense* the heat and light just outside, waiting to score her sensitive skin, scrape at her eyes. "Li Ang?" Wonderingly.

"Good." The warm weight of the Chinoise girl's body rolled away. "They think us dead. We go now."

I was dead. *Perhaps that's beside the point.* She took stock of herself—her arms worked, and her legs. Her hair was a filthy mess, and the ruins of her riding habit were scarcely better. The pain in her chest was a metronome ticking, and she realized the thudding was Li Ang's pulse. The smaller one had to be baby Jonathan's.

Catherine. I am Catherine Elizabeth Barrowe-Browne. I am…alive. No, undead. Something. Robbie shot me.

She groaned, the inside of her skull unhappy with the memory, refusing to contain it. "It's…dawn?"

"Sun soon. There is wagon. Heavy boxes. Yours?" The girl's hands were strong and slim as the rest of her, and she dragged Cat to her feet, wrapping another blanket around her. "Horses, too. My horses better."

Boxes of gold bars. Robbie took them from the claim. Not cursed now, he said. "The boxes…yes. There's…they are important. Li Ang…"

"You save Li Ang and Jin. Li Ang save you. We go now."

"How did you find—"

"Li Ang *quiet*. Not *stupid*." The Chinoise girl trailed off in a spitting, atonal song of curses. Cat stumbled, her broken bootheel throwing her off-balance, and she was evidently much heavier than she had been, for the wagon groaned most unsettlingly when she heaved herself up into the back and collapsed next to the corded trunks. There were scraping sounds, and more cloth settled over her body, merciful dimness easing the pain of inimical daylight.

I shall quite miss the sun. But at least I am alive, and Robbie…

Where had he gone? He was free of the thing in the claim, or so he said. And the gold, its curse lifted, would buy them all breathing room in San Frances.

"Li Ang?" Cat swallowed. The thirst was dreadfully bad, pulling against her veins. "I fear I may not be…quite safe."

"*Jiang shi.*" Li Ang spat as she heaved herself into the wagon's high seat. "You no hurt Jin or Li Ang."

I certainly do not wish to. "No. I would never." But the burning all through her, different than the heavy horrible weight of day, made her not so sure. She was *thirsty*, and the heartbeats were so distracting. Her broken stays grated against her skin, and every inch of her crawled under the weight of drying dirt. At least it did not seem overly warm this morning. The afternoon would likely be a welter of sweat and unpleasantness.

"Good." The Chinoise girl chirruped to the horses and flicked the whip, and baby Jonathan burbled. The wagon jolted, and Cat, wrapped in quilts, found herself tossed about most hideously.

"Li Ang?" There was no answer, just the steady grind of wagon wheels, and Cat closed her eyes under the smother of quilts. It promised to be a *very* long day. And she still had no idea where they were bound. "Li Ang, my dear, where are we *going*?"

"Train," the girl called cheerfully. "You buy ticket. We go Xiao Van-Xi."

It took her a moment to decipher what the Ch[…] meant. Cat let out a half-sobbing sigh of relief. […] Frances, indeed." For Robbie would find her there i[…] somehow separated; they had agreed upon as much [...]

Was it last night? It must have been. And now I am [...]

Cat's fingers crept to her throat. The wounds i[…] were gone, and her charing-charm lay cool and [...] against her skin. And…Robbie's locket, its metal f[…] still tingling with mancy.

Why did he leave me the locket? "Oh, Robbie," she […] and hugged herself under the blankets. The wagon j[…] Jonathan burped and burbled his way to sleep, and [...] while Li Ang began to sing. It was then Cat Barrowe[…] she could not shed a tear.

Whatever clay her body was made of now, it refu[…]

His course had veered, but by the time the jessum trees shook their long tresses in the moonlight, he had an idea of what was waiting for him.

The darkness was more than physical, but when the horse stepped over the invisible boundary of consecration it lifted, and the white gelding discovered his usual ill-temper again. He had to work to convince the damn horse that Jack was the one in charge, and the disdainful laugh from the shadow-figure crouched atop the charterstone at the head of the grave nearly drove the beast out of its mind with fear.

Through it all, Gabe kept the song's measured cadence. When, sweating and shaking, the horse stood with its ugly head hanging and lather dripping from its sides, he let the song die gratefully in his burning throat.

Silence. A faint brush of wind over the new life sprouting amid the ruin and mud.

"You've got a choice," Robbie Browne said, finally.

Jack Gabriel dropped from the saddle with a purely internal sigh of relief. *I just want to get some goddamn rest, kid.* "So do you, Browne. Or is it Barrowe?"

"Both, actually." The boy—or the thing wearing the boy's likeness—shook his head, tossing the forelock with a curiously familiar motion. "Barrowe-Browne. Old names, sir. Not like yours."

My name's old enough. "Where is she?"

"My sister? Far beyond your reach, Sheriff. Which brings us to the choice."

"You ain't Robbie Browne. You're *it*. The thing in the claim."

"A lamentable misunderstanding. The *thing* in the claim lives in me, Jack Gabriel. A marriage of minds, you could call it. Except I'm not willing to give up my bachelor status."

Gabe dressed the horse's reins. If the animal bolted, good riddance. Plus, Joe would likely welcome its return without him. "So who am I talkin' to?"

"Right now, on this ground, it's Robert Browne. The consecration you so thoughtfully performed made *its* hold on me…uncertain." A sigh, as Jack Gabriel's gun cocked with a slight, definite *click*. "If you shoot at me, sir, you shall never see my sister again."

The fear was claws in numb flesh. "I likely never will anyway."

"I wouldn't be so sure. She's been bitten, and buried in ground you so thoughtfully made sacred. For better or worse, dear Cat's just like me now. Little sister, always tagging along behind." Another pause, and the scarecrow-figure shivered atop the charterstone, a quick, liquid, terribly *wrong* movement. "She shouldn't have come."

"Nope." In that, at least, they were in complete agreement. Jack took a single step forward, wet pebbles and sand grinding underfoot. Another. "She ain't fit for this."

"Let me be frank, sir."

"I wish you would be." Another step.

"That's close enough." The light, laughing tone was a warning, and the white horse made a low unhappy sound, shivering. "Here is the bargain, Mr. Gabriel. I shall make you eternal, you shall leave me for daylight and the crows to feast on." Robbie's face was a white dish in the moonlight.

"Now why would you offer me a good deal like that, Browne? You ain't the charitable type."

"I am not. At least, I never was." The boy hopped down from the charterstone, stepping over the freshly turned earth below. "Did you ever have a sister, sir?"

Something's buried there. Buried nice and deep so sunlight won't touch it. "Orphan."

"Ah. Well. Then you don't know." A pause. "Sir, I wish…Catherine is all I have left. I wish for her to be proud of me. I would prefer her not to know I…am as you see me."

"Funny way of showing it."

"I didn't know she would *follow* me. I had to alter my plans rather quickly once she appeared. As usual, you know, she always was rather a disturbance. Now, are you going to be reasonable?"

"There are good people in town dead because of you, Robbie Browne."

"Would you like to add my sister to the list?" The boy's laughter faded, and he reappeared to Jack's left. Quick little bastard, slipping through pools of moonlight and shadow. And he was so damnably tired. "You're Templis, aren't you? The Order of the Redeemer. You know more about what she is than she ever will."

Well, and there it was. His worst fears, confirmed. "The undead at the schoolhouse. They weren't meant for her."

"I knew there was something about you. The thing in the claim recognized you, but it's…distracting, to have that much knowledge. It's like a lumber room; thing wanted often buried—"

Jack *moved*. He hit the boy squarely, the knife sinking into the thin chest, and Robbie Browne laughed. Rolling, wet dirt flying and his exhausted body betraying him, the knife slapped out of his hand and the boy's limbs closing around him like a vise. He struggled, and the prickles of grace burned unholy flesh. Robbie Browne hissed, his breath a sudden foulness…but even though

Gabe's spirit was willing, the flesh enclosing it had endured quite enough. Grace ebbed, and the struggle ended with a greenstick crack as bone in Jack Gabriel's right arm gave way. He screamed, but the thing had its teeth in the juncture of his neck and shoulder. Tearing and ripping, a gout of hot blood down his shoulder, and his left hand was full of the gun he had loaded with charter-blessed ammunition.

Rolling again, the barrel jammed into the boy's ribs. The thing inside Robbie's flesh gapped and leered, and when the gun spoke, the white horse screamed to match Gabe's cries and fled, trumpeting its fear as it tore through shadows and undead mud-substance alike. Another shot, and Gabe's prayer rose like a charter-bell's tolling, grace washing through him in a last hot flood of *in extremis*.

Catherine, he thought, deliriously, and Robbie Browne's body sagged aside.

Jack curled himself into a ball, whisper-screaming as edges of broken humerus grated together. His lower arm had snapped in two places, too, and the pain ate him alive. Everything he had ever thought of eating rose in his throat, escaped in a series of retches.

Robbie's body twitched. It hissed, a viper temporarily dazed. It wouldn't be down for long.

I wish for her to be proud of me.

Me too, Gabe might have said, only he was busy trying to breathe. On his knees, left hand dropping the useless gun, and his fingers scrabbling through dirt for the knifehilt.

He found it, and the thing with Robbie Browne's face glared up at him, its mouth working, black with Jack's blood. "Do…it…" it hissed, and Jack didn't hesitate. The broad blade bit deep, a tide of blackness gouting, and he hacked grimly at the thing's neck until the head fell free, spurts of unholy ichor steaming in the chill night. The jessum trees rattled as they shook their fingers, just like slim graceful women letting their hair down, and the sound of the undead and the mud-creatures outside the consecrated ground falling to bits as the will that had impelled them decayed into dissolution was a whisper fit to haunt nightmares.

There was a brief starry period of blackness, and when Gabe regained consciousness he found himself lying under a cloudless sky, the stars a river and a graying of dawn in the east.

There was a wooden shape to one side, and two slumped corpses that were probably horses, drained to feed Robbie Barrowe's unholy thirst. Jack didn't care. He lay for a little while, until, blinking away dirt and crusted blood and nastier decaying fluid, he found the last gift Robert Barrowe-Browne would ever leave.

It was a second grave, dug just to the side of the freshly turned earth with the charterstone at its head. All Jack had to do was crawl, and pull some of the dirt over himself.

It should be enough. He prayed it would be enough.

His right arm hung useless, and the gun was left behind. He clutched the knife, its blade running with bubble-smoking black ichor, in his left fist as he crawled, scratching along the pan of the flats under Heaven's uncaring vault. In the predawn hush, the scrape and rattle of his boots digging against damp earth were loud as trumpets. When he tumbled into the hole, the sides gave loosely, scattering over him.

It ain't so hard, he told himself. *All you have to do is put the knife in the right place.*

He set the fine-honed edge against his own throat, and arranged his feet. His right arm throbbed and screamed, but he disregarded it. All it would take was a single lunge, jamming the hilt against the side of the grave, and he would bleed out.

But he had to do it before the sun rose.

Jack shut his eyes.

"Cath—" he whispered, and his legs spasmed, pushing him forward.

Chapter 36

Four months later

San Frances was a simmering bowl of smoke, dust, filth, mist, corruption, lewdness, and outright criminality.

It was, Cat reflected, merely Damnation writ large.

Her arms were too thin; she had not yet recovered from the agonizing thirst of the desert. She no longer felt the dreadful heat, and every drop of moisture they had been able to scavenge had gone to Li Ang and little Jonathan. One of the horses had died, so they traveled at night, Cat's boots slipping and sliding as she heaved the wagon along like a mindless undead in a quarry. Next to her, the other horse had lost its fear of her predator's scent, and had merely endured that terrible passage.

The thirst had consumed every excess scrap of flesh, leaving her slim and breastless as a boy. Still, she possessed enough inhuman strength to lift both heavy trunks, and settle them on the wagon. It was a far finer vehicle than the one that had carried them out of the desert; the bars of un-cursed gold from the claim had proven *most* useful. There were even solicitors who could be paid to transact business after dark, and Cat's experience had built a fairly unassailable comfortable independence for a certain Li Ang Cheng Barrowe-Browne, as the widow of one Robert Barrowe-Browne.

How Robbie would laugh.

Not only that, but Catherine Elizabeth Barrowe-Browne and Robert Heath Edward Barrowe-Browne, both deceased, had named Jonathan Jin Barrowe-Browne their heir, and all papers were in order.

Mother would be horrified, and Father might be angry…but it was *right*, Cat thought, that it should be this way. At least the wealth would shield Li Ang and little Jonathan from some of the unpleasantness of life.

Her dress hung on a too-wasted form, scarecrow-thin as Robbie's. Now that the thirst raged through her, she understood a little more of his bitter laughter. She refused to think on the slaking of said thirst, of the lowing of the cattle and the stink of the slaughteryards. Overcoming her disgust at such feedings would help her survive…but dear God, it did not completely erase the terrible burning. Another manner of blood was called for.

Human. It was a mercy her parents were dead.

She sighed as she surveyed her work and found it as proper as she could make it. "It's safest this way, Li Ang."

The Chinoise girl, heavily veiled and mutinously quiet, shook her head. There had been argument, and the throwing of a butcher knife…but really, it had taken only one instance

Another set of racking coughs. Her throat was dry paper, and she suspected that very soon, she would be very thirsty. "Yes." She blinked and recognized the blanket—it was the quilt from her very own bed, and it stopped the terrible burning all over her. She could *sense* the heat and light just outside, waiting to score her sensitive skin, scrape at her eyes. "Li Ang?" Wonderingly.

"Good." The warm weight of the Chinoise girl's body rolled away. "They think us dead. We go now."

I was dead. *Perhaps that's beside the point.* She took stock of herself—her arms worked, and her legs. Her hair was a filthy mess, and the ruins of her riding habit were scarcely better. The pain in her chest was a metronome ticking, and she realized the thudding was Li Ang's pulse. The smaller one had to be baby Jonathan's.

Catherine. I am Catherine Elizabeth Barrowe-Browne. I am...alive. No, undead. Something. Robbie shot me.

She groaned, the inside of her skull unhappy with the memory, refusing to contain it. "It's...dawn?"

"Sun soon. There is wagon. Heavy boxes. Yours?" The girl's hands were strong and slim as the rest of her, and she dragged Cat to her feet, wrapping another blanket around her. "Horses, too. My horses better."

Boxes of gold bars. Robbie took them from the claim. Not cursed now, he said. "The boxes...yes. There's...they are important. Li Ang..."

"You save Li Ang and Jin. Li Ang save you. We go now."

"How did you find—"

"Li Ang *quiet*. Not *stupid*." The Chinoise girl trailed off in a spitting, atonal song of curses. Cat stumbled, her broken bootheel throwing her off-balance, and she was evidently much heavier than she had been, for the wagon groaned most unsettlingly when she heaved herself up into the back and collapsed next to the corded trunks. There were scraping sounds, and more cloth settled over her body, merciful dimness easing the pain of inimical daylight.

I shall quite miss the sun. But at least I am alive, and Robbie…

Where had he gone? He was free of the thing in the claim, or so he said. And the gold, its curse lifted, would buy them all breathing room in San Frances.

"Li Ang?" Cat swallowed. The thirst was dreadfully bad, pulling against her veins. "I fear I may not be…quite safe."

"*Jiang shi.*" Li Ang spat as she heaved herself into the wagon's high seat. "You no hurt Jin or Li Ang."

I certainly do not wish to. "No. I would never." But the burning all through her, different than the heavy horrible weight of day, made her not so sure. She was *thirsty*, and the heartbeats were so distracting. Her broken stays grated against her skin, and every inch of her crawled under the weight of drying dirt. At least it did not seem overly warm this morning. The afternoon would likely be a welter of sweat and unpleasantness.

"Good." The Chinoise girl chirruped to the horses and flicked the whip, and baby Jonathan burbled. The wagon jolted, and Cat, wrapped in quilts, found herself tossed about most hideously.

"Li Ang?" There was no answer, just the steady grind of wagon wheels, and Cat closed her eyes under the smother of quilts. It promised to be a *very* long day. And she still had no idea where they were bound. "Li Ang, my dear, where are we *going*?"

"Train," the girl called cheerfully. "You buy ticket. We go Xiao Van-Xi."

It took her a moment to decipher what the Chinoise girl meant. Cat let out a half-sobbing sigh of relief. "Yes. San Frances, indeed." For Robbie would find her there if they were somehow separated; they had agreed upon as much last night.

Was it last night? It must have been. And now I am…

Cat's fingers crept to her throat. The wounds in her neck were gone, and her charing-charm lay cool and unbroken against her skin. And…Robbie's locket, its metal familiar and still tingling with mancy.

Why did he leave me the locket? "Oh, Robbie," she whispered, and hugged herself under the blankets. The wagon jolted, baby Jonathan burped and burbled his way to sleep, and after a short while Li Ang began to sing. It was then Cat Barrowe discovered she could not shed a tear.

Whatever clay her body was made of now, it refused to weep.

Chapter 35

The moon's cheese-rotten grimace rose through spilled clouds; its sullen light turned the flats into a treacherous chiaroscuro. The plainsong had burned its way through Jack's throat, and he coughed and spat once, breaking the monotony of its rise and fall.

When he did, the shadows pressed close, and he hurriedly took up the thread again, despite the scraping to his voice and the vicious nips of pain all over his body as weary flesh told him just how thoroughly he had abused it. His head tipped forward, and when he glanced up he saw with no real surprise gleams of paired eyes in the ink-black shiftings, oddly colored like beasts' eyes.

He was not merely being watched, for when the massive, ill-tempered white horse pranced restively, some of the shadows would dart in, nipping at the gelding and making him difficult to control. Only the song kept them back, and he heard the sliding sound of mud-beasts rising from the wet earth. By tomorrow, the flats would be a carpet of wildflowers, seeds that had lain dormant springing into brief, gloriously colored life.

His course had veered, but by the time the jessum trees shook their long tresses in the moonlight, he had an idea of what was waiting for him.

The darkness was more than physical, but when the horse stepped over the invisible boundary of consecration it lifted, and the white gelding discovered his usual ill-temper again. He had to work to convince the damn horse that Jack was the one in charge, and the disdainful laugh from the shadow-figure crouched atop the charterstone at the head of the grave nearly drove the beast out of its mind with fear.

Through it all, Gabe kept the song's measured cadence. When, sweating and shaking, the horse stood with its ugly head hanging and lather dripping from its sides, he let the song die gratefully in his burning throat.

Silence. A faint brush of wind over the new life sprouting amid the ruin and mud.

"You've got a choice," Robbie Browne said, finally.

Jack Gabriel dropped from the saddle with a purely internal sigh of relief. *I just want to get some goddamn rest, kid.* "So do you, Browne. Or is it Barrowe?"

"Both, actually." The boy—or the thing wearing the boy's likeness—shook his head, tossing the forelock with a curiously familiar motion. "Barrowe-Browne. Old names, sir. Not like yours."

My name's old enough. "Where is she?"

"My sister? Far beyond your reach, Sheriff. Which brings us to the choice."

"You ain't Robbie Browne. You're *it*. The thing in the claim."

"A lamentable misunderstanding. The *thing* in the claim lives in me, Jack Gabriel. A marriage of minds, you could call it. Except I'm not willing to give up my bachelor status."

Gabe dressed the horse's reins. If the animal bolted, good riddance. Plus, Joe would likely welcome its return without him. "So who am I talkin' to?"

"Right now, on this ground, it's Robert Browne. The consecration you so thoughtfully performed made *its* hold on me…uncertain." A sigh, as Jack Gabriel's gun cocked with a slight, definite *click*. "If you shoot at me, sir, you shall never see my sister again."

The fear was claws in numb flesh. "I likely never will anyway."

"I wouldn't be so sure. She's been bitten, and buried in ground you so thoughtfully made sacred. For better or worse, dear Cat's just like me now. Little sister, always tagging along behind." Another pause, and the scarecrow-figure shivered atop the charterstone, a quick, liquid, terribly *wrong* movement. "She shouldn't have come."

"Nope." In that, at least, they were in complete agreement. Jack took a single step forward, wet pebbles and sand grinding underfoot. Another. "She ain't fit for this."

"Let me be frank, sir."

"I wish you would be." Another step.

"That's close enough." The light, laughing tone was a warning, and the white horse made a low unhappy sound, shivering. "Here is the bargain, Mr. Gabriel. I shall make you eternal, you shall leave me for daylight and the crows to feast on." Robbie's face was a white dish in the moonlight.

"Now why would you offer me a good deal like that, Browne? You ain't the charitable type."

"I am not. At least, I never was." The boy hopped down from the charterstone, stepping over the freshly turned earth below. "Did you ever have a sister, sir?"

Something's buried there. Buried nice and deep so sunlight won't touch it. "Orphan."

"Ah. Well. Then you don't know." A pause. "Sir, I wish…Catherine is all I have left. I wish for her to be proud of me. I would prefer her not to know I…am as you see me."

"Funny way of showing it."

"I didn't know she would *follow* me. I had to alter my plans rather quickly once she appeared. As usual, you know, she always was rather a disturbance. Now, are you going to be reasonable?"

"There are good people in town dead because of you, Robbie Browne."

"Would you like to add my sister to the list?" The boy's laughter faded, and he reappeared to Jack's left. Quick little bastard, slipping through pools of moonlight and shadow. And he was so damnably tired. "You're Templis, aren't you? The Order of the Redeemer. You know more about what she is than she ever will."

Well, and there it was. His worst fears, confirmed. "The undead at the schoolhouse. They weren't meant for her."

"I knew there was something about you. The thing in the claim recognized you, but it's…distracting, to have that much knowledge. It's like a lumber room; thing wanted often buried—"

Jack *moved*. He hit the boy squarely, the knife sinking into the thin chest, and Robbie Browne laughed. Rolling, wet dirt flying and his exhausted body betraying him, the knife slapped out of his hand and the boy's limbs closing around him like a vise. He struggled, and the prickles of grace burned unholy flesh. Robbie Browne hissed, his breath a sudden foulness…but even though

Gabe's spirit was willing, the flesh enclosing it had endured quite enough. Grace ebbed, and the struggle ended with a greenstick crack as bone in Jack Gabriel's right arm gave way. He screamed, but the thing had its teeth in the juncture of his neck and shoulder. Tearing and ripping, a gout of hot blood down his shoulder, and his left hand was full of the gun he had loaded with charter-blessed ammunition.

Rolling again, the barrel jammed into the boy's ribs. The thing inside Robbie's flesh gapped and leered, and when the gun spoke, the white horse screamed to match Gabe's cries and fled, trumpeting its fear as it tore through shadows and undead mud-substance alike. Another shot, and Gabe's prayer rose like a charter-bell's tolling, grace washing through him in a last hot flood of *in extremis*.

Catherine, he thought, deliriously, and Robbie Browne's body sagged aside.

Jack curled himself into a ball, whisper-screaming as edges of broken humerus grated together. His lower arm had snapped in two places, too, and the pain ate him alive. Everything he had ever thought of eating rose in his throat, escaped in a series of retches.

Robbie's body twitched. It hissed, a viper temporarily dazed. It wouldn't be down for long.

I wish for her to be proud of me.

Me too, Gabe might have said, only he was busy trying to breathe. On his knees, left hand dropping the useless gun, and his fingers scrabbling through dirt for the knifehilt.

He found it, and the thing with Robbie Browne's face glared up at him, its mouth working, black with Jack's blood. "Do...it..." it hissed, and Jack didn't hesitate. The broad blade bit deep, a tide of blackness gouting, and he hacked grimly at the thing's neck until the head fell free, spurts of unholy ichor steaming in the chill night. The jessum trees rattled as they shook their fingers, just like slim graceful women letting their hair down, and the sound of the undead and the mud-creatures outside the consecrated ground falling to bits as the will that had impelled them decayed into dissolution was a whisper fit to haunt nightmares.

There was a brief starry period of blackness, and when Gabe regained consciousness he found himself lying under a cloudless sky, the stars a river and a graying of dawn in the east.

There was a wooden shape to one side, and two slumped corpses that were probably horses, drained to feed Robbie Barrowe's unholy thirst. Jack didn't care. He lay for a little while, until, blinking away dirt and crusted blood and nastier decaying fluid, he found the last gift Robert Barrowe-Browne would ever leave.

It was a second grave, dug just to the side of the freshly turned earth with the charterstone at its head. All Jack had to do was crawl, and pull some of the dirt over himself.

It should be enough. He prayed it would be enough.

His right arm hung useless, and the gun was left behind. He clutched the knife, its blade running with bubble-smoking black ichor, in his left fist as he crawled, scratching along the pan of the flats under Heaven's uncaring vault. In the predawn hush, the scrape and rattle of his boots digging against damp earth were loud as trumpets. When he tumbled into the hole, the sides gave loosely, scattering over him.

It ain't so hard, he told himself. *All you have to do is put the knife in the right place.*

He set the fine-honed edge against his own throat, and arranged his feet. His right arm throbbed and screamed, but he disregarded it. All it would take was a single lunge, jamming the hilt against the side of the grave, and he would bleed out.

But he had to do it before the sun rose.

Jack shut his eyes.

"Cath—" he whispered, and his legs spasmed, pushing him forward.

Chapter 36

Four months later

San Frances was a simmering bowl of smoke, dust, filth, mist, corruption, lewdness, and outright criminality.

It was, Cat reflected, merely Damnation writ large.

Her arms were too thin; she had not yet recovered from the agonizing thirst of the desert. She no longer felt the dreadful heat, and every drop of moisture they had been able to scavenge had gone to Li Ang and little Jonathan. One of the horses had died, so they traveled at night, Cat's boots slipping and sliding as she heaved the wagon along like a mindless undead in a quarry. Next to her, the other horse had lost its fear of her predator's scent, and had merely endured that terrible passage.

The thirst had consumed every excess scrap of flesh, leaving her slim and breastless as a boy. Still, she possessed enough inhuman strength to lift both heavy trunks, and settle them on the wagon. It was a far finer vehicle than the one that had carried them out of the desert; the bars of un-cursed gold from the claim had proven *most* useful. There were even solicitors who could be paid to transact business after dark, and Cat's experience had built a fairly unassailable comfortable independence for a certain Li Ang Cheng Barrowe-Browne, as the widow of one Robert Barrowe-Browne.

How Robbie would laugh.

Not only that, but Catherine Elizabeth Barrowe-Browne and Robert Heath Edward Barrowe-Browne, both deceased, had named Jonathan Jin Barrowe-Browne their heir, and all papers were in order.

Mother would be horrified, and Father might be angry…but it was *right*, Cat thought, that it should be this way. At least the wealth would shield Li Ang and little Jonathan from some of the unpleasantness of life.

Her dress hung on a too-wasted form, scarecrow-thin as Robbie's. Now that the thirst raged through her, she understood a little more of his bitter laughter. She refused to think on the slaking of said thirst, of the lowing of the cattle and the stink of the slaughteryards. Overcoming her disgust at such feedings would help her survive…but dear God, it did not completely erase the terrible burning. Another manner of blood was called for.

Human. It was a mercy her parents were dead.

She sighed as she surveyed her work and found it as proper as she could make it. "It's safest this way, Li Ang."

The Chinoise girl, heavily veiled and mutinously quiet, shook her head. There had been argument, and the throwing of a butcher knife…but really, it had taken only one instance of Cat standing over baby Jonathan's new cradle, shaking and dry-weeping with the urge to sink her newfound, pointed and razor-sharp canines into the tiny, helpless pulse, for Li Ang to become convinced of the wisdom of Cat's plan.

Little baby Jonathan, tucked safely in his mother's arms with charter-charms on red paper attached to his swaddling, was fast asleep. Cat stepped back, not trusting herself, and bit her lower lip.

But gently. The teeth she now sported were *provokingly* sharp. "I shall miss you," she said, softly. "The gold shall help, and do *not* let anyone take advantage of you. Especially solicitors. Jonathan is the heir to a fortune in Boston, and you shall be safe enough there. Though I advise you to go overseas."

She had expected Robbie to follow her before now. That he had not, and that he had not met her at any of the appointed times…well, it did not bear thinking of.

If I could survive Damnation, I can very well endure this. She set her chin. "Come now. You shall just make the station, and mind you do not overtip the porters. I shall be watching, to see you off safely."

Li Ang refused to answer. She did accept Cat's help into the wagon, and Cat melded into the shadows as the nervous horses were chirruped to and the whip flicked. *I would have liked to embrace her, at least once more.*

But it was too dangerous, when she could hear the mortal heart working its cargo of precious, delicious fluid through Li Ang's veins.

It was no great thing to pass unnoticed, her shawl over her head, keeping the wagon in sight. She did not ease her vigilance until the veiled woman carrying her baby was helped aboard the huge, steam-snorting train by a solicitous conductor, and Cat moved aimlessly with the crowd at the station, the soft press of their flesh and the many heartbeats a roar of torment until the cry of *Allll aboooooord!* echoed and the metal beast heaved itself forward. Slowly at first, then gathering speed, handkerchiefs fluttered from windows—and there was Li Ang's slim hand, waving a red silken rag that fluttered from her fingers and landed at Cat Barrowe's feet. The woman with the shawl wrapped about her dark, pinned-up hair snatched up the scrap of fabric and held it to her mouth as she watched the train disappear into clouds of steam crackling with stray mancy-sparks.

There was nobody to remark when the shawled woman vanished. One moment there, the next gone, as the next train heaved and screeched its way forward to disgorge its weary passengers.

Chapter 37

It was a fairly respectable boardinghouse, and the rooms were at least clean. Nevertheless, a fastidious hand had been at work among the draperies and at the two beds, and there was a space between a large armoire and the washstand just large enough for a cradle. The marks on the floor showed where the armoire had been pushed aside, no doubt by two strong men.

Or by an entirely different strength.

A key rattled in the lock, and the darkness was complete. It was silent, though the street outside throbbed with catcalls and wagon wheels, clockhorse hooves—for here, the citizenry could afford the pens to marry metal to living equine flesh and bone, instead of the wilderness where plain flesh was good enough.

She sighed as she stepped through the door, locking and barring it with swift habitual motions, and shaking out her shawl. There was a heavy mist from the bay tonight, and its salt-smoke scent clung to her skirts. A dark, unassuming brown, but the cloth was of very good material and the cut was new, if not fashionable.

Quick, decisive tapping bootsteps, crackling and pert. She did have such a distinctive step.

The lucifer hissed as he struck it, and the lamp's sudden golden glow swallowed her indrawn breath.

Her shoulders hit the door behind her, and he stared for a long moment, settling the glass lampshade and turning it down so it wouldn't sting her eyes further. She'd probably been feeding off cattle, and looked like it. Too birdlike-thin, her cheekbones standing out sharply, and the way her throat worked convulsively as she stared at him made him long to speak.

But he'd waited so long. He could wait a little longer.

"Jack?" she whispered.

He nodded, once. "You get into *more* trouble, sweetheart."

The sudden leap of hope in her dark eyes was enough to break a man's heart. "Robbie…" A mere breath of sound, and he could not look away from her lips shaping the two syllables.

"He killed the thing in the claim." The lie came out easily. It should—he'd had plenty of time to practice the words, tracking her down, thinking of what he would say. What he would do, if he ever saw her again. "He…you can be proud, Catherine. He did right."

Her gaze flicked to his chest, where the tin star still gleamed. It was easier to say he was a lawman, and precious few questioned him. Her throat worked again as she swallowed, and he was surprised to find out some things about his body still worked, even if he was technically…undead.

"Are you…" She set herself more firmly against the door. "Are you here to…"

"I'm only here for one thing." Now was the time to rise, the floorboards squeaking sharply underfoot. Measured steps, his spurs striking stray sparks of mancy as intent gathered in the tiny room, the washbasin rattling in its stand. "And that's you, Miss Catherine Barrowe."

"I…" Had he finally struck her dumb? Not likely, because that chin came up, and her dark eyes flashed with familiar fire, through the sheen of phosphorescence on the irises. "I cannot hear your heartbeat, sir."

"Technically, I'm dead. Undead, more like." He shrugged. "Your brother and I agreed it was best."

"Oh, *did* you?" She folded her arms, and he had never been so glad to see the prim mask of politeness. He approached her as carefully as he would a nervous horse, and when he was finally within reaching distance, he stretched out a hand.

Please. He couldn't say it out loud. *I've followed you over half the goddamn earth. I'll follow you over the other half, but give me something, sweetheart.*

Instead, his mouth ran away with him again. "I've been getting what I need from the guilty, sweetheart. There's ways to take what we need and not spread the…not spread the bad mancy. I can do it for both of us, if you like. There ain't no need for you to—"

"It's still murder." Deadly pale. "And you're a sheriff."

I was something else before. His shirt tore, and he tossed the star. It pinged as it hit the floor, rolling under the bed. "I don't *care* about no goddamn law, sweetheart. I care about keeping us both alive. I don't care if we're goddamn cursed. I ain't going to see you die. Not if I can help it."

"Language, sir." But her shoulders dropped, and a trace of color crept into her thin face. "There…Jack, we're *undead*. We're…I don't even know what to call it, unless—"

"I know what to call it. I'll even tell you, if you like. I'll tell you anything you want to know. But you have got to tell me something too, sweetheart."

"Sir." Frosty now, and her hands dropped to her sides, became fists. "Must you address me in such a manner? I hardly think—"

"God *damn* it." That did it. He closed the last bit of space between them, and when he had restrained the urge to shake her, he found himself nose-to-nose with a deathly tired–looking, trembling, paper-pale, absolutely beautiful woman.

Dead, undead, or alive, she was all that remained to him of grace.

"You'd better be willing to marry me," he told her.

"We're *undead*, Jack. Somehow I think the question is moot." But she smiled, and the tips of her long pearly canines dimpled her lower lip, fit to drive him mad. "But if you're proposing—"

"I ain't proposing, sweetheart. I'm *telling* you. Now pack your things. This ain't no fit place for no lady."

The silence stretched between them as she studied his features. The stolen blood in his veins burned, and he didn't care if it turned him to ashes, so long as he immolated right where he was, with Catherine's beautiful, stone-cold hands creeping up around his neck and clasping sweetly.

"Don't you think," she said quietly, "you had better kiss me first?"

In the distance, a train's long mournful whistle sounded. And outside a slumped, barely respectable boardinghouse in the sinks of San Frances, the moon rose higher in a soot-darkened sky.

Finis

Acknowledgments

Thanks to Mel Sanders, who encouraged me to head for the finish line, Miriam Kriss, who encouraged me to consider it for sale, Devi Pillai for not throttling me when I dug in over the brass kettle, and Susan Barnes for sheer good humor. Last but not least, thank you to my dearest Readers. Hopefully you will have as much fun with this one as I did.

extras

orbit

meet the author

Daron Gildow

Lilith Saintcrow was born in New Mexico, bounced around the world as an Air Force brat, and fell in love with writing when she was ten years old. She currently lives in Vancouver, Washington. Find her on the web at www.lilithsaintcrow.com.

introducing

If you enjoyed
THE DAMNATION AFFAIR,
look out for

THE IRON WYRM AFFAIR

BANNON AND CLARE: BOOK ONE

by Lilith Saintcrow

Emma Bannon, Prime sorceress in the service of the Empire, has a mission: to protect Archibald Clare, a newly unregistered mentath. His skills of deduction are legendary, and her own sorcery is not inconsiderable. Yet it doesn't help much that they barely tolerate each other, or that Bannon's Shield, Mikal, might just be a traitor himself. Or that the conspiracy killing registered mentaths and sorcerers alike will just as likely kill them as seduce them into treachery toward their Queen.

In an alternate London where illogical magic has turned the Industrial Revolution on its head, Bannon and Clare now face hostility, treason, cannon fire, black sorcery, and the problem of reliably finding hansom cabs.

The game is afoot...

Prelude

———

A Promise of Diversion

When the young dark-haired woman stepped into his parlour, Archibald Clare was only mildly intrigued. Her companion was of more immediate interest, a tall man in a close-fitting velvet jacket, moving with a grace that bespoke some experience with physical mayhem. The way he carried himself, lightly and easily, with a clean economy of movement – not to mention the way his eyes roved in controlled arcs – all but shouted danger. He was hatless, too, and wore curious boots.

The chain of deduction led Clare in an extraordinary direction, and he cast another glance at the woman to verify it.

Yes. Of no more than middle height, and slight, she was in very dark green. Fine cloth, a trifle antiquated, though the sleeves were close as fashion now dictated, and her bonnet perched just so on brown curls, its brim small enough that it would not interfere with her side vision. However, her skirts were divided, her boots serviceable instead of decorative – though of just as fine a quality as the man's – and her jewellery was eccentric, to say the least. Emerald drops worth a fortune at her ears, and the necklace was an amber cabochon large enough to be a baleful eye. Two rings on gloved hands, one with a dull unprecious black stone and the other a star sapphire a royal family might have envied.

The man had a lean face to match the rest of him, strange yellow eyes, and tidy dark hair still dewed with crystal droplets from the light rain falling over Londinium tonight. The moisture, however, did not cling to her. One more piece of evidence, and Clare did not much like where it led.

He set the viola and its bow down, nudging aside a stack of paper with careful precision, and waited for the opening gambit. As he had suspected, *she* spoke.

"Good evening, sir. You are Dr Archibald Clare. Distinguished author of *The Art and Science of Observation*." She paused. Aristocratic nose, firm mouth, very decided for such a childlike face. "Bachelor. And very-recently-unregistered mentath."

"Sorceress." Clare steepled his fingers under his very long, very sensitive nose. Her toilette favoured musk, of course, for a brunette. Still, the scent was not common, and it held an edge of something acrid that should have been troublesome instead of strangely pleasing. "And a Shield. I would invite you to sit, but I hardly think you will."

A slight smile; her chin lifted. She did not give her name, as if she expected him to suspect it. Her curls, if they were not natural, were very close. There was a slight bit of untidiness to them – some recent exertion, perhaps? "Since there is no seat available, *sir*, I am to take that as one of your deductions?"

Even the hassock had a pile of papers and books stacked terrifyingly high. He had been researching, of course. The intersections between musical scale and the behaviour of certain tiny animals. It was the intervals, perhaps. Each note held its own space. He was seeking to determine which set of spaces would make the insects (and later, other things) possibly—

Clare waved one pale, long-fingered hand. Emotion was threatening, prickling at his throat. With a certain rational annoyance he labelled it as *fear*, and dismissed it. There was very little chance she meant him harm. The man was a larger question, but if *she* meant him no harm, the man certainly did not. "If you like. Speak quickly, I am occupied."

She cast one eloquent glance over the room. If not for the efforts of the landlady, Mrs Ginn, dirty dishes would have been stacked on every horizontal surface. As it was, his quarters were cluttered with a full set of alembics and burners, glass jars of various substances, shallow dishes for knocking his pipe clean. The tabac smoke blunted the damned sensitivity in his nose just enough, and he wished for his pipe. The acridity in her scent was becoming more marked, and very definitely not unpleasant.

The room's disorder even threatened the grate, the mantel above it groaning under a weight of books and handwritten journals stacked every which way.

The sorceress, finishing her unhurried investigation, next examined him from tip to toe. He was in his dressing gown, and his pipe had long since grown cold. His feet were in the rubbed-bare slippers, and if it had not been past the hour of reasonable entertaining he might have been vaguely uncomfortable at the idea of a lady seeing him in such disrepair. Red-eyed, his hair mussed, and unshaven, he was in no condition to receive company.

He was, in fact, the picture of a mentath about to implode from boredom. If she knew some of the circumstances behind his recent ill luck, she would guess he was closer to imploding and fusing his faculties into unworkable porridge than was advisable, comfortable... or even sane.

Yet if she knew the circumstances behind his ill luck, would she look so calm? He did not know nearly enough yet. Frustration tickled behind his eyes, the sensation of pounding and seething inside the cup of his skull easing a fraction as he considered the possibilities of her arrival.

Her gloved hand rose, and she held up a card. It was dun-coloured, and before she tossed it – a passionless, accurate flick of her fingers that snapped it through intervening space neat as you please, as if she dealt faro – he had already deduced and verified its provenance.

He plucked it out of the air. "I am called to the service of the Crown. You are to hold my leash. It is, of course, urgent. Does it have to do with an art professor?" For it had been some time since he had crossed wits with Dr Vance, and *that* would distract him most handily. The man was a deuced wonderful adversary.

His sally was only worth a raised eyebrow. She must have practised that look in the mirror; her features were strangely childlike, and the effect of the very adult expression was…odd. "No. It *is* urgent, and Mikal will stand guard while you…dress. I shall be in the hansom outside. You have ten minutes, sir."

With that, she turned on her heel. Her skirts made a low, sweet sound, and the man was already holding the door. She glanced up, those wide dark eyes flashing once, and a ghost of a smile touched her soft mouth.

Interesting. Clare added that to the chain of deduction. He only hoped this problem would last more than a night and provide him further relief. If the young Queen or one of the ministers had sent a summons card, it promised to be very diverting indeed.

It was a delight to have something unknown, but within

guessing reach. He sniffed the card. A faint trace of musk, but no violet-water. Not the Queen personally, then. He had not thought it likely – why would Her Majesty trouble herself with *him*? It was a faint joy to find he was correct.

His faculties were, evidently, not porridge *yet*.

The ink was correct as well, just the faintest bitter astringent note as he inhaled deeply. The crest on the front was absolutely genuine, and the handwriting on the back was firm and masculine, not to mention familiar. *Why, it's Cedric.*

In other words, the Chancellor of the Exchequer, Lord Grayson. The Prime Minister was new and inexperienced, since the Queen had banished her lady mother's creatures from her Cabinet, and Grayson had survived with, no doubt, some measure of cunning or because someone thought him incompetent enough to do no harm. Having been at Yton with the man, Clare was inclined to lean towards the former.

And dear old Cedric had exerted his influence so Clare was merely unregistered and not facing imprisonment, a mercy that had teeth. Even more interesting.

Miss Emma Bannon is our representative. Please use haste, and discretion.

Emma Bannon. Clare had never heard the name before, but then a sorceress would not wish her name bruited about overmuch. Just as a mentath, registered or no, would not. So he made a special note of it, adding everything about the woman to the mental drawer that bore her name. She would not take a carved nameplate. No, Miss Bannon's plate would be yellowed parchment, with dragonsblood ink tracing out the letters of her name in a clear, feminine hand.

The man's drawer was featureless blank metal, burnished to a high gloss. He waited by the open door. Cleared his throat, a low rumble. Meant to hurry Clare along, no doubt.

Clare opened one eye, just a sliver. "There are nine and a quarter minutes left. Do *not* make unnecessary noise, sir."

The man – a sorceress's Shield, meant to guard against physical danger while the sorceress dealt with more arcane perils – remained silent, but his mouth firmed. He did not look amused.

Mikal. His colour was too dark and his features too aquiline to be properly Britannic. Perhaps Tinkerfolk? Or even from the Indus?

For the moment, he decided, the man's drawer could remain metal. He did not know enough about him. It would have to do. One thing was certain: if the sorceress had left one of her Shields with him, she was standing guard against some more than mundane threat outside. Which meant the problem he was about to address was most likely fiendishly complex, extraordinarily important, and worth more than a day or two of his busy brain's feverish working.

Thank God. The relief was palpable.

Clare shot to his feet and began packing.

Chapter One

A Pleasant Evening Ride

Emma Bannon, Sorceress Prime and servant to Britannia's current incarnation, mentally ran through every foul word that would never cross the lips of a lady. She timed them to the clockhorse's steady jogtrot, and her awareness dilated. The simmering cauldron of the streets was just as it always was; there was no breath of ill intent.

Of course, there had not been earlier, either, when she had been a quarter-hour too late to save the *other* unregistered mentath. It was only one of the many things about this situation seemingly designed to try her often considerable patience.

Mikal would be taking the rooftop road, running while she sat at ease in a hired carriage. It was the knowledge that while he did so he could forget some things that eased her conscience, though not completely.

Still, he was a Shield. He would not consent to share a carriage with her unless he was certain of her safety. And there was not room enough to manoeuvre in a two-person conveyance, should he require it.

She was heartily sick of hired carts. Her own carriages were *far* more comfortable, but this matter required discretion. Having it shouted to the heavens that she was alert to the pattern under these occurrences might not precisely frighten her opponents, but it would become more difficult to attack them from an unexpected quarter. Which was, she had to admit, her preferred method.

Even a Prime can benefit from guile, Llew had often remarked. And of course, she would think of him. She seemed constitutionally incapable of leaving well enough alone, and *that* irritated her as well.

Beside her, Clare dozed. He was a very thin man, with a long, mournful face; his gloves were darned but his waistcoat was of fine cloth, though it had seen better days. His eyes were blue, and they glittered feverishly under half-closed lids. An unregistered mentath would find it difficult to secure proper employment, and by the looks of his quarters, Clare had been suffering from boredom for several weeks, desperately seeking a series of experiments to exercise his active brain.

Mentath was like sorcerous talent. If not trained, and *used*, it turned on its bearer.

At least he had found time to shave, and he had brought two bags. One, no doubt, held linens. God alone knew what was in the second. Perhaps she should apply deduction to the problem, as if she did not have several others crowding her attention at the moment.

Chief among said problems were the murderers, who had so far eluded her efforts. Queen Victrix was young, and just recently freed from the confines of her domineering mother's sway. Her new Consort, Alberich, was a moderating influence – but he did not have enough power at Court just yet to be an effective shield for Britannia's incarnation.

The ruling spirit was old, and wise, but Her vessels...well, they were not indestructible.

And that, Emma told herself sternly, *is as far as we shall go with such a train of thought*. She found herself rubbing the sardonyx on her left middle finger, polishing it with her opposite thumb. Even through her thin gloves, the stone prickled hotly. Her posture did not change, but her awareness contracted. She felt for the source of the disturbance, flashing through and discarding a number of fine invisible threads.

Blast and bother. Other words, less polite, rose as well. Her pulse and respiration did not change, but she tasted a faint tang of adrenalin before sorcerous training clamped tight on such functions to free her from some of flesh's more...distracting...reactions.

"I say, whatever is the matter?" Archibald Clare's blue eyes were wide open now, and he looked interested. Almost, dare she think it, intrigued. It did nothing for his long, almost ugly features. His cloth was serviceable, though hardly elegant – one could infer that a mentath had other priorities than fashion, even if he had an eye for quality and the means to purchase such. But at least he was cleaner than he had been, and had arrived in the hansom in nine and a half minutes precisely. Now they were on Sarpesson Street, threading through amusement-seekers and those whom a little rain would not deter from their nightly appointments.

The disturbance peaked, and a not-quite-seen starburst of gunpowder igniting flashed through the ordered lattices of her consciousness.

The clockhorse screamed as his reins were jerked, and the hansom yawed alarmingly. Archibald Clare's hand dashed for the door handle, but Emma was already moving. Her arms closed around the tall, fragile man, and she shouted a Word that exploded the cab away from them both. Shards and splinters, driven outwards, peppered the street surface. The glass of the cab's tiny windows broke with a high, sweet tinkle, grinding into crystalline dust.

Shouts. Screams. Pounding footsteps. Emma struggled upright, shaking her skirts with numb hands. The horse had gone avast, rearing and plunging, throwing tiny metal slivers and dribs of oil as well as stray crackling sparks of sorcery, but the traces were tangled and it stood little chance of running loose. The driver was gone, and she snapped a quick glance at the overhanging rooftops before the unhealthy canine shapes resolved out of thinning rain, slinking low as gaslamp gleam painted their slick, heaving sides.

Sootdogs. Oh, how unpleasant. The one that had leapt on the hansom's roof had most likely taken the driver, and Emma cursed aloud now as it landed with a thump, its shining hide running with vapour.

"*Most* unusual!" Archibald Clare yelled. He had gained his feet as well, and his eyes were alight now. The mournfulness had vanished. He had also produced a queerly barrelled pistol, which would be of *no* use against the dog-shaped sorcerous things now gathering. "*Quite* diverting!"

The star sapphire on her right third finger warmed. A globe-shield shimmered into being, and to the roil of smouldering wood, gunpowder and fear was added another scent: the smoke-gloss of sorcery. One of the sootdogs leapt, crashing into the shield, and the shock sent Emma to her knees, holding grimly. Both her hands were outstretched now, and her tongue occupied in chanting.

Sarpesson Street was neither deserted nor crowded at this late hour. The people gathering to watch the outcome of a hansom crash pushed against those onlookers alert enough to note that something entirely different was occurring, and the resultant chaos was merely noise to be shunted aside as her concentration narrowed.

Where is Mikal?

She had no time to wonder further. The sootdogs hunched and wove closer, snarling. Their packed-cinder sides heaved and black tongues lolled between obsidian-chip teeth; they could strip a large adult male to bone in under a minute. There were the onlookers to think of as well, and Clare behind and to her right, laughing as he sighted down the odd little pistol's chunky nose. Only he was not pointing it at the dogs, thank God. He was aiming for the rooftop.

You idiot. The chant filled her mouth. She could spare no words to tell him not to fire, that Mikal was—

The lead dog crashed against the shield. Emma's body jerked as the impact tore through her, but she held steady, the sapphire now a ringing blue flame. Her voice rose, a clear contralto, and she assayed the difficult rill of notes that would split her focus and make another Major Work possible.

That was part of what made a Prime – the ability to concentrate completely on multiple channellings of ætheric force. One's capacity could not be infinite, just like the charge of force carried and renewed every Tideturn.

But one did not need infinite capacity. *One needs only slightly more capacity than the problem at hand calls for*, as her third-form Sophological Studies professor had often intoned.

Mikal arrived.

His dark green coat fluttered as he landed in the midst of

the dogs, a Shield's fury glimmering to Sight, bright spatters and spangles invisible to normal vision. The sorcery-made things cringed, snapping; his blades tore through their insubstantial hides. The charmsilver laid along the knives' flats, as well as the will to strike, would be of far more use than Mr Clare's pistol.

Which spoke, behind her, the ball tearing through the shield from a direction the protection wasn't meant to hold. The fabric of the shield collapsed, and Emma had just enough time to deflect the backlash, tearing a hole in the brick-faced fabric of the street and exploding the clockhorse into gobbets of metal and rags of flesh, before one of the dogs turned with stomach-churning speed and launched itself at her – and the man she had been charged to protect.

She shrieked another Word through the chant's descant, her hand snapping out again, fingers contorted in a gesture definitely *not* acceptable in polite company. The ray of ætheric force smashed through brick dust, destroying even more of the road's surface, and crunched into the sootdog.

Emma bolted to her feet, snapping her hand back, and the line of force followed as the dog crumpled, whining and shattering into fragments. She could not hold the forcewhip for very long, but if more of the dogs came—

The last one died under Mikal's flashing knives. He muttered something in his native tongue, whirled on his heel, and stalked toward his Prima. That normally meant the battle was finished.

Yet Emma's mind was not eased. She half turned, chant dying on her lips and her gaze roving, searching. Heard the mutter of the crowd, dangerously frightened. Sorcerous force pulsed and bled from her fingers, a fountain of crimson sparks popping against the rainy air. For a moment the mood of the crowd threatened to distract her, but she closed it away and concentrated, seeking the source of the disturbance.

Sorcerous traces glowed, faint and fading, as the man who had fired the initial shot – most likely to mark them for the dogs – fled. He had some sort of defence laid on him, meant to keep him from a sorcerer's notice.

Perhaps from a sorcerer, but not from a Prime. Not from me, oh no. The dead see all. Her Discipline was of the Black, and it was moments like these when she would be glad of its practicality – if she could spare the attention.

Time spun outwards, dilating, as she followed him over rooftops and down into a stinking alley, refuse piled high on each side, running with the taste of fear and blood in his mouth. Something had injured him.

Mikal? But then why did he not kill the man—

The world jolted underneath her, a stunning blow to her shoulder, a great spiked roil of pain through her chest. Mikal screamed, but she was breathless. Sorcerous force spilled free, uncontained, and other screams rose.

She could possibly injure someone.

Emma came back to herself, clutching at her shoulder. Hot blood welled between her fingers, and the green silk would be ruined. Not to mention her gloves.

At least they had shot her, and not the mentath.

Oh, damn. The pain crested again, became a giant animal with its teeth in her flesh.

Mikal caught her. His mouth moved soundlessly, and Emma sought with desperate fury to contain the force thundering through her. Backlash could cause yet more damage, to the street and to onlookers, if she let it loose.

A Prime's uncontrolled force was nothing to be trifled with.

It was the traditional function of a Shield to handle such overflow, but if he had only wounded the fellow on the roof she could not trust that he was not part of—

"*Let it GO!*" Mikal roared, and the ætheric bonds between them flamed into painful life. She fought it, seeking to contain what she could, and her skull exploded with pain.

She knew no more.

CPSIA information can be obtained
at www.ICGtesting.com
Printed in the USA
FSOW01n1508300617
35786FS